A
SIMPLE
FAVOR

A
SIMPLE
FAVOR

A NOVEL

DARCEY BELL

HARPER

An Imprint of HarperCollins*Publishers*

HarperCollins books may be purchased for educational, business, or sales promotional use. For information, please email the Special Markets Department
at SPsales@harpercollins.com.

FIRST EDITION

Designed by Fritz Metsch

Library of Congress Cataloging-in-Publication Data

Names: Bell, Darcey, author.
Title: A simple favor : a novel / Darcey Bell.
Description: First edition. | New York, NY : Harper, 2017.
Identifiers: LCCN 2016032303| ISBN 9780062497772 (hardback) | ISBN
    9780062497796 (ebook)
Subjects: LCSH: Single mothers—Fiction. | Bloggers—Fiction. | Female
    friendship—Fiction. | Missing persons—Fiction. | Deception—Fiction. |
    Psychological fiction. | BISAC: FICTION / Suspense. | GSAFD: Suspense
    fiction.
Classification: LCC PS3602.E45255 S86 2017 | DDC 813/.6—dc23 LC record
available at https://lccn.loc.gov/2016032303

International ISBN: 978-0-06-266633-8

17 18 19 20 21   RRD   10 9 8 7 6 5 4 3 2 1

PART
ONE

———

My mother used to say: Everyone has secrets. That's why you can never really know anyone else. Or trust anyone. It's why you can never know yourself. Sometimes we even keep secrets from ourselves.

Growing up, I thought that was good advice, although I didn't completely understand it. Or maybe I did, a little. Kids have secrets. The imaginary friends, the things they'd get in trouble for if a grown-up ever found out.

Later I discovered that Mom was speaking from personal experience. And I wonder if she was not just preparing me but programming me for secrecy and mistrust. Did she sense that I would grow up to have darker and more shameful secrets than anyone else's? Secrets I mostly manage to keep—even from myself?

1

STEPHANIE'S BLOG

URGENT!

Hi, moms!

This is going to be different from any post so far. Not more important, since all the things that happen with our kids, their frowns and smiles, their first steps and first words, are the most important things in the world.

Let's just say this post is . . . MORE URGENT. *Way* more urgent.

My best friend has disappeared. She's been gone for two days. Her name is Emily Nelson. As you know, I don't ever *name* friends on my blog. But now, for reasons you'll soon understand, I'm (temporarily) suspending my strict anonymity policy.

My son, Miles, and Emily's son, Nicky, are best friends. They're five. They were born in April, so they both started school a few months later and are a little older than the other kids in their class. I'd say more mature. Miles and Nicky are everything you'd want your child to be. Decent, honest, kind little people, qualities that—sorry, guys, if any guys are reading this—are not as common in boys.

The boys found each other in public school. Emily and I met picking them up after school. It's rare that kids become friends with their moms' friends' kids, or that moms become friends with their kids' friends' moms. But this time it clicked. Emily and I were lucky. For one thing, we're not the youngest moms. We had kids in our midthirties, when our mom clocks were ticking away!

Sometimes Miles and Nicky make up plays and act in them. I let the boys film them on my phone, though I'm usually careful about how much time I let the kids spend on the electronic devices that make modern parenting such a challenge. One amazing skit they did was a detective story, "The Adventures of Dick Unique." Nicky was the detective; Miles, the criminal.

Nicky said, "I'm Dick Unique, the world's smartest detective."

Miles said, "I'm Miles Mandible, the world's most evil criminal." Miles played it like a villain in a Victorian melodrama, with lots of deep *ho ho ho*s. They chased each other around our yard, pretending to shoot each other (no guns!) with their fingers. It was awesome.

I only wished that Miles's dad—my late husband, Davis—could have been here to see it!

Sometimes I wonder where Miles gets his theatrical streak. From his dad, I guess. Once I watched Davis give a presentation to potential clients, and I was surprised by how animated and dramatic he was. He could have been one of those goofy-charming, attractive young actors with floppy, shiny hair. With me he was different. More himself, I guess. Quiet, kind, humorous, thoughtful—though he did have some very strong opinions, mostly about furniture. But that seemed natural—after all, he was a successful designer-architect.

Davis was a perfect angel. Except for once. Or twice.

Nicky said his mom helped them come up with the idea for Dick Unique. Emily loves detective stories and thrillers. She reads them on the Metro-North commuter train to Manhattan when she doesn't have to prepare for a meeting or a presentation.

Before Miles was born, I read books. Every so often now I'll pick up something by Virginia Woolf and read a few pages to remind myself of who I used to be—of who, I hope, I still am. Somewhere under the playdates and school lunches and early bedtimes is the young woman who lived in New York City and worked at a magazine. A person who had friends, who went out for brunch on weekends. None of those friends had kids; none moved to the suburbs. We've lost touch.

Emily's favorite writer is Patricia Highsmith. I can see why Emily likes her books; they're page-turners. But they're too upsetting. The main character is a usually a murderer or stalker or an innocent person trying not to be killed. The one I read was about two guys who meet on a train. They each agree to murder someone as a favor for the other.

I wanted to like the book, but I didn't finish it. Though when Emily asked, I told her I adored it.

The next time I came over to her house, we watched the DVD of the movie Hitchcock made from the novel. At first I worried, what if Emily wanted to talk about how the movie differed from the book? But the movie drew me in. One scene, on an out-of-control carousel, was almost too scary to watch.

Emily and I were sitting at opposite ends of the massive couch in her living room, our legs stretched out, a bottle of good white wine on the coffee table. When she saw me watching the merry-go-round scene through my splayed fingers, she smiled and gave me a thumbs-up sign. She liked it that I was frightened.

I couldn't help thinking: What if Miles was on that merry-go-round?

After the movie ended, I asked Emily, "Do you think real people would ever do things like that?"

Emily laughed. "Sweet Stephanie. You'd be amazed by what people will do. Things they'd never admit to anyone—not even to themselves."

I wanted to say that I wasn't as sweet as she thought. I'd done some bad things too. But I was too startled to speak. She'd sounded so much like my mother.

Moms know how hard it is to get a good night's sleep without having scary stories rattling around in our heads. I always promise Emily I'll read more Highsmith books. But now I wish I hadn't read that one. One murderer's victim was the other guy's wife.

And when your best friend disappears, that story is not what you want to dwell on. Not that I think that Emily's husband, Sean, would harm her. Obviously, they've had problems. What marriage hasn't? And Sean's not my favorite person. But (I think) he's basically a decent guy.

Miles and Nicky are in the same kindergarten in the excellent public school I've blogged about many times. Not the school in our town, which has funding issues due to the (aging) local population voting down the school budget, but the better school in the next town over, not far from the New York–Connecticut border.

Because of zoning regulations, our kids can't ride the school bus. Emily and I drive our boys in the morning. I pick up Miles every day. Emily works half day on Fridays so she can get Nicky at school, and often she and I and the boys do fun things—get burgers or play miniature golf—on Friday afternoons. Her house is only a ten-minute drive from mine. We're practically neighbors.

I love hanging out at Emily's, stretched out on her couch, talking and drinking wine, one of us getting up every so often to check on the boys. I love the way her hands move as she talks, the way the light winks off her beautiful diamond and sapphire ring. We talk a lot about motherhood. We never run out of things to say. It's so thrilling to have a real friend that I sometimes forget how lonely I was before we met.

During the rest of the week, Emily's part-time nanny, Alison, picks Nicky up after school. Emily's husband, Sean, works late on Wall Street. Emily and Nicky are lucky if Sean *ever* gets home in time for dinner. On those rare days when Alison calls in sick, Emily texts me, and I fill in. The boys come back to my house until Emily can get home.

Maybe once a month Emily has to stay late at work. And twice, maybe three times, she's had to be out of town overnight.

Like this time. Before she disappeared.

Emily works in public relations for a famous fashion designer in Manhattan whose name I've also been careful not to mention. In fact she's the *director* of public relations for a *very* famous designer. I try to be conscious about brand names on the blog because of trust issues involved and also because name-dropping is *so* unattractive. That's also why I've resisted accepting advertising.

Even when she's late, or at meetings, Emily texts me every few hours. She calls when she gets a minute free. She's that kind of mom. Not helicopter, not hands-on, not any of those negative expressions society uses to judge and punish us for loving our kids.

When Emily gets home from the city, she always makes a beeline from the station to pick Nicky up. I have to remind her to stay under the speed limit. When her train is going to be late, she texts me. Constantly! What station they're at, her ETA, until I text her back: NO WORRIES. BOYS FINE. GET HERE WHEN U GET HERE. SAFE TRAVELS.

It's been two days since she hasn't shown up or gotten in touch with me or returned my texts or calls. Something terrible has happened. She's vanished. I have no idea where she is.

Moms, does Emily sound like the kind of mother who would leave her child and disappear for two days and not text or call or answer my texts or calls? If nothing was wrong? *Seriously?*

Okay, got to run now. I smell chocolate-chip cookies burning in the oven. More soon.

Love,

Stephanie

2

STEPHANIE'S BLOG

WHERE WE LIVE NOW

Hi, moms!

Until now I've tried not to mention the name of our town. Privacy is so precious—and there's so little of it these days. I don't mean to sound paranoid, but even in a town like ours, hidden cameras might be watching to see what brand of canned tomatoes you buy. Especially in our town. People assume it's a rich town because it's in that part of Connecticut, but it's not all that rich. Emily and Sean have money. I have enough to live on from what my husband, Davis, left me, another reason I can afford to blog without running it as a business.

But because Emily's disappearance changes everything, and because someone who lives near us may have seen her, and because I'm frantic, I feel I need to *out* Warfield. Warfield, Connecticut. It's about two hours from Manhattan on Metro-North.

People call this the suburbs, but I grew up in the suburbs and lived in the city, so it's always felt like country to me. I've blogged about how Davis had to drag me kicking and screaming up here from the city. I'd spent years getting *out* of the suburbs. I've blogged about how I fell in love with country life, how fantastic it feels to wake up with the sun streaming into the eyebrow colonial that Davis restored without sacrificing any of its period details, and how I love drinking tea while the rainbow machine (a kind of prism you put in the window) my brother Chris gave us for a wedding present scatters brightness all over the kitchen.

Miles and I adore it here. Or anyway, I used to.

Until today, when I was feeling so anxious about Emily that everyone— the moms at school, nice Maureen in the post office, the kid who bags groceries—they all seemed sinister, like in those horror movies where everyone in town is a cult member or a zombie. I asked a couple of my neighbors, fake-casually, if they'd seen Emily around, and they shook their heads no. Was it my imagination that they gave me funny looks? Now you moms can *really* see how crazy-making this is.

Moms, forgive me. I got distracted and just blabbed on, as always.

I SHOULD HAVE PUT THIS EARLIER!!!

Emily is around five foot seven. She has blond hair with dark streaks (I never asked if they were real) and dark brown eyes. She probably weighs around a hundred and twenty pounds. But that's a guess. You don't ask your friends, How tall are you? How much do you weigh? Though I know some men think that women never talk about anything else. She's forty-one, but she looks thirty-five, at the most.

She has a dark birthmark underneath her right eye. I only noticed it when she asked me if she should get it removed. I said no, it looked fine and that women in the French court (so I'd read) painted those "beauty spots" on.

Emily always wore a perfume that I guess you could call her signature scent. She said it was made from lilacs and lilies, by Italian nuns. She orders it from Florence. I love that about Emily, all the elegant, sophisticated things she knows about that would never have crossed my mind.

I've never worn perfume. I always think it's a little off-putting when women smell like flowers or spices. What are they hiding? What's the message they're sending? But I like Emily's perfume. I like it that I can always tell from the scent when she's nearby, or when she's been in a room. I can smell her perfume in Nicky's hair, after she's held him tight and hugged him. She's offered to let me try some, but it seemed too weird, too intimate, the two of us smelling like creepy smell-twins.

She always wears the diamond and sapphire ring that Sean gave her when they got engaged. And because she moves her hands a lot when she talks, I think of the ring as a sparkling creature with a life of its own, like Tinker Bell flying out in front of Peter Pan and the Lost Boys.

Emily has a tattoo: one of those delicate crown-of-thorn bracelets around her right wrist. That surprised me. She didn't seem like someone who would get a tattoo—especially one that couldn't be covered up unless she wore long sleeves. At first I thought it was some fashion-industry thing, but when I felt I knew her well enough and asked, Emily said, "Oh, that. I got it when I was young and wild."

I said, "We were *all* young and wild. Once upon a time."

It felt good to say something I could never say to my husband. If he'd asked what I meant by *wild* and I told him, life as we knew it would have ended. Of course, that life ended anyway. The truth has a way of coming out.

Wait. The phone's ringing! Maybe it's Emily. More soon.

Love,

Stephanie

3

STEPHANIE'S BLOG

SIMPLE FAVORS

Hi, moms!

It wasn't Emily on the phone. It was a robocall telling me I'd won a free trip to the Caribbean.

Where was I? Oh, right:

Last summer, sunning at the community pool while the boys splashed in the baby pool, Emily said, "I'm always asking you for favors, Stephanie. And I'm so grateful. But can I ask for just one more? Could you take care of Nicky so Sean and I can get away, for Sean's birthday weekend, to my family's cabin?" Emily always calls it "the cabin," but I imagine that her family vacation home on the shore of a lake in northern Michigan is a bit fancier than that. "I was amazed Sean agreed, and I want to nail this down before he changes his mind."

Of course I said yes. I knew what a problem it was for her to lure Sean away from his office.

"On one condition," I said.

"Anything," she said. "You name it."

"Can you put suntan oil on this hard-to-reach spot on my back?"

"Gladly." Emily laughed. As I felt her small, strong hand rubbing the oil into my skin, I remembered the fun of going to the beach with my friends in high school!

The weekend that Emily and Sean went away, Miles, Nicky, and I had a great time. The pool, the park, a movie, and burgers and veggies on the grill.

Emily and I have been friends for a year, since our boys met in pre-K. Here's a picture of her I took at Six Flags, though you can't see her all that well. It's a selfie of the four of us, boys and moms. I scanned the kids out. You know I have strong opinions about posting images of one's kids.

I don't know what she was wearing the day she disappeared. I didn't see her when she dropped Nicky off at school. She was a little late that day. Usually the buses arrive and unload all at once. The teachers have a lot going on, greeting the kids, herding them inside. I don't blame them for not noticing what Emily was wearing or whether she seemed like her cheerful normal self or anxious in any way.

Probably Emily looked like she always looks when she's going to the office: like a fashion executive (she gets designer clothes at a huge discount) heading to work in the city. She'd called me early that morning.

"Please, Stephanie, I need your help. *Again.* An emergency's come up at work, and I have to stay late. Alison has a class. Can you get Nicky at school? I'll come get him in the evening, nine at the latest."

I remember wondering: What counts as an "emergency" in the fashion business? The buttonholes are too small? Someone sewed a zipper in backward?

I said, "Of course. I'm totally happy to do you a favor."

A simple favor. The sort of simple favor we moms do for each other all the time. The boys would be thrilled. I'm pretty sure I remember asking Emily if she wanted Nicky to sleep over. And I'm pretty sure she said no thanks. She'd want to see him at the end of a tough day, even if he was asleep.

I picked up Nicky and Miles after school. They were in heaven. They love each other in that puppyish way little boys do. Better than brothers, who fight.

They played nicely in my son's room and on the swings where I could watch them from the window. I made them dinner. We had a healthy meal. As you know, I'm a vegetarian, but Nicky will only eat burgers, so that's what I cooked. I can't count how often I've blogged about how hard I try to balance the good nutritious stuff with what they'll actually eat. The boys discussed an incident at school: a boy got sent to the principal's office for not listening to the teacher even after he got a time-out.

It got late. Emily didn't call. Which seemed weird. I texted her, and she didn't text me back. Which seemed even weirder.

Okay, she said *emergency*. Maybe something happened at a factory in one of the countries where the clothes are made. Sewn by *slaves* is my impression, but that could never be mentioned. Maybe there's another scandal involving her boss, Dennis, who's had some well-publicized substance-abuse episodes. Emily has had to do some heavy damage control. Maybe she was at a meeting and couldn't get out. Maybe she was somewhere with no cell phone reception. Maybe she'd lost her charger.

If you knew Emily, you'd know how unlikely it is that she would lose her charger. Or that she wouldn't find a way to call in and check on Nicky.

We moms are so used to being in touch. You know how it feels when you need to reach someone. It's like you're possessed. You keep calling and texting and trying to keep yourself from calling and texting again *because you just called and texted*.

Each time, my calls went to voice mail. I heard Emily's "professional" voice—perky, crisp, all business. "Hi there, you've reached Emily Nelson. Please leave a brief message, and I'll get back to you as soon as I can. Talk soon!"

"Emily, it's me! Stephanie! Call me!"

It got to be bedtime for the boys. Emily still hadn't called. This had *never* happened. I got those stomach butterflies of fear. Terror, really. But I didn't want to let the kids know, especially Nicky . . .

I can't write any more, moms. I'm just too upset.

Love,

Stephanie

4

STEPHANIE'S BLOG

GHOSTS FROM THE PAST

Hi, moms!

You all remember how often I blogged about not letting Miles see how grief stricken I was when his dad—Davis—was killed in the same accident with my brother, Chris.

It was a beautiful summer Saturday afternoon. Davis lost control of our vintage Camaro, and they hit a tree. Our whole world changed in one minute.

I lost the only men who ever mattered to me, not counting my dad, who died when I was eighteen. And Miles lost his father and his beloved uncle.

Miles was only two, but he could sense my grief. I had to be strong for his sake and not fall apart until after he was asleep. So you could say I had good (if you could call that *good*) preparation for not freaking out or letting the boys suspect how worried I was about Emily.

After I put the boys to bed, I had another glass of wine to calm my nerves. The next morning, I woke up with a headache, but I acted as if everything was fine. I got the kids dressed. It helped that Nicky had slept over so often, it didn't seem strange. Nicky and Miles are about the same size, so Nicky could wear Miles's clothes. That was another way I knew that Emily had meant to pick Nicky up last night; she always sends a change of clothes when he's going to stay.

Emily still hadn't called. I was approaching full panic mode. My hands shook so much that when I poured the kids their Cheerios, crispy O's skidded all over the kitchen table and onto the floor. I don't think I ever missed Davis so much—someone to help me, advise me, calm me down.

I decided to drop the kids off at school and then try to figure it out. I didn't know who to call. I knew Sean—Emily's husband, Nicky's dad—was in Europe somewhere, but I didn't have his cell number.

I can hear all the moms out there thinking I've broken my own rules. NEVER HAVE ANOTHER CHILD OVER FOR A PLAYDATE WITHOUT BACKUP CONTACT INFORMATION!!! Both parents' home and work and cell numbers. A close relative or someone empowered to make medical decisions. The name and phone number of the child's health care provider.

I did have the nanny's—Alison's—number. She's a responsible person. I trust her, though you know I worry about kids being raised by nannies. Alison said that Emily told her Nicky was having a sleepover with Miles. Good news! I didn't ask how long Emily said he'd be staying. I was afraid it would make me seem . . . not together, and you know how sensitive we moms are about competency issues.

You moms will think I'm not only irresponsible but insane for not having Nicky's dad's cell phone number. There's no excuse. I can only ask you not to judge me.

When I dropped the kids off at school, I told Mrs. Kerry, their fantastic kindergarten teacher, that I'd kept the kids overnight. I had the craziest feeling, *like I'd get Emily in trouble* if I said she hadn't come back and hadn't called. As if I . . . as if I was *telling on her.* Ratting her out for being a bad mom.

I said I couldn't reach Emily but I was sure that everything was okay. We must have gotten our signals crossed about how long Nicky would be staying. But just in case, could the school give me his dad's—Sean's— cell number? Mrs. Kerry said Emily had mentioned that her husband was spending a few days in London on business.

Miles's teachers like me. They all keep up with my blog. They appreciate how positively I blog about the school, how often I send them major love and hugs for the great job they're doing with our kids.

Mrs. Kerry gave me Sean's number. But I could see (over the top of my phone) that she was looking at me with a slightly mistrustful expression. I told myself that I was being paranoid, again, that she was trying to seem concerned but not worried. Trying not to judge.

I felt better having Sean's number. I should have called him right away. I don't know why I didn't.

I did call Emily's company in the city.

Dennis Nylon Inc. There. I've said it. To me and a lot of you moms, Dennis Nylon is what Dior or Chanel was to *our* moms. An unapproachable, unaffordable, all-powerful fashion god.

I asked the young (everyone who works there but Emily is practically a child) man who answered the phone to connect me to Emily Nelson's office. Her assistant, Valerie, asked me for the thousandth time who I was, exactly. Okay, I get it. Valerie has never met me. But does she have that many Stephanies in her life? Does Emily?

I said I was Nicky's best friend's mom. Valerie said she was sorry but Emily had stepped out of the office for a moment. I said no, *I* was sorry. Nicky had slept at my house last night, and Emily hadn't come to pick him up. Was there someone I could speak to? I was thinking how every mom should have a Valerie of her own. An assistant! There are so many things we do—so much we need help with.

Davis had two assistants, Evan and Anita. Talented young designers. Sometimes I feel like I'm the only person in the world without an assistant. I'm kidding, of course. We have so much more than most people, but still . . .

I could tell that something wasn't right. Valerie said that someone would call me right back. But no one ever called.

I've blogged about the silly, hurtful divisions that often come between working moms and stay-at-home moms. I've kept it secret, but I've always been a teensy bit jealous of Emily's career. The glamour, the excitement, the practically free clothes! The celebrities' unlisted numbers, the runway shows . . . all the cool things Emily does while I'm home making peanut butter sandwiches and wiping up spilled apple juice and blogging. Not to underestimate how happy and grateful I am to be able to reach out to (by now) thousands of moms worldwide. I also know that Emily is missing out on a lot of things, on the ordinary fun stuff Miles and I do every afternoon.

Now no one at Emily's company seems to be concerned. She's worked there almost since she got out of college. Dennis should be going on the news and pleading with someone to find her.

Relax, Stephanie. Calm down. It hasn't been all that long.

Thanks, moms. It comforts me just to know you're out there reading this.

Love,

Stephanie

5

STEPHANIE'S BLOG

ALL MY FAULT?

Hi, moms!

What a typical mom I am! By now I've almost convinced myself that the whole misunderstanding is my fault. Emily must have asked me to keep Nicky for a couple days instead of for the evening. Then why do I remember her saying that Nicky *wasn't* going to sleep over, that she would get him by nine?

Many of us have shared on this blog about how hard it is for moms to feel they've got a grip on reality—what day it is, what's expected of us, what someone said or didn't. Nothing is easier than convincing a mom that something's her fault. Even when it isn't. *Especially* when it isn't.

By that afternoon, I had myself so psyched that I half expected to see Emily waiting under the big oak tree near the entrance to the school where she always is on Fridays. I was so positive she'd be there that, for a split second, I imagined I saw her.

It couldn't have been her. For one thing, it was Wednesday. I had that sinking feeling—you can't find your kid anywhere, and in the lifetime it takes to find him, you feel like your heart is going to explode. There was a period when Miles loved to hide from me, and I flipped out every time . . .

Wait. I have a plan. More soon.

Love,

Stephanie

STEPHANIE'S BLOG
A VISIT TO EMILY'S

Hi, moms!

Normally, I wouldn't go over to Emily's house without calling. I did try her landline. No one answered. Emily had given me her keys and asked for the keys to my house. I'd been so impressed because it seemed like such a sensible, grown-up, mom thing to do. Plus it meant we were really friends. We could use the keys in an emergency. Or even if we just arrived early for a playdate and the other wasn't home. *This* was an emergency. I didn't want to invade Emily's privacy, but I had to make sure that she hadn't fallen or hurt herself, or that she wasn't ill and in need of my help.

I couldn't bring the boys. What if I found something dire? My imagination was running wild. I imagined her house smeared with blood, Charlie Manson–style. I pictured her in a bathtub full of blood.

I decided to stop by Emily's on my way to pick up the boys at school.

Just pulling into her driveway felt dangerous and spooky. It was raining slightly; a wind was shaking the trees, and I felt like the branches were

saying, Don't go there. Don't go there. I'm joking. I'm a sensible mom. I
don't hear the trees talking.

I felt a lot better when I spotted Emily's housecleaner Maricela's car
in the driveway. Maricela told me she was just finishing up, which was
comforting. If Emily were dead or lying helpless somewhere in the house,
Maricela would have noticed.

Maricela is an angel. I only wish she worked for us, but Miles and I can't
afford her.

She said, "The senora said she'd be gone four days. She said I should
come to clean and then again to see if the plants need water."

Four days! What a relief!

"Have you heard from her?"

"No. Why would I?" Maricela asked sweetly. "Senora, are you all right?
Would you like something to drink? Food? The senora left beautiful fruit in
the fridge."

Beautiful fruit was a good sign. Emily meant to return. I asked for a glass
of water, and Maricela went to get it.

It felt strange to sit on the couch where I'd spent so many hours with Emily.
Her big, comfy sofa felt suddenly lumpy and strange, like something
you could sink into and never climb out of. Like a Venus flytrap couch. I
considered searching the house for clues.

Why hadn't Emily said she'd be gone four days? And why didn't she return
my calls? I knew my friend. Something awful had happened.

Being in Emily's house made me feel even more jumpy and scared. I kept expecting her to walk in and ask what I was doing. First I would feel relieved, overjoyed to see her, and then maybe guilty, even though she'd given me plenty of reason to drop by.

Where is she? I felt like whining, like a child.

I looked above the mantelpiece at the photograph of the twins. There were so many gorgeous things in Emily's home: Persian rugs, Chinese vases, iconic design pieces, masterpieces of midcentury modern furniture. Davis would have loved her house, if only he'd lived to see it. But Emily made a point of showing me the black-and-white photo of the two girls in their party dresses and hair bands, so oddly beautiful and so haunting, half smiling at some secret knowledge.

Emily said, "That photo cost more, and I love it more, than anything in the house. If I told you how we got it, our friend in the auction house would have to kill me. Which twin do you think is the dominant one?"

It was almost like déjà vu or a memory of another life. *My* other life—when I lived in the city and worked at a magazine. A home-decorating magazine you can buy at the supermarket checkout counter, but a magazine nonetheless: a cover, paper, text, photos. I used to have a life in which I met people who made odd comments and asked interesting questions and had beautiful, unexpected objects in their houses. People who talked about something besides what after-school lessons their kids were taking and whether you could know if the tomatoes were really organic. People who had fun!

"I don't know," I'd told Emily. "Which twin do *you* think?"

She said, "Sometimes I think one, sometimes the other."

"Maybe neither," I said.

"*That* never happens," she said. "There's always a dominant one, even in a friendship."

Was Emily the dominant friend? I looked up to her, I know . . .

Now my friend was gone. And there were the twins, still looking at me with their tender, inscrutable little faces.

The living room was perfect. Naturally. Maricela was here. On the coffee table—Davis would have known what midcentury modern genius designed it—was a paperback book. A Patricia Highsmith novel. *Those Who Walk Away.* Sticking out from the pages was a bookmark from our local bookstore. That was when it occurred to me—not quite in a flash, more like a flicker—that Emily might have walked away. Left her son with me and taken off. People walk away. It happens. Their friends and neighbors and family members say they never *ever* suspected.

I decided to read the Highsmith book for information I might have missed. Information about Emily. I couldn't take her copy. When she came back, she'd be annoyed. I'd order a copy if the library didn't have it. If I could just keep cool and stay reasonable, everything would work out. All this would turn out to be a bad dream, a mistake, a misunderstanding that Emily and I could laugh about, later.

Maricela brought me water in a polka dot vintage glass. The perfect glass. Even the glass was so Emily!

"Drink," Maricela said. "You'll feel better."

I drank the cold clear water. But I didn't feel better.

I thanked Maricela and left the house. I checked my phone. No texts or emails. I was sure that Emily wasn't one of "those who walk away." Something was very wrong.

I should have called the police. But I was still in denial, blaming myself for getting my facts wrong, for hearing my friend say something she didn't say.

Since then my subconscious has gone into overdrive, running horror movies about carjacking, kidnapping, murder, the corpse in the ditch, the blow to the head that's left Emily wandering around, amnesiac. Maybe someone has found her. Maybe someone will bring her home.

Which is why I'm posting this. We've all heard about those miracles that are the upside of the internet. They are the very best thing about social networking and blogging! So I'm asking the moms community to keep its naturally extra-sharp mom eyes open. If you see a woman who looks like Emily, ask her if she's okay. If you see a woman who looks like Emily and she seems injured or lost, text me immediately at the number at the bottom of the screen.

Thanks, dear moms!

Love,

Stephanie

7

STEPHANIE'S BLOG

(THE NEXT DAY)

SECOND THOUGHTS AND A CALL TO SEAN

Hi, moms!

Fitful sleep. Weird dreams. When I woke at six, I didn't know what was wrong. Then I remembered that Emily was gone. Then I remembered the rest of it, and I was scared to look at my phone. I'd given out my private number and asked my readers to report any woman who looks like Emily, who—to be honest—looks like lots of blond, thin, pretty, gym-toned moms. Her tattoo and ring might narrow it down, but lots of moms have tattoos. Who knows if she's wearing her ring? What if she's been robbed?

Thank heaven the moms community is so sensible. I only got two texts. Both Emily sightings from places (one from Alaska, one from the north of Scotland—it's amazing how far my little blog has reached) so distant that I didn't see how Emily could have gotten there in the (*short*, I keep telling myself) time she's been gone.

I actually thought of changing my phone number, in case thousands of moms started contacting me, trying to be helpful. Still . . . while we always need to be careful about keeping our personal information safe, it's the only number that Emily's got, and I'm still hoping she'll call. Nicky and I need her to be able to get in touch.

The second night, at dinner, Nicky was starting to get antsy. Any kid would. I'm sure he was picking up on my anxiety. Until now he'd never stayed for two nights in a row, not counting the weekend when his parents went away and everyone had such a good time and no one was nervous. Now Nicky started asking me when his mom was coming to get him. He ate his veggie burger and immediately threw up. I stroked his head and told him that his mom would be back soon and I was calling his dad.

It was seven when I called Sean in England. I was so desperate that—stupidly—I forgot the time difference. He sounded groggy.

"Did I wake you up? I'm so sorry!" Why was I apologizing? His wife had gone missing!

"You didn't wake me," he said thickly. "Who is this?"

I had the weirdest temptation to giggle because I always wondered if Sean would still have the tony British accent if you woke him from a deep sleep. He did.

"Emily's friend," I said. "Stephanie."

"Stephanie," he repeated. He had no idea who I was, though he'd met me many times. "What is it, Stephanie?"

"I don't mean to be alarmist," I said, "But Emily left Nicky with me, and I was wondering . . . where she is and when she's planning to come home. I must have heard her wrong. I didn't know Nicky would be staying—"

I could practically hear his patience run out. Snap!

"She's traveling on business," he said evenly. "She'll be gone for a couple of days." Very definite, very clear.

"Oh," I said. "That's a relief. I'm so sorry I bothered you."

"Not a problem," he said. "And do feel free to call again if you need me . . . Stephanie."

Only after we hung up did I realize that he hadn't asked how Nicky was. What kind of father was he? What kind of husband? Wasn't he even a little worried about his wife? But why should he have been worried? They were both away on separate business trips. That was how they lived. Did I believe that a husband and wife had to talk every single night?

Besides which, I'd woken him. Lots of men can stay half-conscious for a long time after they wake up. Another luxury that single moms can't afford.

Emily didn't return that night. I didn't call Sean back, and once more I pretended that everything was all right. A normal evening with the kids. Nicky cried, on and off. I let the boys climb into my bed and watch cartoons on TV until it was time for them to go to sleep. I pushed the bad stuff to the back of my mind, which is something moms learn to do. I just had to be patient. Give it a day. There was nothing to do but wait.

Emily still hadn't returned by the next evening when Sean got back from England. He phoned me from the airport. Now he sounded nervous too. He dropped his stuff at home, where he must have hoped (or feared!) to find Emily. Then he drove straight to my house.

As soon as Nicky heard his dad's voice, he came flying out of Miles's room. He flung his arms around his father. Sean picked his son up and kissed him and hugged him against his chest.

Somehow Sean's being in my house, holding his frightened but brave little boy, made my watery fears turn to solid ice.

This is real. My friend has disappeared.

Moms everywhere, please help.

Love,

Stephanie

8

STEPHANIE

Everyone has secrets, my mother used to say. Not a great thing to tell a daughter you want to grow up into a healthy person who can have healthy relationships with other healthy people. But Mom certainly had her reasons.

Four days after my father passed away, when I was eighteen, a stranger knocked on our door. My mother looked out the window and said, "Look, Stephanie! It's your father."

I'd heard the expression "crazy with grief," but Mom was perfectly sane. Of course, she was heartbroken about my dad. They'd loved each other very much. At least as far as I knew.

Maybe neither of us really believed that Dad was gone. He'd traveled a lot, so for a while after his heart attack on the golf course near our home in a pleasant suburb of Cincinnati, it seemed as if he might still be on a business trip. He'd been a pharmaceutical company exec who attended conferences and meetings all over the country.

Anyway, what my mother really meant was, "Look. It's your father when he was twenty-four. The year we got married."

I looked out the window.

The young man on our doorstep was the groom in my parents' wedding photo.

I'd never seen him before, yet I felt that I'd been looking at him every day of my life. Actually, I had. I'd lived with him in the framed photograph on the dusty upright piano.

The only difference was that the stranger was wearing jeans and a denim jacket instead of a white tuxedo, and his dark hair was stylishly cut instead of slicked back, Elvis-style, like my dad in the wedding photo.

My mother said, "Ask him in." He was so good looking I couldn't stop staring. My dad had been handsome before the traveling and excessive drinking and airport food caught up with him.

Mom told the young man, "Just stand there. Don't say a word." She grabbed her wedding photo off the piano and handed it to him. He stared at the photo. He seemed shocked. Then he laughed out loud. We all laughed.

He said, "I guess we can skip the DNA test."

His name was Chris. He lived in Madison, Wisconsin. My dad was his father. They used to see each other every six months; my dad rerouted his trips so he could come through Wisconsin and visit his other family: Chris's mom and Chris.

Chris had seen my dad's obituary in the online version of our local paper. It had shown up in his Google Alert, which made me think that he'd wanted (poor guy!) to keep tabs on my dad. *His* dad. His mother had died of heart failure, a year before. Of course, Chris wasn't mentioned in Dad's obituary, but we were. And we were listed—that is, my dad was listed—in the phone book.

The fact that this hot guy was my half brother took a while to sink in. I still kept expecting him to say that he was a distant cousin who happened to resemble my dad.

There was another weird detail I should add: At that point, I looked almost exactly like my mother when she was around my age. (I still resemble her, though less than I used to.) I looked like her in the wedding photo, and my newfound brother Chris looked like my—*our*—dad. And there we were, the happy bridal couple, straight off the top of the wedding cake, cloned and reanimated twenty years later. What can I say? It was hot.

I was wearing jeans and a T-shirt, but I was conscious of holding my body just like Mom in her wedding gown, my elbows tight against my sides and my hands curled at my chest, like chipmunk paws. When I made myself lower my arms and stand like a normal person, I saw Chris glance at my breasts.

Had my mother suspected the truth? Was that why she talked about everyone having secrets? I could never make myself ask, even—especially—after Chris entered our lives.

She invited Chris to sit down at the kitchen table, and she served him a plate of cold cuts left over from my dad's funeral. We'd ordered way too much, and though the shock of Dad's death was magnified by the shock of meeting a brand-new brother, the physical fact of Chris sitting in Dad's seat and calmly eating mortadella made everything seem almost normal. Almost right.

My mother said, "Chris, we're so sorry for not inviting you to the funeral!"

Why was *Mom* apologizing? Because she always did, just like women are supposed to. Everything is always our fault! Even though I felt sorry for Mom, I wanted her to shut up.

Chris said, "Gosh, why would you? You didn't know about me."

We must all have been thinking that it was Dad's fault. But it was a little late to blame *him*.

Chris said, "I'm the one who should apologize."

"For what?" my mother said.

"For showing up like this," he said. "And I guess . . . for existing."

Chris had a beautiful smile. We all laughed again. It was more laughing than Mom and I had done since Dad died.

"Have more," my mother said, and refilled his plate without waiting for him to answer. I loved watching how he ate, appreciative and voracious.

Would my whole life have been different if my mom hadn't said it was too late for Chris to start out on the long drive home? If she hadn't invited him to spend the night?

What happened was going to happen. Chris and I stayed up all night talking. I don't remember what we talked about. Our lives, our hopes, our fears. Our childhoods, our dreams for the future. What did I have to say for myself? What did I know? I was eighteen. A kid.

In the morning, Chris took my cell number. The next afternoon, he called. He hadn't left for Wisconsin. He was staying at a motel not far from our house.

I already had a boyfriend. I'd gone to the senior prom with him not long before. I'd had sex with him a few times. He was the first guy I'd had sex with, and I wondered what all the fuss was about.

I wasn't thinking about my boyfriend. I was thinking about how fast I could drive to Chris's motel without getting a ticket.

Chris had told me what room he was staying in. I shivered as I knocked on the door, and I didn't stop shaking as I walked into his room and shyly kissed him hello and looked for a place to sit. There was a rickety chair beside a desk. His clothes were piled neatly on the chair. We both knew I was going to sit on the bed.

He sat down next to me. The back of his hand grazed my breast.

"Come over here," he said, though I was already there.

I can still hear him say it, and when I do, I feel breathless and my knees get weak, just like they did then. After that, I understood what sex was supposed to be about. Why people would do anything for it. Die for it. Once I knew, I couldn't get enough. There was no going back. Chris and I couldn't stay away from each other. I wanted, I *needed* to be there: that thrilling, intensely pleasurable, intimate place we could get to, together.

I have to be careful when and where I let myself remember being with Chris. I can't think about it when I'm in public, certainly not when I'm driving. That same liquid desire runs through me. My eyelids get heavy, sleepy with longing. I close my eyes against the heat, and I feel myself melting into a puddle of pure *wanting*.

———

THE NIGHT SEAN got home from London, I put the boys to bed in Miles's room. Nicky cried and didn't want to go to bed because his dad was home. And (no one had to say) because his mom wasn't. But Sean went in and stayed with him until he fell asleep.

I asked Sean if he wanted a drink.

"I've never wanted a drink so badly in my life," he said. "A strong one. But I don't think it's a great idea to be smelling like a brewery when the police come."

I was relieved when he called the cops. It meant he was taking this seriously. I hadn't felt it was my place to call and report a missing friend. I'd been waiting for Sean.

I don't know why they sent the state troopers, who, in our area, mostly do traffic stops. That's *their* field of expertise. And the occasional domestic dispute.

How strange that the cops should have been the ones who looked guilty when they walked in. Sergeant Molloy had red hair and a red mustache like an old-school porn star. Officer Blanco's lipstick (were female cops allowed to wear *that* much makeup?) was smeared. It crossed my mind that they'd been fooling around in the patrol car when Sean's call came in.

Maybe that was why they seemed confused. At first they thought I was Sean's wife, so why had he reported his wife missing? And then they thought that my house was Sean's house . . . It took a while to get things straight: Sean was the husband, I was the friend. When Sergeant Molloy asked how long Emily had been gone and Sean had to look at me for the answer and I said six days, Sergeant Molloy shrugged, as if to say that his wife—he was wearing a wedding ring—was always taking off for weeks at a time without telling anyone. Officer Blanco gave him a funny look, but the sergeant was staring at Sean, as if he was wondering why Sean needed to ask *me* how long his wife had been gone. Or why we'd waited so long to report her missing.

"Sorry," said Sean. "I'm a bit jet-lagged."

"Been traveling?" asked Sergeant Molloy.

"I was in London," said Sean.

"Visiting family?" Brilliant deduction, Sherlock. The accent was the tip-off!

"Business," said Sean.

The troopers exchanged a long look. They'd probably learned in the police academy that the husband is always the first suspect. But they must have missed the class that explained what to do if the husband was on the other side of the Atlantic when the wife went missing.

"Give it another couple days," said the sergeant. "Maybe she just wanted a little time off. A little holiday from her life."

"You don't understand!" I said. "Emily left her son with me! She'd *never* go away and leave him and not call or get in touch."

"All the more reason," said Officer Blanco. "I got three kids, and believe me, there are days when I dream about how sweet it would be to take a break, check into some nice, comfy spa somewhere, and have a little *me* time."

I spaced out for a moment, thinking about my blog and about how I heard things like that from moms all the time. But Emily wasn't like that. How could I make them understand that something was really wrong?

Meanwhile the cops had moved on to asking Sean if he'd tried to contact any of her friends and family.

"*I'm* her friend," I said. "Her best friend. *I'm* the one she would tell if—"

Sergeant Molloy cut me off. "Family? Close relatives?"

"Her mom's in Detroit," said Sean. "But I'm sure that Emily wouldn't have gone there. She and her mother have been estranged for years."

I was shocked. Emily had led me to believe that she and her mother had a loving—though not particularly close—relationship. Emily had been so sympathetic when I told her about my mom and dad.

"Any idea why?" asked Officer Blanco. What relevance could that possibly have to Emily's disappearance? They must have assumed that their badges and uniforms gave them license to ask any nosy question they wanted.

"My wife didn't like to talk about it," said Sean. "There were problems from the distant past that have never been resolved. Anyway, her poor mum is suffering from dementia. According to my wife, she isn't even always sure who or where she is. She drifts in and out of reality. She thinks her husband—who's been dead for a decade—is still alive. If it weren't for her caretaker . . ."

"Even so," said Officer Blanco. "People in trouble often head for their childhood home, their first place of safety."

"I can guarantee you that my wife isn't there. That was definitely not where she felt safe. And why would my wife be in trouble?"

Was it possible that Sean was lying? Emily never mentioned the fact that her mother was in poor health. The only complaint she'd ever voiced was that her mother hated the birthmark under her eye and had campaigned to have it removed. Emily had resisted—mostly to defy her mother—but the conflict had left her with a lifelong complex about that little dark spot.

And I'd always believed that we told each other everything.

The troopers couldn't wait to get out of there and write up their report. Or maybe they were just eager to resume making out in the patrol car. They told us to let them know if we heard from Emily, and that the detectives would contact us in a day or two if she still hadn't turned up. A day or two? *Seriously?*

The doorbell rang again. It was Sergeant Molloy.

"One more thing," he said, like Peter Falk in old *Columbo* reruns. I almost laughed. "I hope you aren't planning any more trips to Europe in the near future," he told Sean.

"I'll be right here," said Sean coldly. "I mean at my home. Taking care of my son."

After I heard the patrol car pull out of the driveway, I said, "I guess we'll be wanting that drink."

"Definitely," said Sean.

I poured us each a double bourbon, and we sat at the kitchen table, sipping our drinks, not saying anything. It felt almost pleasant, drinking, not talking, having a man in the house after so long. But then I remembered why Sean was there. And I was terrified all over again.

I said, "Maybe you *should* call her mother."

At least we would be doing *something*. And I wanted to be there when Sean called. Either Emily had left out some important information about her life, or she had lied to Sean. Or Sean had lied to the police. None of it made sense. Why would he lie about something like that? Why would *she*?

"Sure," he said. "It's worth a try. At least I can talk to her mum's caretaker."

Sean dialed. I wanted to ask him to put the call on speakerphone. But that would have seemed too bizarre.

"Hi, Bernice," he said. "I do so hate to bother you. But have you heard from Emily, by any chance? Oh, of course. I thought not. No, everything's fine. I think she's traveling for the company. And I just got home. Nicky's fine, he stayed with a friend. I don't mean to alarm you . . ." There was a silence. Then Sean said, "Sure, I'll talk to her if she wants. I'm glad to hear she's having one of her good days."

Another silence, then, "Good evening, Mrs. Nelson. I hope you're well. I'm wondering if you might have heard from your daughter?"

Silence.

"Emily. Well, no, I thought so. Do give her my love if you see her. And you take care. Bye-bye."

There were tears in Sean's eyes when he hung up. And I felt awful for having been so mean-spirited and suspicious. Whatever mixed feelings I'd had about Sean, Emily was his wife. Nicky's mom. Sean loved her. And we were in this together.

"Oh, that poor old woman," said Sean. "She asked me, 'Daughter? Which daughter?'"

Hearing that, I was almost glad that my mother had died suddenly, mercifully, before I had to watch her disappear in stages.

"What about the family cabin on the lake?" I said. "Up in Michigan. Where you guys went for your birthday. Do you think she might have gone there?"

Sean gave me a swift, searching look, as if he was wondering how I knew about the cabin, as if he didn't *want* me knowing about the cabin. Didn't he remember that I was the one who'd taken care of Nicky when he and Emily stole away for their romantic birthday weekend?

"No way," he said. "She loved being there. But not alone. Never alone. She was afraid that the place was haunted."

"Haunted how?" I said.

"I don't know," said Sean. "I never asked. Once she said it was full of ghosts."

I wondered how close Sean and Emily's marriage could have been if she'd said the family cabin was haunted and he never asked what she meant.

"She told me that her parents were very cold, controlling, rejecting people, and that the tough times she went through in her early twenties were a reaction to what she'd endured in a loveless home. I always thought that was one of the things we had in common. Our childhoods were a mess."

Emily's disappearance and, I guess, the bourbon had enabled Sean—normally so British and reserved—to speak more freely than I'd ever heard him speak. Actually, before this, we'd never exchanged more than a few words, so maybe I mean more freely than I'd *imagined* him speaking. I wanted to say that my childhood had also been a mess. But a different kind of mess. It seemed neat and orderly when I was growing up. It was only later that I learned how messy it had been.

But I didn't say any of that. Not only because there were things about me that Sean didn't need to know, but also because I was afraid of seeming as if I was competing with him and Emily for who had the messiest childhood.

One afternoon, not long after, Sean called and asked if I'd pick up Nicky after school. The detectives had asked him to come into the station house in Canton. He was leaving work to get there, but he didn't know how soon he would get home.

It was six by the time he arrived at my house. He'd been questioned by two detectives, again by a man and a woman, Detectives Meany (Could I *believe* that was her name?) and Fortas. He said they seemed only marginally more competent than the troopers who had come to my house that night.

At least they'd taken the trouble to contact the police in Detroit, who'd visited Emily's mother and gotten the same response Sean did. No, Mrs. Nelson hadn't seen her. No, Mrs. Nelson had no idea where her daughter was. Actually, they'd mostly spoken with her caretaker. Mrs. Nelson was having one of her "bad days" and could hardly remember her daughter's name.

All during his conversation with the detectives, Sean said, he felt as if they were following instructions from a textbook: Interview with Husband of Missing Wife 101. Still, it had been grueling. They'd asked him the same questions over and over. Did he know where Emily might have gone? Was their marriage happy? Any arguments? Any reason she might have been dissatisfied? Any possibility that she might have been having an affair? Any history of alcoholism or substance abuse?

"I said she'd experimented with drugs, briefly. Like we all did, in our twenties. I smiled at them, like an idiot. But the joke was on me. They weren't smiling back. No fooling around in their twenties for them. It went on for hours. The dreary interrogation room. They'd go away, then come back. Just like all those BBC detective procedurals I always liked and Emily didn't. And yet . . . I never felt as if they really suspected me of anything. Quite honestly, Stephanie, I felt as if they didn't really believe that Emily is in trouble. I don't know why, how they dared to presume they knew anything about us. About my marriage. But I got the impression they thought that Emily just picked up and left. Ran away. They kept saying, 'In the absence of a body, in the absence of any sign of foul play . . .'

"And I kept wanting to shout at them: *What about Emily's absence?!*"

"What about it?" I'd been hanging on Sean's every word and at the same time thinking that his remark about Emily not liking the detective procedurals was the first complaint I'd ever heard him make about her. She'd had plenty of complaints about him. He didn't listen to her. He made her feel stupid. Every wife in our town could have said the same about her husband. I could have said it about Davis.

A few days later, Detective Meany phoned. I was glad Sean warned me about her name, so I didn't snicker or say something stupid when she introduced herself. She said I could come to their office any time that was convenient for me. They would work around my schedule. That was nice. But was I imagining the slightly contemptuous, ironic note in her voice when she said *schedule*?

I drove to the Canton station house after I dropped Miles at school. I'll confess I was nervous. It seemed to me that everyone looked at me as if *I'd* done something wrong.

Detective Meany and the much younger Detective Fortas asked me some of the same questions they'd asked Sean. They mainly wanted to know if Emily had been unhappy. All the time I was talking, Detective Fortas kept checking his phone, and twice he sent a text that I knew had nothing to do with me.

I said, "She loved her life. She would never do this. A devoted wife and mom has gone missing, and you guys are doing nothing!" Why was I the only one standing up for my friend? Why hadn't her husband said what I was saying? Maybe because Sean was British. He was too polite. Or maybe he felt that this wasn't his country. This one was on me.

"All right." Detective Fortas sounded as if he was doing me a big favor. "We'll see what we can find out."

That weekend, the detectives showed up at Sean and Emily's house and asked if they could look around. Fortunately, Nicky was with me— playing with Miles—so Sean let them in. He said their search was tentative, cursory. He almost felt as if they were real estate agents, or house hunters thinking of buying the place.

They asked for pictures of Emily. Sean collected some snapshots that he handed over. Luckily, he called me first, and I suggested that he not give them any photos with Nicky in them. He agreed that was a good idea.

Between the two of us, we gave the detectives a complete description—the tattoo on her wrist, her hair, her diamond and sapphire ring. Sean cried when he told them about the ring. I had to keep myself from mentioning her perfume. It didn't seem like something you'd say to a detective on the trail of a missing person. Lilacs? Lilies? Italian nuns? Thanks for your help, ma'am. We'll call you if we need you.

Finally Emily's company woke up from its deep fashionista slumber. Their silence wasn't surprising. She was the public voice of Dennis Nylon Inc., and without her, nobody there knew how to speak.

Dennis Nylon was her boss's seventies club-kid name. He'd risen from punk street fashion to become one of the world's most chic and expensive designers. Wearing his signature skinny black suit, the Dennis Nylon unisex suit, he appeared on the six o'clock news to say that his company was fully cooperating and supporting the efforts of the detectives to find Emily Nelson, their beloved employee and cherished friend. He wore a tie with the company logo, which (to me) was tacky. But maybe no one else noticed.

Actually, what he said was "to find out *what happened to Emily Nelson.*" That he seemed so sure that *something had happened to her* gave me the chills. At the bottom of the screen was a number to call if you had any information. It looked like an infomercial with a number to call if you wanted to order the tie. Still, his TV appearance did get the case more attention, at least for a while. I heard, from the detectives, that the company made a sizable contribution to the police department—to help inspire the detectives to go that extra mile.

Dennis Nylon Inc. volunteered to make flyers and put them up around the area. The company sent up a busload of fashion interns, and for an entire day, our town was swarming with underweight androgynous young people, all with asymmetrical haircuts and skinny suits, carrying armloads of flyers, staple guns for the telephone poles, and double-sided tape for shop windows. HAVE YOU SEEN THIS WOMAN? I wasn't sure *I* had, because the glam head shot of Emily—full makeup, blown-out hair, the little birthmark photoshopped out of existence— looked so little like my friend that I'm not sure *I* would have recognized her. Seeing the photos everywhere upset and comforted me at the same time—they were a constant, distressing reminder of our loss, along with a small consolation: at least someone was doing *something*.

Anyway, something or someone got Detectives Meany and Fortas off their asses long enough to consult the geeks who monitor CCTV footage. They followed Emily's trail to JFK, where she kissed Sean goodbye outside the terminal. But she never checked in for the San Francisco flight on which she was booked. Neither Sean nor I had any idea that she was planning to go out West.

It had been Sean's impression that she was on her way into Manhattan, that she'd caught a ride to JFK with his car service so she could keep him company and say goodbye. After that, he thought, she was going to work and then away on business. The people at Dennis Nylon knew nothing about a business trip to the West Coast.

The security cameras caught her leaving the terminal, then showing up at a rental car agency, where she leased a full-size four-door sedan. She took the first thing they offered, a white Kia. The cops questioned the rental agent, but he didn't remember anything except that Emily seemed very definite about not wanting a GPS. That hadn't seemed unusual. Lots of people don't want to pay extra for a navigational system when they already have one on their phones.

That sounded right to me. Emily has a great sense of direction. Whenever we went anywhere, even just to the town pool, I drove, and she mapped our route on her phone. She knew how to figure out if there was traffic, though there never was any traffic in our town, unless you were going to the train station at rush hour. Which I never am—and she was, five days a week.

Where was she going in that car? Why didn't she text or call me?

Good news: The genius detectives discovered that the car rental company had a corporate E-ZPass, and they tracked it to a toll station about two hundred miles west of Manhattan on the Pennsylvania Turnpike. Bad news: That's where they lost her. Emily seems to have left the thruway and taken smaller roads—and dumped her phone and vanished off the map. Into the dead zone.

Sean and I asked the detectives to alert the local and state police near where she was last seen, but they'd already done that. If she'd run away, she could be anywhere. There were endless dead zones on the smaller roads. They would have to see what new leads came in.

Dead zones. Just the words gave me the creeps.

The next surprise was that Emily had withdrawn two thousand dollars in cash from the bank. That certainly suggested that she was planning some sort of trip.

You can't get that much from an ATM, at least not in our town. The police said that the closed-circuit camera footage from the bank showed her at the teller's window—alone. On several successive days. It seemed possible (to paranoid me) that a criminal or carjacker was waiting for her outside, threatening to hurt her or her family if she signaled for help. I could never understand why the cops never seemed to take this scenario seriously. Didn't they watch the news? Innocent moms were being abducted from mall parking lots practically every day.

Sean told his company that he couldn't travel until his wife was found. He offered to go on unpaid leave. But they understood, and they put him on half-time. He'd be assigned to a local project so that he could work from home with only occasional trips from Connecticut into the city.

Sean was *so there* for Nicky. So caring and so fully present that it was beautiful to see. He brought Nicky to school every morning and picked him up every afternoon. He had frequent conferences with Mrs. Kerry, in part to keep her updated on the progress of the investigation, though probably she already knew everything—or at least a lot—about it.

At first there was some publicity, thanks (I think mostly) to Dennis Nylon. Connecticut mom disappears! Sean, the brave, anguished husband, went on TV and asked anyone who might have seen Emily to please contact the authorities. He was entirely convincing, and I'm sure everyone believed him. But it was only the local news, and already our story had stepped down from the attention-grabbing segment starring Dennis Nylon.

When the detectives found out that Emily had rented a car and made a sizable bank withdrawal, the case seemed even more like a story about a runaway wife. The media interest gradually leaked away, and the reporters moved on. The husband's alibi checked out. There were no new clues, no leads, no evidence, and Emily was still missing.

If Nicky hasn't fallen apart, it's because of us. Sean and I work together. Nicky and Miles have lots of playdates. I gave Sean the name of the therapist to whom I took Miles after his dad and uncle died, when Miles was constantly hiding from me in public places so I couldn't find him, and then laughing when I went crazy with worry. The therapist had said that lots of children played that game. He said children are always testing us. That's how they learn. I shouldn't blame it on the tragic loss of Miles's dad and uncle, though obviously that had been extremely traumatic.

The doctor said that I should calmly ask Miles to stop hiding, and he would. He said that Miles had a conscience. I liked hearing that, just as I like the feeling I have now: that Sean and I are doing everything we can to make this as easy as possible on Nicky. Not that it could *ever* be easy.

Miles had stopped hiding, and now I tell myself that Nicky will stay strong. We'll get through this together.

We've kept Nicky away from the reporters. His photo never appeared with the pictures of Emily and Sean. He stayed at my house during those first days when his dad had interviews with media people and meetings with the detectives.

The rental car was never located. Sean had to fill out a ton of paper-work to get Emily declared a missing person, which voided the rental agreement. I think he got help from the lawyers at his firm.

Sean and I are a team. Nicky is our project. We have long talks when Sean brings Nicky to play with Miles, and when we meet outside school in the afternoon. I give Sean support and encouragement for insisting that the police keep searching for Emily. We both agree that it's way too early to tell Nicky that his mother might be dead—or even to suggest it. Nicky will ask when he wants to know, and we will tell him that there is still hope.

Until there isn't.

Before Emily disappeared, I hadn't spent any time with Sean. Maybe if Davis had lived, we might have been couple-friends. We might have invited them over for dinner. But Davis had been dead for two years by the time I met Emily. Sean always seemed to be at work or traveling for business, so Emily and I had a pure mom friendship.

Though it's hard for me to believe now, I hadn't much liked Sean. I guess I saw him as a snobby upper-class British frat boy, a wannabe master of the universe. Tall, handsome, entitled, self-assured—totally not my type. He works in the international real estate department of a major Wall Street investment firm. Though I'm still not entirely sure what his job involves.

It's always a blessing when you find out that someone is a much nicer person than you'd thought. I wish I could have found that out about Sean without Emily having had to disappear.

Emily used to complain about him. She said he was never home, he left all the childcare to her, he didn't respect her intelligence, he criti-cized her, he made her feel flaky and irresponsible, he didn't appreci-ate how much she did, he undervalued her contribution to the family, not only in terms of childcare but financially too. He had no respect for what she did at her job. He thought the fashion industry was nothing more than a lucrative bit of fluff. She liked books, and he liked TV.

Sometimes (and Emily would only say this after the second glass of wine) she thought that Sean wasn't nearly as smart as he thought he was. Not nearly as smart as *she* thought he was when they met.

She did say that sex with Sean was great. Life-changingly great. She said that the sex made everything else seem less important. Life-changing sex was another thing that I tried not to envy about my best friend's perfect life.

Anyway, Emily said Sean wasn't cheating on her or drinking or gambling or being violent or doing any of the things that really terrible husbands do. The truth is, I liked it when Emily grumbled about her marriage. I loved Davis with all my heart and soul. I still miss him every day. But it wasn't as if we hadn't had issues. Every marriage does, and the pressures and demands of raising a small child certainly don't help.

Davis often made *me* feel stupid, even when I was sure, or almost sure, that he didn't mean to. He knew so much about architecture and design, and he had so many *opinions*. It got to the point where, when we went into a store, I was afraid to say I liked this or didn't like that for fear of the withering look he'd give me (unconsciously, I knew) when he didn't agree. Which was almost always. It got to be sort of a bore.

But as I've blogged about so many times, being a widow means that unless you are in a support group—which I never have been, though I understand why so many women find them helpful—none of the married women I meet will even mention her husband, not even to complain. I guess they're afraid of making me feel worse because I don't have a husband to complain about. As if I needed to hear a woman gripe about her husband's snoring to make me miss Davis.

I hadn't liked my phone conversation with Sean when I'd reached him in England early on, when Emily hadn't come to get Nicky. He'd sounded not only sleepy but annoyed. Well, sorry if your wife has disappeared. Sorry I woke you. He didn't seem to know who I was, though he pretended in that phony-polite British way. Oh, Stephanie, yes, of course.

I got the feeling that Sean didn't remember meeting me, which was not very flattering. I've blogged about how many people (mostly, but *not only,* men) can't tell one mom from another, maybe because the only thing they see is the stroller. When Sean said that Emily had planned to be away for a few days on business, he'd made it sound as if I was the flaky one.

Sean didn't take Emily's disappearance seriously until he got home from England and she wasn't there. And that's when he drove right over. I've blogged about how seeing him and Nicky in my house made Emily's absence finally seem real.

But I *definitely did not* blog about how Sean was so much taller and better looking and more attractive than I remembered. To be honest, I felt disloyal for even noticing.

He said he'd thought she'd been in Minnesota, but now he wondered if she'd said she was going to Milwaukee.

"I'm sorry, I'm English," Sean said. Meaning he couldn't be expected to tell one Midwestern location starting with an *M* from another? I got the sense that he pulled that "Sorry, I'm English" routine whenever he hadn't been paying attention. His wife was in some Midwestern "M" place, but he didn't know which one.

Which is all to say that I wasn't predisposed to like him. But since Emily disappeared, I've begun to sympathize with and respect him. It feels good to talk about Nicky. I like knowing that Sean trusts me enough to ask what *I* think about how his son is doing, about what we should tell Nicky. It's a compliment because it must mean he admires how I'm raising Miles.

There's something sexy about being in a state of perfect harmony and understanding with an extremely handsome single dad. What makes it less sexy is that this is not some random dad but the husband of my disappeared best friend.

If I want to be able to live with myself, if I want to keep thinking of myself as a decent human being and not a monster, I will have to do everything possible to ignore, to resist, to not even acknowledge the spark of *something* between us. Which is also sexy, in its way. So there's a dilemma, one of those things you don't blog about—not if you're in your right mind.

I guess that's why I keep thinking about the day Chris showed up at my mom's, why being around Sean reminds me of the day my half brother entered my life. There's that same jolt of attraction to someone inappropriate. Someone *very* inappropriate. That tingle of pure excitement.

I'd been attracted to the guy in my parents' wedding photo. And now I was drawn to the husband of my friend. I wouldn't have picked these men, but there it is. Does that make me a pervert or a criminal? Or simply a bad person?

9

STEPHANIE'S BLOG

ONE NEWS FLASH AFTER ANOTHER

Hi, moms!

First of all, I want to thank moms everywhere for your words of sympathy, love, and support. It's in times of crisis like this that we have each other's back and make our voices heard. The quiet moms who have been reading the blog and clicking through the comment threads without posting are now writing to say that their prayers are with me and Sean, Nicky, and Miles. In this sad time, it would seem gross and vulgar to tell you how many distinct hits on the site I've gotten in the last weeks.

Meanwhile I feel like the bad friend who flakes out when you need her or when you're worried about her and you want to know what's happening. I haven't posted in a while, though I know how concerned you've been. But my life has been in chaos as I've struggled to keep up the search for my friend and to work alongside her husband to make sure that their little boy feels as safe as he can under the circumstances.

I know from your messages that many of you were following Emily's story when it was in the news. Sean and I drew the line at trying to interest one of those creepy TV "investigative reports." It would be too traumatic for

Nicky in case he ever found it on YouTube. Still, we know those shows have sometimes located a missing person.

Some of you may be thinking that I am writing this now because of what you may have been reading lately in the tabloids or seeing on TV. I mean now that a new element (money!) has made the authorities more interested in our case than they were when it was just a story about a beautiful wife and mother who left for work one day and never came home.

As some of you have probably heard, just one month before Emily's disappearance, a two-million-dollar life insurance policy was taken out in her name, payable to Sean.

Moms, do you see what's happening here? Real life is starting to sound like one of those ripped-from-the-headlines TV shows, a script you probably can't get made anymore because it's been done too often. Husband takes out mega-insurance policy. Wife disappears.

Before they found out about the policy, the police questioned Sean. Briefly. Standard procedure. The husband is always the prime suspect, as everyone who owns a television knows. But his alibi checked out completely.

He'd been in England, where practically every moment of your day is monitored and recorded on CCTV. His snooty hotel was reluctant to cooperate, but when someone from the embassy there insisted, they surrendered the footage that showed Sean entering and leaving his hotel room. On the night Emily vanished, there's footage of Sean having a drink in the hotel bar with a couple of the real estate developers he'd gone to the UK to meet. And then he went off to bed. Alone.

That Emily's life insurance policy took so long to surface shows you the level of efficiency we are dealing with here, which you moms already know if you have ever tried to file a health insurance claim or register your child for pre-K. When the policy finally came to light, the cops came back for another (suspicious) look at Sean.

The truth is that the policy slipped Sean's mind because he'd been under such stress. Which in my opinion *proves* he's innocent. What kind of cold-blooded wife killer takes out a policy and then forgets about it? *Seriously?* But the police have it backward. They believe this suggests that he *is* guilty, that he's pretending to have forgotten because the truth looks bad. So what are they thinking? That Sean took out the policy and hired someone to kill his wife? That he and I are in this together?

None of that happened.

Perhaps you moms will forgive me for not having posted for so long now that you know how much has been going on in my life, starting with this unfortunate and maddening development. The police have twice picked up Sean and held him without charging him. Is there justice in this country? Don't we have laws against this? Even when you know your rights and have enough money and an excellent lawyer, as Sean does, and a Wall Street firm behind you—even that isn't enough to scare some old-fashioned common sense into these small-town detectives.

Each time Sean is taken down to the police station, Nicky—who has been a brave little soldier until now—becomes nearly inconsolable, and I have to drive over to their house, whatever the hour of the day or night, and pick him up and bring him home and rock him to sleep on my lap and put him in Miles's bunk bed. Sometimes I stand in the doorway of Miles's room and watch them sleep and listen to their sweet, snuffly snoring, and I think how angelic our children are, how much they trust us, and how—try as we might—there's no way we can protect them from the horrors that life may have in store for them.

Anyhow, this seems like a good moment to get back to blogging and tell the moms community that an innocent man is being persecuted and harassed. It's hard for me to explain how I know he is innocent. But I do. I know it with every cell of my body. During this anxious time that Emily has been gone, Sean and I have worked together to maintain our morale, to keep up the search, and most importantly to bolster the spirits of a courageous little boy.

You moms will understand that this hasn't been easy for Miles. Knowing that his best friend's mother could vanish into thin air has (naturally!) made him a little clingy. He's reluctant to be left for a sleepover with Nicky. But once he gets past the separation anxiety, he loves it.

Several times I've had to drive away from Emily's house (I still think of it that way) with my child's sobs echoing in my ears. But I know Miles will be fine. He'll have fun. And the reason I know this is because of the closeness and trust I have felt, over these difficult weeks, with Nicky's dad. Do you think I would leave my child with a credible suspect in a murder investigation?

Anyhow, there's been no murder. What keeps destroying the police's nonexistent case is the absence of a body or any evidence of foul play. First Emily was driving in Pennsylvania; then she wasn't. There's no indication that she didn't wake up one day and decide she'd had enough of motherhood, enough of the fashion industry, of Connecticut, of Sean. Of the whole package. Even Nicky. It's possible that she took off to start a new life under an assumed name. The cops say it happens all the time.

This wasn't the friend I thought knew! But if Sean has turned out to be the opposite of what I'd thought, couldn't Emily as well? It's crazy-making to find out that you could have been so wrong about someone. It's hard to know what to feel. Should I be angry at her? At myself? Should I feel betrayed? Tricked? Honestly, I just feel very sad.

To end this post on a less gloomy note, I'm linking to the post in which I talk about my friendship with Emily. I wrote it when I was still calling her E. But by now you know who I mean, even as I begin to think that maybe I never really knew who she was or what I meant to her. Or whether she really was my best friend, after all.

It's going to make me cry to read this.

But I'm posting it anyway.

Love,

Stephanie

10

STEPHANIE'S BLOG

(BLOG POST LINK)

FRIENDS FOR LIFE

What is it that keeps us moms from becoming true friends? Do we resent other moms because we always wind up talking about our kids, as if we no longer have our own needs and hopes and desires? Do other mothers make us feel guilty for thinking about anything besides our kids? Or are we too competitive with other moms? How can we be friends with someone who tells us that her nine-month-old is walking when our ten-month-old hasn't started to crawl?

I won't lie about how lonely I was, staying home and taking care of my son. Until I had Miles, we lived in the city. I had a job at a woman's magazine writing copy about new designs in furniture and decor, about household hints and shortcuts, storage tricks, spot removal, that sort of thing. Now that I *have* a household, I can't remember one helpful hint.

My husband insisted that the city was no place to raise a child. It took a lot of persuading, but in the end I saw his point. I thought that living in the suburbs—the country, actually—would be fun, and it has been. The minute my husband saw our house, he fell in love with it, though I couldn't see the potential, at first. But again, he convinced me, and now I love it more than I can say.

I went through a bit of a crazy time right after we moved. I forgot who I was. The only thing I cared about was being a superwife and supermom. I was living a nightmare from the 1950s. I made all my own baby food from scratch. I cooked elaborate dinners for my husband that he was too tired to eat when he got home from work, or else he was too full because he'd been taken to some fancy lunch while I snacked on the leftovers from last night's dinner. And though I tried to be understanding and patient, we'd bicker.

As soon as my son was old enough, I enrolled him in all sorts of classes and programs. Toddler yoga. Baby dance. Swimming lessons. I was doing it so he would learn and have fun and meet other kids. But I also wanted to meet other moms, make friends, find caring women who were having the same mixed feelings, the same rewards and challenges, that I was.

But I could never get anything going with the Connecticut moms. They all seemed to have closed ranks, circled the wagons, and turned back into the mean girls they'd been in junior high. When I tried to start conversations, they'd look at each other and practically roll their eyes. They'd stare at me just long enough to be polite, then go back to talking to each other.

That's why I started this blog—to reach out to other women who feel isolated, mothers everywhere dealing with the demands of parenting. Some of you may find it strange that a mom who can't make friends in the real world would start a blog and give advice and share with friends in the virtual world. But what helped me get past my self-doubt was realizing that I couldn't be the only mom feeling friendless and alone.

Being a widow makes everything—including motherhood—harder. My husband is gone. He's the first thing I think of when I wake up in the morning, the last thing I think of before I go to bed. Wait—no, not the first thing. There are always a few blissful seconds when I wake up and forget and feel almost okay—and then I notice that his side of the bed is empty.

For months after the accident, I thought I was going to die of grief. And maybe I would have done something stupid—self-harming and irreversible—if I hadn't had my little boy throwing me the life preserver of his love, keeping me from going under.

My brother was gone too, so I couldn't rely on him. And that was a whole other kind of sorrow. I became an expert on the different varieties of pain.

My mother had died, not long after my dad. And I didn't want to go like she did: dead of a broken heart. There was no one I could talk to. My friends in the city had moved on with their own lives, and I sometimes thought they looked down on me for getting married and having a child— for caving in and moving to the suburbs.

Everyone in our town knew about the accident that killed my husband and brother. I would have gained fifty pounds if I'd eaten all the casseroles and sandwich platters my neighbors brought over, all the cakes they left on my doorstep. But after a while, it was as if some kind of rebound effect set in. People began to avoid me, as if tragedy was contagious.

I got through it. Blogging helped a lot, as did the wonderful responses I got from moms all over the country and eventually the world: smart, brave, together women. I even heard from a few widows, and we poured our hearts out online. What did moms do before the internet?

And then, a few months after my son started pre-K, I met E.

It was a drizzly, unseasonably warm Friday afternoon in October. We'd come to pick up the kids at school. I'd forgotten my umbrella and was waiting in the rain—unlike the other moms, who wouldn't get out of their cars if they thought a cloud might threaten their salon blowouts. E. beckoned me over to where she was standing, under the oak tree where she always waited for her son on Fridays. She had a huge umbrella, more than big enough to keep the two of us dry. It was a very distinctive umbrella, clear plastic over a layer of some kind of liquid in which happy yellow cartoon ducks swam around.

I'd seen her there before. I'd noticed because she always looked more natural and real than a woman you'd expect to be wearing such obviously expensive clothes.

She said her name was E. before she said that she was N.'s mom. Her son was in school with my son; they were friends. So right away we had that in common. The boys had worked that out.

Unlike the other shifty-eyed mothers, she looked straight at me. And I felt that she *saw* me.

I said, "Maybe I should blog about how we should always remember to bring an umbrella." I could see that she was interested in the fact that I blogged.

She said, "Take this one. Keep it. It was a one-off. A prototype. My boss had it made by the franchise people, and then he didn't like it and canceled the order."

"I couldn't," I said. "Especially if it's the only one like it."

"Please," she said. "Take it. Look . . . are you busy this afternoon? Why don't you come to our place. It's nearby. The boys can play. I can make them hot chocolate. We could have a glass of wine. My husband won't be home for a couple of hours."

I followed her in my car to her house, a few miles from school. Her home looked like a house in a magazine, though much more elegant and stylish than the houses in the magazine I used to work for. It was a big old Georgian, rather grand, and filled with museum-quality mid-century modern furniture. On the walls were prints and paintings by famous artists.

Over the mantel was a photograph of two twin girls. I won't say who the artist was because I never drop household names on this blog. I thought it was a strange choice to have at the center of your living room. But E. was proud of it, and it was way more interesting than anything I'd seen in our town. For a house in which a small child lived, the place was extremely neat, almost like a stage set. I was relieved when I saw that her son's room was just as messy as my son's room.

E. said that her housecleaner, M., was responsible for keeping things in such good shape. E. said she didn't know what she'd do without her.

E.'s home-decorating choices would have pleased my late husband. Every knife and fork, every glass, every place mat and napkin had been selected with thought and care. I marvel at people like that. How they know exactly what to buy and how to make their homes so perfect. My husband had made those decisions for us, and I'd been glad to let him. My mom would have had plastic slipcovers over the couches, like *her* mom had, if my dad and I hadn't teased her.

The boys went off to play. E. and I opened a bottle of wine, and we began the conversation that has lasted throughout our friendship.

She'd moved here a year ago. Her husband, who is British, works on Wall Street. She and her husband and son used to live on the Upper East Side. But she couldn't stand the other moms, the playdates, the constant competition over who had more money and fancier clothes and who vacationed in more exclusive ski resorts and Caribbean islands. She and her husband hoped that life would be less stressful for them and healthier for their son in the country. And they were right. I think.

When she asked what my husband did and saw the look on my face, she said—before I had to say a word—"Oh, I'm so sorry!" She could tell that something tragic must have occurred, but she'd moved here too recently to have heard about the accident. So I felt that I was starting fresh and could choose when and where and what I wanted to say about my family's catastrophe.

It was just before Thanksgiving when I told her. E. and I were watching the kids cut out cardboard turkeys and paste paper feathers on them when I told her my tragic story. She began to cry for my loss—tears of sympathy and grief. She told me she wished she could invite me over for Thanksgiving, but they were using her son's vacation time to visit her husband's mother in England.

"That's okay," I said. "Miles and I will still be here when you get back."

And that's how it's been ever since. I admire E. for working hard and being a fabulous mother and trying to be a good wife and a good friend—and for doing it all not only with grace but also with glamour. And I know she admires my blog. I haven't had a friend like this since I was in grade school. Only some people—the lucky ones—have a gift for friendship, and it turns out we both do. We finish each other's sentences and laugh at the same jokes. We like the same Fred Astaire and Ginger Rogers movies. I read, or try to read, the detective stories she loves—when they aren't too scary. My whole life seems brighter. I have more patience with myself and my son when I can look forward to sharing the everyday satisfactions and stresses with another grown-up.

On the surface we must seem very different. E. has a stylish, expensive haircut. I get my hair cut by a lovely young woman in town who used to work in the city, but sometimes I go between haircuts so long that my hair looks as if I cut it myself. E. dresses in designer clothes, even on weekends. Whereas I am more likely to order comfy stuff—long skirts and tunics—online. Yet underneath all that, on a much deeper level, E. and I are very much the same.

Naturally, she reads my blog, and she's full of praise for my writing. For the bravery and generosity of what I am willing to share about the amazing adventure of motherhood. I tell her things I never even told my husband. It's such a great feeling: letting go, after you've been keeping things bottled up inside for so long. To know that there is someone who will understand and not judge.

Having a friend like E. has restored my faith in our superpowers: the ability we moms have to be there for each other. We can be friends. Real friends.

And so I'd like to dedicate this blog to my best friend, E.

So here's to you, E.

Love,

Stephanie

11

STEPHANIE

When I put up the link to my blog post about becoming friends with Emily, I tried not to read it. But I couldn't help myself. And just as I'd feared, it made me cry.

There was one little thing I remember now that I hadn't paid attention to back then. I remember Emily saying that the umbrella she gave me—the umbrella with the ducks, which I've now put away in a back closet because the reminder of those early days is so painful—was one of a kind. But when I got to her house that afternoon, I noticed, in the front hall, an umbrella stand in which there were a dozen duck umbrellas. It looked almost like an art piece. Of course I didn't ask her about it at the time—we'd just met. And then I forgot about it. But now it makes me wonder. Was I *already* misunderstanding her, hearing her wrong? Was she lying about the umbrella? But why would she tell a lie that would be exposed the minute I walked in the door?

Anyway, that was the least of the things that bothered me. Reading the post, I felt horribly guilty. Because I was beginning—just beginning—to have feelings for Emily's husband.

There is that period of time when you're pretty sure you're going to have sex with someone, though you haven't yet. Everything is clogged with desire. Everything feels like that hot, thick air that weighs so heavily on your skin on the swampiest day of summer. Especially when it's someone whom, for lots of good reasons, you're not supposed to have sex with.

Maybe one problem with my marriage was that we never had that sense of anticipation, that gradual buildup of desire. Someday I will tell Miles all the reasons not to have sex on the first date. Like his mom and dad did. Though I won't go into the specifics.

My first date with Davis wasn't even a date. It was supposed to be an interview. We met in a coffee shop in Tribeca, near Davis's studio. His firm was called Davis Cook Ward, which was his name, all three of them. His architecture and design career was going extremely well. He designed houses for rich people and, for fun, beautiful but affordable garden furniture from recycled materials. He'd designed some wooden furniture that was going to be featured in the magazine I worked for. We had coffee, then lunch. Then we went to his loft, where we stayed until the next morning, when I had to go back to my East Village apartment and get changed and go to the office.

My relationship with Davis was comfortable. It was fun. It was easy. But there was never a moment when I felt that I would die if I couldn't have him. Maybe because I'd already had him. The long, slow, delicious waiting had ended before it began.

Or maybe my problem was that it was safe. Maybe I need that thrill of the forbidden, the taboo, that sense of doing something that I know is wrong.

One evening Sean came to pick up Nicky and stayed for dinner. During dinner, a violent thunderstorm began. I invited Sean to spend the night in the guest room instead of going out in the weather. And he agreed.

Sean and I talked until it was so late and we were so tired that our eyes were closing. We exchanged a freighted but chaste little peck on the cheek. He went to his room, and I went to mine. As soon as I got into bed, I was wide awake. The thought of him there in the dark, in my house, was almost like having sex. I masturbated, thinking about him. I wondered if he was doing it too, thinking about me.

Just knowing he was a few rooms away was like phone sex without a phone. It took every ounce of self-control not to go to his room. Meanwhile I was still telling myself that nothing was going to happen, that I wasn't the sort of person who sleeps with the husband of her disappeared best friend.

I knew that even if we could do it without anyone finding out, we would feel so guilty that the next time we saw the police, they would pick up on it and maybe mistake it for guilt about something else. I knew this was ridiculous, but still . . .

But there it is: desire in the air. Everything is soaked in it, even though I know that Sean and I are both thinking: your wife's best friend, your best friend's husband. Emily loves and trusts us. What kind of people are we? And the fact that we both feel that guilt and desire, and know the other is feeling it, makes everything hotter—and more confusing.

Many nights now Sean and Nicky come for dinner and stay late. Nicky falls asleep in Miles's room, and Sean carries him out to the car and drives him home. Sean and I have been staying up, drinking brandy, and talking, and amid all the sexual tension, or maybe *because* of it, Sean has been opening up. He's told me about his horrid childhood, his alcoholic upper-class British mother, whom his college-professor father left for a colleague when Sean was twelve and who has come way down in the world but not in her social ambitions and her illusions about herself.

I talk a lot about Davis and Miles. I don't mention my blog. It's interesting to me that I so wanted Emily to respect and admire my blog, but I don't want Sean to even read it. I'm proud of what I write. But I avoid the subject. Maybe I don't want Sean thinking I'm just another over-involved supermom with a laptop. He makes fun of mothers who project that semi-aggressive competence and always have the latest baby equipment. He calls them Captain Mom. I don't want him to see me as another Captain Mom. Maybe I worry he'll compare me unfavorably with Emily and her glamorous career in fashion.

We talk a lot about Emily. He's told me how they met, which—oddly, now that I think about it—never came up when Emily was talking about her life. Usually you exchange those stories early on in a friendship. Her fashion company and his investment firm were cochairing a benefit for a relief organization that works to bring clean water to women in Africa. The dinner was at the Museum of Natural History, which—with the flowers and candles and the mood lighting—was terribly romantic.

Emily introduced the person who introduced the person who introduced her boss, Dennis Nylon. And when Sean saw her on the podium, in a simple but stunning black evening dress, and he saw—on the giant screen monitors around the room—the tears in her eyes when she spoke about the charity and about the hard lives of the women they were helping, he decided then and there that he was going to marry her.

It made perfect sense to me. I knew how moving Emily's tears could be. I'd seen her cry for me and my husband and my brother. Sean's account of their meeting and courtship was one of those beautiful stories that I wish I could tell about *my* own life, my own marriage.

Talking about Emily helps us both. It makes us feel more hopeful about the possibility that she is still alive and will be found. And it defuses the tension between us, as if she were actually there, reminding us that she's the person we love—and not each other.

One night Sean told me that there were a few things about Emily that I probably didn't know. Things she'd kept secret. I held my breath because I still believed—even though it seemed clear now that I was wrong—that I knew everything about her. Or almost everything.

It turned out that she'd been abused by her grandfather when she was a little girl. Her parents never admitted it, which was part of the reason she'd been estranged from them. Also (possibly as a result) she'd had a drinking problem during her twenties; she'd also had a brief flirtation with painkillers and Xanax back then and spent a month in rehab. But she'd been clean ever since.

I was shocked, not by what he told me but by the fact that I hadn't known. Was this what she'd meant when she talked about the "wild days" when she got her tattoo? In all the conversations and confidences we'd shared, why had those traumatic things not come up? I'd trusted her with secrets I'd never told anyone. Why hadn't she trusted me?

I'd never seen any evidence of the problems Sean described. She always drank sensibly around me. Even after they beat their addictions, people with drinking problems are always weird around alcohol. And Emily wasn't. Once, at her house on a Friday afternoon, I almost went for a third glass of wine, and she gently reminded me that I had to drive Miles home.

But every day was making it more obvious that unless she'd been injured or killed, she'd left us on purpose. She wasn't the person Sean thought she was, the person *I* thought she was.

Where was she going in the rental car headed west? Whom was she going to see? Was there someone in her past? Someone she'd recently met? Some dark mystery she needed to solve, some unfinished business?

I read the Patricia Highsmith novel that Emily left when she disappeared. It's about a man who is trying to kill his son-in-law, in Rome and in Venice, because his daughter has committed suicide and he blames his son-in-law. Nobody ever knows why the girl killed herself, though the husband gives some reasons that don't make sense. Something about her loving sex or hating sex and being too much of a romantic to live in the real world. I couldn't figure it out, and even though we know the grieving husband is innocent, there were moments when I didn't blame the father-in-law for nursing his smoldering, deadly rage. I wondered if the book was a message from Emily, a hint that she planned to kill herself and that no one would ever know why.

In which case we could only wait for her body to turn up. In the

Highsmith novel, the murderous father-in-law is always expecting his son-in-law's body to wash up by the side of a canal. But the young wife who kills herself does it in the bathtub. There's a body and blood—no question about what happened. But with Emily, there were mysteries leading to more mysteries, questions upon questions.

I think about Sean all the time. I put on makeup and my most attractive outfits (I try to keep it subtle) whenever I know he's coming over with Nicky. I always offer to collect Nicky from school, in theory so Sean can get some work done but in truth so I'll have an excuse to see him. I love his charm, his attention, his easy natural laugh. I've always had a weakness for men with beautiful smiles.

Sean has begun staying for dinner more often. I've found out what foods he prefers. Steaks and roasts mainly. After all, he's British. I've learned to make them the way he likes. Burned. Miles couldn't have been more delighted when I stopped trying to persuade him to eat vegetarian meals.

I've been eating red meat for the first time since Chris and Davis died. I'm amazed (and a little disappointed in myself) by how much I still love that rich, salty, juicy, bloody taste. And I've started to associate that delicious taste with being around Sean. I feel almost as if we're vampires on a sexy TV series where the undead with their fangs and perfect bodies zoom across the screen to have sex.

I'd stopped eating meat for personal and ethical reasons, but I can hardly expect to get credit for being ethical about animals when I'm being so unethical about humans: wanting to sleep with the husband of my best friend.

I could never blog about this. Never. The moms would never forgive me. They need to think of me as a loving mother who would never want an animal to be hurt for my sake but who isn't so rigid that I won't make hamburgers if that's all the kids will eat. Some of them might disapprove if I stopped being a vegetarian. But they would never *ever* forgive me for putting myself to sleep at night by having sexual fantasies about my friend's husband. They would know what a terrible person I am, and they would send out a firestorm of furious hating posts, which I would deserve. And when they finished venting their anger at me, they would stop reading my blog.

Most nights, Sean and I drink wine with dinner. I've started buying good wine, the best I can afford, because it makes everything so much more elegant and mellow. In case I ever doubted Sean about Emily having had a drinking problem, all I have to do is watch the way he scrutinizes me whenever I drink. I sip my wine, and I always make sure to leave a few drops in my second glass. Do I secretly want to let him know that life with me would be better than it was with Emily?

Usually Sean stays and helps me clean up. The kitchen is steamy and warm, and the windows fog up, hiding us from the world out-side, creating a private space where we feel safe and alone, shut off and protected from everyone and everything. I'd never realized how sexy doing the dishes could be.

Sometimes the tension is almost overwhelming. On those nights when Sean picks up Nicky before dinner and goes home—he says he's been learning to cook, but I suspect that they grab a pizza on the way—I'm glad to take a break. It's a relief when it's just Miles and me, having our meal in peace.

Miles seems to like his new life. He enjoys hanging out with Nicky's dad, and after all this time, I think it's good for him to have a man—a father figure, even if it's his friend's father—around the house.

When Miles was a baby, I used to stare into his eyes all the time, but you can't do that with a five-year-old. So I've taken to staring at Miles when he is asleep and noticing (as everybody says) how much he looks like me. But what they don't say is that he's a million times more beautiful than I am.

And so my attraction to Sean has become another secret I can't tell anyone. Sometimes when I'm missing Emily, I think I could tell *her*.

Then I realize that she would be the last person I could tell about being infatuated with her husband.

It only makes me feel more lonely, more desperate to see Sean. And to see Emily. A vicious circle, as they say. Though the truth is that the more I long to see Sean, the more my desire to see Emily starts to fade.

Once, when Sean left his iPod on my kitchen counter, I checked his playlist and bought CDs of his favorite music—mostly Bach and the White Stripes and old-school British bands like the Clash—even though my own taste runs to Ani DiFranco and Whitney Houston. When he and Nicky are around, I play his music instead of mine. When the kids are asleep in Miles's room, we binge on TV series like *Breaking Bad*. Sean already watched all five seasons, but he wants me to see it with him. It would have been way too violent for me to think about watching before I met him, but it makes me happy to know that there is something he cares about and wants to share with me.

Sean has talked about how, when he was growing up in the UK, his ideas about the United States came entirely from Charles Bronson films and TV series like *That '70s Show*. And now he sometimes wonders if there are kids like him in other countries who think the US is still the Wild West, full of high school science teachers batching meth in RVs and killing Mexican drug lords. I stare at him, rapt with interest. And it isn't fake. I think what he says is practically the most fascinating thing I've ever heard anyone say.

When he told me that he'd watched the series before, I tried not to imagine him watching it with Emily. I try never to think about Sean saying the same things to her that he says to me. I try not to wonder if she thought what he said was as interesting as I think it is. It was Emily who read books, Sean who watched TV. I try not to think about her complaining that he made her feel stupid. I try to concentrate on the fact that he wants *me* to see it. I've begun to think that he cares about me as more than just as a friend, or a friend of his wife's, or his son's best friend's mom.

Sometimes I try not to think about Emily, and sometimes I try not to think about anything *but* Emily, as if thinking about her could work magic. One day she will simply show up, and everything will go back to how it used to be. Except that I may have fallen in love with her husband.

None of this makes me feel good about myself, but it does make me strangely happy. I feel as if I'm walking around on my own little cloud or swimming in my own little pool of warmth and light and heat, though the winter is coming on, and the weather has been awful.

I don't know what's worse. The disloyalty, I guess. Or maybe the most shameful part is that I've turned my son into a little spy. When Miles comes home from Nicky's, I ask, fake-casually, if Nicky's dad said anything about me. Is Alison still working for them? Are she and Nicky's dad friendly? Does Sean talk a lot on the phone?

Miles says he never sees Alison. He doesn't think that Alison is Nicky's nanny anymore now that Nicky's dad is home all the time and his mom is gone.

Poor Miles.

One night, putting him to bed, I said, "Honey, do you want to talk about Nicky's mom being gone? I mean, how you feel about it—"

"No, thanks," he said. "It just makes me sad. Everyone is sad. Especially Nicky."

Tears welled up in my eyes, and I was glad that, in the glow from the night-light, Miles couldn't see me well enough to notice.

I said, "We're all really, *really* sad. But sadness is a part of life. Sometimes it can't be avoided."

"I know, Mom," said my wise, beautiful child. The next thing I knew, he was fast asleep.

One evening, when Miles and I were alone at dinner, Miles said, "Last night, when I stayed over at Nicky's, his dad was talking about you."

"What did he say?" I tried to keep my voice level.

"He said I was lucky to have such a nice, generous mom."

"Was that all? Did Nicky's dad say anything else?"

"That was it," said Miles.

It wasn't so much what he said—*nice* and *generous* were compliments, but maybe not what I wanted to hear—that made me happy. It was the fact that Sean *wanted* to talk about me, that he'd talked about me to my son. He was thinking about me when I wasn't there.

I feel as if I'm betraying everyone. Emily especially, but also myself.

Sean and I haven't even done anything yet! But I already feel guilty. If that's not a sign that I have a conscience, what is? I've blogged about how women in general and moms in particular are always made to feel guilty, but now it's occurring to me, as it has in the past, that there might be times when we *should* feel guilty. *I* should, anyway.

Another thing I feel guilty about is that I never felt this same crazy, passionate, out-of-my-head yearning for my husband. Sex with Davis was good. It wasn't great. It was just what I needed. Davis was what I needed: a truly nice guy. I'd been having a rocky time. A nice guy like Davis didn't need to know about my problems in the past, and I never felt the need to tell him. Being with him was comfortable. I used to think, This is like going home. This is how going home is supposed to feel. And being with Davis answered a lot of unresolved questions for me—questions about my future. Or so I thought at the time.

I got pregnant with Miles by accident. But so does everyone, right? I think it happened after a wedding that was much more romantic than ours.

Davis and I got married at City Hall when his office was on lunch break. His assistants, Evan and Anita, were our witnesses, and afterward we went out for lunch to the best dumpling house in Chinatown. Davis knew about things like that—where to get the best dumplings.

We'd been very pleased with ourselves, how hip and cool we'd been to get married in such an offhand, casual way, as if it was nothing. Just another day. But not long after that, Evan and Anita had a big, fancy wedding outdoors on an estate in Dutchess County. Under a bower of white roses, in a rolling meadow leading down to the Hudson River.

It was so gorgeous, it made me feel as if I'd been tricked. As if we'd tricked ourselves into not caring about something we should have cared about. I wondered if Davis felt the same way. Even if he was having similar regrets, he'd make fun of me if I asked him. I couldn't help looking enviously at the table loaded with wedding presents. All Davis and I got was a check for a thousand dollars from Davis's mom. Though if we'd gotten all those gifts, Davis would have insisted on returning them so he could pick out things that were more to his taste.

We both got drunk at the wedding and had the best sex we'd ever had. I'm pretty sure we conceived Miles that night, more to prove that we were still one step ahead of the newlywed young couple than because we wanted a baby.

How wrong I was about not wanting a child with all my heart! I fell in love as soon as Miles was born. Davis fell in love with him too. It was as if the three of us were madly in love with each other.

Not long afterward, Davis moved us to Connecticut and mostly worked from home except for meetings in the city or site visits around the country. He restored our house and designed the gorgeous light-filled addition. The house was almost completely finished, everything but the attic in the old part of the house, when Davis and my brother Chris were killed in the car wreck.

Sean is nothing like Davis. Sean is dark and tall, rugged, and muscular. Davis was a fair-haired beanpole. But sometimes when I walk into the kitchen and Sean is standing by the window, I have a moment when I think it might be Davis. I'm always happy to see him. But then when I realize that it's Sean, I'm happier. Like it or not, that's a fact.

But obviously there are . . . doubts. Doubts about Sean, doubts that I'd never confide in another human being. Doubts about who he is, what he knows about Emily's disappearance—and whether he knows something that he's not saying.

I wonder if every woman in love has doubts. I never had doubts about Davis, and I was in love with him, or so I told myself. I know some women fall in love with convicted killers, but I'm not that type of person. I have a son to protect. I'm not stupid. It's only reasonable to ask myself if there is the slightest chance that Sean could be involved in Emily's disappearance.

I keep up a solid front for the blog, and for the police, and the world, but I take pride in not being such a "woman in love" that I don't watch Sean closely and allow myself to ask if some tiny unconscious thing he does seems . . . not right. When we talk about Emily, I search his face for a sign of irritation, resentment, or guilt, anything to indicate trouble. But even when he's told me about her problems—the drinking, the pill addiction, the estrangement from her parents—there's never anything in his face or voice but love and sorrow that she's gone.

It's simple common sense that my watchfulness should shoot up to the code-red (well, maybe code-orange) level after I heard about the life insurance policy that would pay Sean two million dollars if Emily died. But the second Sean got off the phone with the insurance company, he answered all my questions. It wasn't as if he was playing for time to concoct a plausible story. The naturalness and simplicity with which he explained the situation was reassuring. His company had offered the option of life insurance for employees and their spouses for an extra few dollars a month to be deducted from Sean's (sizable) paycheck. It was too small a deduction to make the tiniest difference. So he'd checked the box that said MAXIMUM and promptly forgot the whole thing.

I don't believe he did anything wrong. I keep looking for something that doesn't add up, some detail that doesn't make sense. But I never get the slightest clue that he's hiding something or lying. And as someone who has hidden things and lied in her life, I like to flatter myself into thinking I'm pretty good at detecting the signs and symptoms.

Anyway, it's not a matter of clues. You can't say exactly how you know this kind of thing. You can't explain why you're sure. But you are. You know it in your bones. I know that Sean is innocent as much as I have ever known anything. *Ever.*

12

STEPHANIE'S BLOG
A HOLDING PATTERN

Hi, moms!

Looking at my life from the outside, you might think it looks a lot like my life before Emily disappeared. Minus our friendship, obviously, but with a lot of other elements back in place. Me and Miles, our house, his school, this blog. You might have picked up the hints that Nicky and his dad have become more a part of our lives. But that is only natural, given what they're going through. What *we're* going through.

Again I want to thank you for all the love and support. It means a great deal to me. Judging from your messages and knowing how intuitive moms tend to be, I can tell you know that all this appearance of normalcy is just a Band-Aid over a gaping wound. Our lives have been torn apart and will never be glued back together. They have been shredded by the disappearance of a mother, a wife, a friend. We continue to miss her and to live in the hope that she is alive.

So you could say that we are in a holding pattern, stalled in midair, waiting for something to decide our destination and promise a safe, if turbulent, landing.

Nicky is beginning to show the strain. He's been refusing to eat anything but guacamole and chips, which Emily used to make for him, though never when I was there. At times he seems angry at me. He says that I'm not his mother, that he wants his mother. And even though I understand, it's stressful. The poor child.

All I can do is be there for him and help him and his dad whenever I can. I can only cherish the time I have with Miles and be grateful for this precious gift of life, which can be taken at any moment.

Continue to wish us well. Beam all your love to Nicky. And hope and pray for Emily, wherever she may be.

In the immortal words of Tiny Tim, God bless you, one and all.

Love,

Stephanie

13

STEPHANIE

One afternoon Sean phoned me from home.

He said, "Oh, thank God you're there, Stephanie. I'm driving over. *Now.*"

Something about the way he said *now* made my heart pound. Okay, this was it. He wants me as much as I want him. I haven't been imagining it. He's coming to tell me that he wants us to be together.

"I have news," he said.

I could tell from the sound of his voice that it wasn't good news, and I was ashamed of the hasty conclusion I'd jumped to.

"What kind of news?"

"Terrible news," he said.

I watched from the window as he got out of the car, walking slowly, like someone weighed down by a burden. He seemed to have aged years in the hours since I saw him last. When I opened the door, I saw that his eyes were red rimmed and his face was ashen. I threw my arms around him and hugged him, but it wasn't one of the freighted, lingering, lust-infused embraces with which we had been saying good-bye lately after our evenings together. It was a hug of consolation, of friendship, and—already—sorrow. Somehow I knew what I was about to hear.

"Don't talk," I said. "Come in. Sit down. Let me make you some tea."

He sat on the sofa, and I went into the kitchen. I was shaking, and I splashed boiling water on my wrist, but I was so preoccupied that it didn't hurt—until later.

Sean took a sip of tea, then shook his head and put down the cup.

He said, "The police called today. Some fishermen in northern Michigan found a badly decomposed body. It had washed up on the shore not far from Emily's family's cabin. Apparently the body is in such bad shape they're not even asking me to come out there and identify it. They say there would be no point. They've asked me to FedEx Emily's toothbrush and hairbrush because they're going to have to rely on the DNA tests to—"

He broke down sobbing. His voice was thick with tears when he said, "It wasn't supposed to happen this way. I was sure she was still alive. I was positive that she was going to come home."

What did he mean? How *was* it supposed to have happened? What did he know that he wasn't saying? Or did he just mean that Emily wasn't supposed to die so tragically, so young?

The police estimated that she'd drowned not long after she went missing, though it was hard to determine the precise date. Oh, and some hikers found the rental car a mile away in the woods. There were no signs of a struggle. She'd been alive when she drowned. There were only two sets of fingerprints in the cabin. One of them, they assumed, was Emily's. The other was Sean's, which made sense; he'd been there for his birthday. (The cops had taken his fingerprints soon after Emily disappeared, the first time they brought him in for questioning.)

Neither Sean nor I could find words for what we were feeling. I could still hear Emily asking me to take care of Nicky so she and Sean could get away. Asking me to do her a simple favor. I had no idea what Sean was thinking. Perhaps he was remembering their hot stolen weekend.

I said, "Maybe it's not her . . . Maybe there's been some horrible mistake."

"The ring," he said. "They found the ring. My mother's diamond and sapphire ring. It was still on her finger. It had somehow gotten wedged . . ."

And then we both began to cry. We held each other and sobbed. Separately and together.

14

STEPHANIE'S BLOG
VERY SAD NEWS

Hi, moms!

I have sad news to report. The police in Squaw Lake, Michigan, the site of Emily's family's cabin, have found a body that they believe to be hers. Because of the absence of any evidence of injury, or any signs of a struggle or violence, and because the cause of death is drowning, they are ruling the death either a suicide or an accident. There is no way to know what was in Emily's mind when she walked into that lake. Maybe she swam out too far, maybe . . .

Emily's husband, Sean, has gone out to meet with the authorities and bring Emily home. Apparently the police called Emily's mother in Detroit, but her caretaker said it would be better to wait until she was having one of her "good days" to give her the bad news.

Like the pain of childbirth, the pain of grief and the sheer amount of *work* that death involves are things we forget. But I went through it with my mother and later with Davis and Chris. Chris helped me with my mother's death. He'd been there to give me support. But mostly I did it alone.

Now I've been trying to remember who that person was, the young woman and then the young mom who was strong and resourceful enough to do what had to be done: the calls to make, the notice to place in the paper, the decisions about the mountains of possessions a person accumulates during a lifetime, even a short one. I still have all of Davis's things, some of Chris's, and even a lot of my mom's stuff in the barn here in Connecticut.

What to do with Emily's things? It's too soon to decide. And how are we going to tell Nicky? Sean and I agree that Sean should tell him right after breakfast on a Sunday when he'll be coming over to play with Miles later in the day.

If Nicky wants to stay home with his dad all day, that will be fine. And if he chooses to be distracted . . . he can play with my son, who will feel genuinely sad for what Nicky is going through. After all, Miles's dad died, even if Miles was too young to remember. Sean and I trust Miles to make Nicky feel better. Even though he's only five, that's who he is. A good little person.

Not long after we got the news about Emily's death, Sean and I found Nicky, after a long and frightening search, hiding in her closet among her clothes. When Sean brought this up with Nicky's therapist, he suggested that we begin to move some of her stuff out of the house. (I hope you moms will forgive me if this is oversharing.) If that was what had to be done, I suggested a storage space.

Sean was adamant. He refused to get rid of a single one of her things. Once when we were discussing it, he became overwrought and said, "When she comes back—" and then caught himself. That was how I knew that he still refused to accept the fact that she was dead.

I was just as glad not to have to undertake the awful job of going through the possessions of the dead. And it seemed wrong to give a closetful of

Dennis Nylon clothes to the Salvation Army. I certainly couldn't wear them. Aside from the facts that I'm probably fifteen pounds heavier than Emily and a little shorter, her clothes are not my style. I'd feel like I was playing dress-up, a crunchy stay-at-home mom pretending to be a fashionista career woman. Besides, there's that part of you that always thinks, What if the person *isn't* dead? What if she returns and is mad at us for giving away her beautiful clothes? Such feelings are especially common in cases like this, when there is no real closure. No loving deathbed farewell, no proper funeral.

It's all so terribly sad. Every time I think about my friend, I cry inconsolably, and I can tell how hard and how bravely Sean has been trying not to break down. Especially in front of Nicky.

No matter what the authorities conclude or don't conclude, it is our deeply held conviction that Emily's death was an accident. Sean and I do not believe that she meant to kill herself. We knew her. She loved life. She loved her husband and son. She loved me. She would never have chosen to leave us.

We assume she needed a break, that the pressures of work and marriage and motherhood had gotten to her so badly that, despite the hard-won years (decades!) of sobriety, her old demons—the substance issues she'd so valiantly overcome—resurfaced. She saved up some pills, bought some booze, went to her family cabin to unwind and spend a couple of days by herself. It's not what I would have expected of her, but it's possible all the same.

She went swimming. She swam out too far. She miscalculated. She drowned.

According to Sean, she was an okay swimmer, but no more. And the toxicology reports showed evidence of alcohol and prescription pain and antianxiety medication. Enough to impair her judgment and cognition. To seriously affect the common sense that was one of the things I'd loved about her.

I am praying that you all will understand and not judge. Not everyone is strong. We can go a little crazy and do things we shouldn't do. It could happen to any of us.

And this is one of those tragic cases in which the person didn't hurt anyone but herself.

And us. Her husband, her son, her best friend.

So please be forgiving. Let me mourn my friend. I know that your love and prayers are with us. Thank you in advance for your heartfelt words of comfort and condolence.

Love,

Stephanie

15

STEPHANIE

I can't remember which of us—Sean or I—was the first to say that, despite what the police report said, we didn't think Emily killed herself. I honestly believed that her death had been an accident, and I'm pretty sure Sean did too. Having her death ruled an accident rather than a suicide would be much better for Nicky when he got old enough to understand.

And if it was an accident, as we believed it was, the insurance company owed Sean and Nicky the two million dollars that they wouldn't have had to pay if it was a suicide committed less than two years after the policy was taken out. I looked this up online and mentioned it to Sean, but I sensed that he already knew.

I had to wonder about Emily. Anyone would have had questions. And one of those questions had to do with the Patricia Highsmith novel that she was reading, in which the beautiful young woman kills herself for no reason that anyone ever finds out.

For Sean and I and Nicky and Miles, the reason and the way that Emily died was important. But it was only a detail. The main thing was that Emily was gone. She wasn't coming back.

Sean and Nicky scattered her ashes in the woods behind their house. I don't think Nicky understood what they were doing. And Sean didn't make it easier by telling him that they were throwing his mom's spirit to the wind. Later Sean told me that Nicky kept asking, "Where is Mom's spirit supposed to be? Where is Mom? And there isn't any wind."

Sean had read about the ritual on a Buddhist website, which I thought was really beautiful and not anything one would expect from a handsome, hypermasculine British guy who works on Wall Street. It made me think that his hidden sensitive side was part of what Emily loved about him. And it was certainly part of what I loved.

Sean asked if Miles and I wanted to be there when they scattered Emily's ashes. I would have liked to, more than anything, but I felt that it would be better for Nicky if we weren't. Maybe I'm superstitious. Maybe I wouldn't have felt right about scattering the ashes of a woman whose husband I might be in love with.

Sean showed me a copy of the autopsy report. He told me to look at the "findings" that described severe liver damage suggesting heavy, long-term use of alcohol and opiates. Not only scars, but ongoing damage. Apparently that had tipped the coroner toward the suicide verdict, but even so they couldn't be sure.

I said that it wasn't possible. One of us would have known if Emily was drinking heavily and abusing drugs. Sean insisted that it was highly possible. When he was at university, four of his most brilliant classmates were serious junkies. Two of them graduated at the top of their class, with firsts. And no one ever knew.

"*You* knew," I pointed out.

"I was their roommate," Sean said. "I must be drawn to those sorts of people."

It bothered me to hear Emily described as a *sort of people*. But what sort of person was she? How could you know someone as well as I thought I knew her and not know the most basic things about her? Some people beat the odds and lead high-functioning, productive lives while maintaining a habit. Emily had kept it together. Work, a job, a child, a family. A well-organized and even (on the surface) glamorous life.

I went over every conversation I'd ever had with Emily, every afternoon we'd spent together. What had I failed to see? What had she been trying to tell me and I hadn't been able to hear?

What kind of best friend had I been?

———

THE FIRST TIME Sean and I had sex I remembered what I had been missing. The pure, crazy pleasure. One of his hands cupped my breast, while the fingers of his other hand trailed lightly up my thigh. He flipped me over so he could kiss the back of my neck and all the way down my spine, then turned me back over again and put his head between my legs. I was shocked by how good he was in bed, but why should I have been surprised? Our skins and our bodies, it all felt so good, nothing else existed except the rush of feeling—of gratitude and yes, of love—for someone who could make you feel like that. The desperately wanting to come and the desperately wanting the sex to never end.

At the time, I wasn't thinking about anything except how good it felt. But afterward, it came back to me: everything I'd forgotten or put out of my mind when I'd been with Davis. I realized what I had settled for, what I had been willing to live without, to give up in return for a comfortable marriage, a respectable widowhood, and a life in which I put Miles's needs above my own. Now that I remembered, I refused to live without that pleasure and joy again. I had needs, my body had needs, that weren't all about Miles. It was as if sex with Sean had made me remember that I was a person.

I tried not to think about Emily saying that sex had always been the best part of her marriage, that it made everything else seem less important. That she could deal with Sean's absences, with his obsession with work, with his subtle put-downs and his failure to appreciate her if he just came home and (her word) fucked her.

Most of all, I tried not to think about how Emily would have felt if she knew.

Strangely enough, our affair began with one of Nicky's meltdowns.

He'd begun throwing tantrums, crying and screaming. About

nothing, it seemed. But of course it wasn't about nothing. His mother was dead. How could his tears not break my heart?

Sean was taking Nicky to the therapist who had seen Miles after Davis's death. Dr. Feldman was soothing and reassuring, as he had been before. But he had no real suggestions except to be patient and wait it out. He told us he'd be happy to see Nicky once a week, but Nicky refused to go that often, and the doctor said it was better not to force him.

The first night I had sex with Sean, we were all eating dinner at my house. Miles and Sean and I were having steak. Nicky was playing with his guacamole and chips, angrily scooping up the mashed avocado and jamming the chips into his mouth. The creamy green goo dripped down his chin.

Suddenly Nicky shoved his plate to the middle of the table and stared at the platter of steak, sliced, sitting in a pool of blood and juice.

Nicky said, "That's my mom. That's her. You've killed her and cooked her"—now he was glaring at me—"and we're eating her. Like in that movie I saw."

It hurt my feelings, especially after how much I've done for Nicky, how much I care about him. I reminded myself that he was a little boy who had lost his mom, a boy in unimaginable pain. And really, it had nothing to do with me . . . or with my (still repressed) feelings for his dad.

"What movie?" Sean asked Nicky. He didn't look at me to see how I'd reacted to Nicky's accusation. Ordinarily, that might have hurt my feelings too. But because the intensity of Sean's focus on Nicky showed how deeply—and instinctively—he cared about his son, it made me love and respect him even more.

"I saw it with Miles on his TV. We sneaked into the den and watched it after his mom was asleep," Nicky said defiantly, daring me to contradict him.

Sean and I looked at each other, smiling slightly, but concerned. It was as if the part about their watching the (probably forbidden) movie had erased the part about my killing and cooking Nicky's mom.

"You're busted," I said to Miles. Miles laughed.

Then Nicky threw himself on the floor and began to scream. It seemed almost as if he was having a seizure. Thank God we don't have near neighbors. What if this were happening in a city apartment? Oh, poor Nicky!

First Sean held him; then I took over and tried to calm him down. But Nicky didn't want me touching him, and he squirmed out of my arms and went back to his dad. Neither Sean nor I lost patience. Not for one second. We never gave up. It was as if Nicky was our child, our son, and we were helping each other be the best parents we could be. I stroked Nicky's arm while Sean stroked his hair, and Miles tried to hold his hand, even though Nicky was trying to punch his father's shoulder.

"Sweetie," I told Miles. "Leave Nicky alone. He's sad."

Miles didn't need to see this, but it felt wrong to make him leave the room. I decided to let him watch cartoons on my iPad, which I try not to do very often.

It was a solution. Not a great solution, but a solution. Even Nicky calmed down a little. As I settled Miles in the comfortable chair, his dad's old chair which I still have, and set him up with the cartoon, I could feel Sean watching me and liking what he saw. Knowing that he was admiring my skills as a mom was weirdly hot, but the truth was that—given the way I felt about Sean, no matter how much I tried to overcome those feelings—anything would have been hot.

Nicky was exhausted. He passed out in Sean's arms. Sean held him sleeping for a while and then carried him to Miles's room and lowered him into the bottom bunk bed and gently tucked him in.

"It's bedtime," I told Miles.

"Not for another half hour."

"Now," I said. "We're tired. Nicky's having a hard time."

"We all are," said Miles.

Sean and I exchanged glances that said, Miles is a beautiful kid.

Miles was right. We were all tired, all having a hard time. Nicky's meltdown had stripped us bare and left us raw and defenseless.

I put Miles to bed and made sure both boys were all right. Then

Sean and I slumped onto the couch and collapsed, and Sean searched for the next episode of *Breaking Bad*. We'd stopped watching it after we'd gotten the news about Emily's death—the violence and the darkness were too much for us—but we'd recently started again.

Just our luck, it was the sexiest episode, maybe the only romantic segment in the series. Jesse Pinkman and his girlfriend are falling in love. It was like a date movie in the midst of all that meth-cooking and gore and murder, except that his girlfriend's a junkie.

I sat close to Sean. He put his arm around me. I leaned my head on his shoulder.

We were trembling. We both could feel it, though it was unclear which of us was shuddering.

We started kissing. He kissed my neck, then my shoulders, then lifted my shirt and kissed my breasts.

That was how it began.

There were so many questions we should have asked, questions we needed to ask. But during those first weeks, we were so happy to be together and do what we (or anyway, I) had been dreaming about for so long that we didn't ask any questions that weren't about sex and what felt good.

We were careful. The boys never knew. We agreed that we would do it only when the boys were in school. Sean slept over less often than before. Having him in the house and not being with him was torture.

We didn't have a name or words for what we were doing. We didn't ask if it would last or what we planned to do next. We didn't ask, What about Emily? Are we betraying her memory? We hardly spoke. Even though the house was empty, we tried not to make any noise.

Did I worry that Sean was thinking of Emily when he was with me? No, I didn't. He couldn't have been. I would have known. No one is that good.

Now, at night, alone in my bed, I don't sleep well. As soon as I lie down, I fall into a slumber so heavy I feel drugged, but after three or four hours I wake up and lie awake until the light comes up and it's time to get Miles (or Miles and Nicky) ready for school.

There's something so ecstatic about the present moment—about my affair with Sean. But what about the future? Can the four of us go on living together like this, as an unofficial family?

Sean could go back to his office. I could drive the boys to school and pick them up every day. Nicky will get over his grief. Everyone does, sooner or later. Even if they never forget the pain, they don't feel it every minute.

Sometimes I think that the affair is totally sinful and wrong. I torment myself. I think, Sean and I have to stop. But one thing I've learned about myself is that I'm not good at stopping something I want to do, especially when that something involves sex. And besides, who are we hurting?

God knows what Sean is feeling. Does he feel guilty about having sex with his wife's best friend so soon after his wife's death? Or does he think it doesn't matter because Emily's dead and she can't know or care what he does anymore? Or is he doing it to get back at Emily? Does he secretly wonder if she killed herself? I've been reading a lot about suicide, and I know how often the survivors are enraged at the person who died, furious in ways they can't admit to themselves or even understand.

I would hate to think that Sean was sleeping with me because he's angry at Emily. Whenever that thought creeps into my mind, I push it away by reminding myself that we were attracted to each other before we knew she was dead.

And then I feel guiltier than ever.

16
———

STEPHANIE'S BLOG
DRAFT POST (NEVER POSTED)

Emily's ghost follows Sean from his house to mine. She is always there, watching and listening. She knows when we meet for breakfast in the diner after we've spent nights at our own houses.

We concentrate on Nicky. That's what Emily would have wanted, though you might ask why someone who cared so deeply about her child would take massive doses of pills, wash them down with alcohol, and go for a swim in the lake.

17

STEPHANIE'S BLOG
EVERYDAY GRIEF

Miles knew when Nicky and his dad were going to scatter Nicky's mom's ashes. Though Nicky might not have understood, Miles did. Maybe because he had more experience with death. He said that he and I, in our own backyard, should have a quiet moment on the afternoon when Nicky and his dad were giving Nicky's mom's spirit back to the woods.

For a long time Miles and I stood with our heads bowed and our eyes closed. I crouched down and leaned over so we could put our arms around each other.

You moms all know how strange it is, our children growing up. Just yesterday Miles was a baby in my arms. Now he is still a child, but he's also a little man I can lean on. I would never put that sort of burden on him, but he is my little rock. We've had practice dealing with grief. We've learned that it will pass. Maybe Miles told Nicky that. Maybe it made their bond stronger.

For months after my husband and brother were killed, I cried every day. Sometimes I cried on and off all day. I remember looking at strangers and thinking they were suffering and I couldn't see it, just as they couldn't tell what agony I was enduring. But if there were some version of luminol, the stuff they use to find blood at crime scenes, to detect the presence of grief, half the people we pass on the street would light up like Christmas trees.

I don't remember when the constant suffering eased up. But it did. I can't remember how I first got through the day without tears. I can't remember the first morning I awoke without wanting to go straight back to bed. Forgetfulness is kind.

I miss my husband and brother and now my best friend. Sometimes the pain is so sharp that I groan out loud. I hear myself, and I think that someone else must have made that heart-wrenching noise. But there is never a day when I'm afraid that I can't live through it.

Having Miles means everything. I've learned to put myself aside and live for my son. Which isn't to say I've forgotten, or that I don't remember every second of the day when my husband and brother died. Every minute of that afternoon is seared into my brain.

My husband and my half brother always disliked each other, though they pretended not to. They were both proud and decent and kind, and it was important to them both that they appear to get along. But that was impossible. Both were alpha males: Chris in his street-macho way, and Davis in his equally hard-headed old-family WASP way.

When we lived in the city, Davis hired Chris, who had become a builder, to contract out the Fort Greene renovations he was doing then. The tension between them improved somewhat when Davis and I moved to Connecticut and they stopped working together. My brother would visit every month or so. Miles adored his uncle. Chris and Miles had special names for each other that Davis and I were not allowed to know.

It was a pity that Davis and Chris didn't get along. They had a lot more in common than you might think. They liked boxing and baseball. They knew a lot about cars. They both cared about me, though I know that was a big part of the problem.

One summer afternoon we were all sitting on the front porch of our house in Connecticut and drinking lemonade. A showy vintage car drove down the road.

Davis said it was a Hudson from a certain year, and Chris said no, it was a Packard from another year. They were both positive that they were right, and the discussion got heated. Finally they made a bet.

"Okay," said Davis. "Here's the deal. Let's check it out in my vintage auto encyclopedia. Then we'll drive to the butcher shop. The loser pays for the ribs and steaks. If we're both wrong, we'll split it." They'd been planning to barbecue. They both got a kick out of grilling, though neither one knew his way around a kitchen or a stove.

"Deal," said Chris. "I'm thinking porterhouse. That's how sure I am."

Davis told Miles, "Go get Daddy's book, Buddy." I hated it when he called our son Buddy. Chris volunteered to go with Miles, who was way too small to carry the heavy volume. His dad was joking about him being able to get it.

All three of my guys leaned over the book as they looked for the mystery car. Miles was so excited. You would have thought that he could read, though he was only two.

Finally Chris said, "Aha! There you go!"

Chris was right. Davis was wrong.

"You win, man. The steak's on me," my husband said. "Let's buy something great." He kissed me, just a casual peck, and went to get his keys.

Were those the last words I heard him say? *The steak's on me. Let's buy something great.*

Davis was driving the 1966 Camaro he took out for fun drives in the summer. Chris was riding shotgun beside him.

I know what the last words they heard from me were. They were always the last words that anyone in my family heard from me before they left the house. I couldn't let them leave without saying: *I love you. Drive safely.*

To this day I thank God every waking moment that I put my foot down and refused to let Miles go along with them. He wanted to be a big boy, to go for a ride with his dad and his uncle. But he needed to take a nap if he was going to make it through dinner. And I thought the guys might have more fun if they didn't have to worry about him, if they didn't have to buckle and unbuckle him from his car seat, if they could skip all the fun stuff I did all week.

Later the cops would say that a truck came barreling up Route 208, way too close to their side of the road. Davis swerved to avoid it and lost control, and they slammed into a tree head on.

Just like that.

Treasure every moment you are lucky enough to spend with your loved ones because we never know what will happen just a few heartbeats later.

I just looked down and noticed that there are tears on my keyboard. So I guess the healing process hasn't progressed quite as well as I thought. As I'd like to think.

Thank you, sweet moms, for listening and responding.

Love,

Stephanie

18

STEPHANIE

What happened was nothing like that. Well, not nothing. My husband and brother drove off in a car. They were going to buy something to grill. Their car hit a tree, and they were both killed instantly. That was what happened, but not *how* it happened.

They didn't just dislike each other. They hated each other. They had always hated each other.

They couldn't have been more different. Chris was down to earth, and Davis was up in the clouds. They had such different senses of humor that sometimes Chris would say something that he meant as a joke and Davis took it as an insult—or vice versa. If they hadn't been related—through me—they would never have spent five minutes in the same room. They had only one thing in common: me. And Miles, I guess. Devoted father. Doting uncle.

There were always fights that got nasty and mean, arguments that blew up. I don't recall what started it that day. They often argued about the make and year and model of some vintage auto they saw. It could have been that. It hardly mattered. The two guys went from zero to sixty in ten seconds. Faster than a Maserati.

It got loud and ugly. Fast. The same old things got said. One of them accused the other of thinking he knew everything, and the other one called him a fraud. One said he was sick to death of the other's shit, and the other said . . . I don't know. They fought like brothers, except that they were brothers-in-law. If Cain and Abel had been related by marriage, instead of blood, things might have turned out even worse, though it's hard to imagine what worse could have happened.

It had been like that for so long, I knew exactly how it would go. One of them would stalk out of the room, and there would be a few moments of peace. Then the other would follow him, as if something was finally going to be settled. And they'd start shouting again. Or else it was so quiet I could feel the tension all through the house. It made me want to scream.

Miles heard every word. I don't think he understood much. But he heard the tone of it. His dad and his uncle were mad. Miles began to cry.

I blogged about how the two guys decided to get some meat to grill. But again, that's not quite true. I was the one who suggested that they take a ride to the butcher's. I will never forgive myself, not for the rest of my life.

I said, "Why don't you go for a ride? Cool off. Go to the Smokehouse and get something delicious for dinner."

The Smokehouse! That got their attention.

The Smokehouse was one of the things we loved most about living here. It's an old-fashioned German butcher. They make their own sausage and cold cuts and have the best cuts of meat. Cheerful blond German girls wait on you and, regardless of what you order, say, "You got it!" Davis and I adored it. Even when I was trying to cut back on eating meat, I'd break down and go there and get a warm homemade-liverwurst sandwich on a kaiser roll.

Brokering an accord between my husband and my brother was like breaking up a dog fight. There was a lot of cursing and snarling, but finally both Davis and Chris were relieved (as they always were) that things hadn't gotten physical. They'd never come to blows. But the two men I loved most in the world despised each other and didn't care who knew. They wanted me to know it. They didn't want me to forget.

They were glad for a chance to get out of the house, even with each other. It was a safe, easy way to end the fight, a way for them both to save face.

Davis grabbed his keys and kissed me a quick goodbye.

"Drive safely," I said. "I love you."

"See you," my brother said.

They didn't come home. They didn't come home. They didn't come home. *Where were they?* They didn't answer my texts or calls. Had they gone out for a drink? Miles took a nap and woke up grumpy. Hungry. Where were his dad and his uncle? When was dinner?

When the police came to the door, my first thought was that my husband and brother had gone into town and started fighting again and been arrested. How would Miles and I get them out of jail?

It took forever to understand what the cop was saying.

The officer must have been used to dealing with people in shock, but still he looked at me oddly when I said, "Was there meat in the car? Did they even get to the Smokehouse?"

"Meat?"

It was at that moment that I became a vegetarian.

The cop asked if there was someone—a family member, a close friend—I could call. Officer Something-or-Other (I didn't catch the name) could stay with me until someone arrived. He motioned toward the police car in the driveway, at a woman in a police hat in the passenger seat.

I was holding Miles, who started to cry. The officer gave him a pitying look. Poor little fella just lost his dad.

I said, "No, thanks, you can go. It's fine. I'll call my mother."

Nothing was fine, and my mother had been dead for five years. I just wanted them out of there.

That it was *my idea* for the guys to get meat to grill would be tough for anyone to live with—and stay sane.

After the police left, I spent a long time trying to calm Miles, who was crying his head off, even though he couldn't understand what had happened. I was so busy with him I didn't have time to go to the bathroom. Mothers of small children learn to postpone or ignore their most basic needs.

Miles and I lay down on my bed. Miles drifted off to sleep, and I slipped off into the bathroom, keeping the door open so I could hear if he woke up.

I saw a piece of white printer paper taped with Band-Aids to the bathroom mirror. The Band-Aids were at odd angles and the whole thing looked psycho, like the way serial killers decorate their lairs on TV crime shows.

It was Davis's handwriting, except that Davis's handwriting was normally, like everything about him, orderly and neat. This was the way Davis might have written if he'd taken bad drugs. Hasty. Careless. Angry. Scrawled. I had to read it several times, not only because it was hard to decipher but also because I was still in shock.

The note said: *I'm sick of all the lying.*

On the sink was a photograph of me and Chris standing and talking in our backyard. Laughing. Davis had torn the photo down the middle, and a jagged rip separated me and my half brother.

I knew that it was a suicide note or that someone might see it that way. I burned it in the bathroom sink. I didn't want anyone thinking that Davis had killed himself. On a practical level, we had insurance to consider. It would affect how Miles and I lived from then on. Miles didn't need to know. Davis's mom didn't need to know. I didn't want or need anyone to know.

I must have blacked out for a moment. The next thing I knew, I was sitting on the bathroom floor. I must have hit my head on the edge of the sink.

As I pressed a washcloth against my forehead to stop the bleeding, I heard Miles crying in the bedroom. When he saw me, with blood trickling down my face, he began to scream.

I thought: You're right to cry, my darling boy. You're right to be afraid.

Your mother is a monster.

19

STEPHANIE

I knew what Davis meant. I knew what he meant by "lying."

Chris and I had been in love ever since that day he walked into my mother's house. There was never a moment when we didn't know we were doing something wrong, just as there was never a moment when we thought that our love affair wasn't going to happen or when we believed it was going to end. We would swear off each other; we'd promise ourselves that we'd stop. Then Chris would call or drop by, and it would start again.

When I went to college, Chris left Madison and rented an apartment near my dorm. Because he was a carpenter, and good at it, he could pretty much find work anywhere. After I got out of class, I'd go to his place and wait for him to come home. We'd spend the late afternoon and early evening on his bed, just a mattress on the floor of his cold room, as the New England winter sun went down early and the light turned charcoal, then blue. We were so happy being together, naked skin against naked skin. We were each other's drug and each other's dealer.

People who wonder why we couldn't stay away from each other and behave like decent human beings—why we couldn't get over it and move on—all I can say is that they never had something like that happen to them. It lasted—on and off—for years. Things got crazy. There were a couple of months when just looking at my mom and dad's wedding photograph would get me hot. How sick is that? Is there a twelve-step group for this? There is probably a group for survivors of everything that has happened in my life. Not that I would have gone.

Chris and I would agree: This isn't right. This isn't healthy. We're hurting people, hurting ourselves. We'd end it again, for as long as we could hold out.

It was during a period when we were actually keeping our promise that I met Davis. The ultimate nice guy, as long as you didn't cross him about a paint color or where the couch goes. How solid and sane and large-hearted he was! He cared about the planet, the future. He wanted a family, a house. He was so earnest, so sincere. He seemed to live in a bright, shiny world where people did the right things and didn't have sex with their half brothers.

I could even imagine—*almost* imagine—that Davis would be forgiving if I ever told him the truth about Chris. Assuming our affair was over. But I didn't tell Davis. And it wasn't over.

It would have seemed suspicious for him not to meet my brother. And he knew the story—*some* of the story—of how Mom and I learned that Dad had another family.

I decided their first meeting should be in a public place, which is what you're advised to do when there might be some kind of scene or conflict. I don't know why I thought there would be. The conflict was all in my head.

We went out to dinner at an old-fashioned Italian red-sauce restaurant in Brooklyn that Davis liked because it was authentic. Unchanged since Christopher Columbus.

Chris had a girlfriend, tall and blond like all the women he dated at the time. I think her name was Chelsea. Those girls couldn't have looked less like me. Maybe my brother was trying to show me that he'd gotten over me. But he was always so distant and cool with those girls;

I was never fooled. I knew how he acted when he was turned on. When he *cared*. I wasn't even slightly jealous, though he wanted me to be.

Davis was not the kind of person who would imagine someone, his wife, a woman he thought he knew and loved, having sex with her half brother. And that evening, nothing happened that would have made anyone suspicious. Chris and I had gotten good at being undetectable.

Still, he and Davis got into a stupid argument about—of all things!—Frank Lloyd Wright. Davis was going on and on about what a genius Wright was.

Chris said, "Sure, he was a genius. But a real genius would have cared if his clients' roof leaked. And Wright told them to put a pail under the leak or move the furniture."

I agreed with Chris on that one. I was imagining what it might be like to live in a gorgeous, leaky house. But it would have been unwise to take my brother's side.

How easily that could have been a friendly conversation, a bonding thing. They both knew about Frank Lloyd Wright; they both had strong opinions. They knew about architecture and construction, though from different angles.

I looked around for the waiter. More wine! Where the hell was our pasta?

Finally, Chris said, "What if we agree to disagree?"

"Fabulous!" I shot a grateful look at my brother.

Later, at home, Davis said, "If he wasn't your brother, I'd say the guy was a moron."

"He is my brother," I said. "So you'd better watch what you say." We laughed, and I thought: I've dodged a bullet. For now.

One night, when Davis was in Texas visiting the site of a museum that his office was competing to design, Chris came over, uninvited. I swear I didn't call him, so it was like some sixth sense, some intuition that let him know I was alone.

He walked in the door. We looked at each other. He hugged me hello. The hug turned into a kiss. And once again, it was *on*.

My affair with Chris stopped when Davis and I got pregnant with Miles, and Chris and I relapsed only once (and not for long) after Miles was born. I didn't want my precious son raised by an incestuous adulterer. Me.

The only time Davis ever asked me directly about Chris was not long before he died. It was after a backyard barbecue we gave for his office staff.

I'd asked Davis if I could invite Chris so I could have someone to talk to. Our guests would mostly discuss design and office gossip, with a polite question about Miles thrown in to acknowledge that I was the one who'd made the potato salad and bought the hot dogs. And had the boss's child. Not that any of them had any real interest in Miles—or me. It was all about Davis—the genius, the star.

Davis said, "Sure, why not? Ask Chris."

He must have thought it was better than having me complain afterward that everyone had ignored me. It was risky having Chris there. But I hadn't seen him for a while, and I knew that I wouldn't be bored if I could just look at him from across the yard.

For the first hour of the party, I noticed Davis watching me. He must have seen that I was half there, half somewhere else—until Chris showed up.

I was at the food table. Chris came up behind me. When I turned around, there he was. My happiness, when I saw him, was more than brother-sister happiness. It seemed so obvious. I looked across the lawn and saw that Davis had seen it too.

That night Davis said, "Stephanie, I need to ask you something. Maybe this is going to sound weird, but . . . is there anything . . . unusual about your relationship with Chris? Maybe I'm just being paranoid, but sometimes I get the feeling that you guys are a little . . . too close. And sometimes it kind of freaks me out. Your bond is so intense, it's almost like you're lovers."

I was sitting in front of the bedroom mirror, brushing my hair. I pretended I'd dropped something on the floor so I wouldn't have to meet his eyes.

"Hey, I thought I was supposed to be the paranoid one in this marriage," I said. "Because that's ridiculous. We're just close. Maybe because we're siblings who missed out on our childhood together, we're making up for lost time."

Davis knew that I was lying. He knew in that way that people know and don't know things that they don't *want* to know about the person they love. But he knew just the same.

We had some dinner plates—off-white with bands of jade—that Davis was very fond of. He had laboriously selected them, one by one, from a bin of vintage crockery at a store on lower Broadway.

That night, when I refused to admit that my relationship with Chris was anything more than ordinary family affection, Davis went into the kitchen. I heard a crash, then another. I ran into the kitchen to find that he'd thrown several plates against the wall.

"What was that for?" I asked.

"I don't know," he said. "Maybe *I'm* just making up for lost time."

That was unlike him. It was more in character for him to do what he did then: He apologized and vacuumed up the broken pottery shards.

I thought that my having Miles, that *Davis and I* having Miles, would change things. I thought it would make Chris and me come to our senses. But it had only driven us further underground, where the air was closer and steamier and hotter.

On the day that the two of them died, the summer heat was suffocating. I was in the backyard by the pool, with Miles splashing in the baby pool beside me, and Davis was farther down toward the deep end, under an umbrella. He was fair skinned and sunburned easily, unlike my brother and me.

Late in the afternoon I heard the sound of Chris's truck pulling up in front of the house. I stared at Miles so I wouldn't be looking for

Chris as I heard him come up the walk. I couldn't look at Davis. He would have seen everything on my face.

There was nothing to do but exchange a hasty hug and kiss. Davis was watching us.

He knew. And I knew that he knew.

I closed my eyes so my husband couldn't see the desire in them. I went to get Chris a beer. Then the three of us sat around and watched Miles, who was taking his plastic monkey for a ride in an orange plastic boat.

On the day they died, after the argument, when the two men got in the car, I remember wondering, Where do we go from here? The truck coming straight at them and the tree they struck answered my question for me.

Davis was buried in New Hampshire, in the country cemetery near the house where his mother's family has lived forever. I left Miles with his grandma's housekeeper so he wouldn't have to see his father's shroud lowered into the ground. Unbeknownst to me, Davis had left a will requesting a green burial and leaving everything (including the future income from his design products) to me.

There were lots of people at the service. His whole office staff had come up from Manhattan, as had some of the clients who lived in the houses he'd built and renovated: strangers who had worked with him and grown fond of him. Plus he had a huge family all over New England, aunts and uncles and cousins I'd never met, a whole clan assembled to say goodbye, and (some of them) to meet me for the first and last time.

At the reception at Davis's mom's house, there were cold cuts and a wheel of hard cheese that no one could hack into. Crackers and carrot sticks. Coffee. Tea. That was it. I thought: Are there people in the world who don't know that people *really* need a drink on a day like this? It explained a lot about Davis, but it was too late for me to be helped by—or to care about—a new take on how my husband's upbringing had formed him.

The next day I left Miles with his grandmother and flew to Madison for Chris's funeral. I was the next of kin. There was no one to help me make any of the decisions that had to be made, but I was so numb that I got through it on automatic. I assumed that Chris (who didn't have a will) would have wanted to be buried next to his mom. It took a little sleuthing to track down her grave, but I was grateful for the distraction.

It was a very different service from Davis's. No relatives except me. No aunts or uncles or cousins. But Chris had had a lot of friends. An announcement appeared in the Madison paper, and a couple of Chris's friends posted it on Facebook. It seemed as if half the class of his large public high school was there.

They'd all loved him, and—except for one guy named Frank who had worked in construction with Chris and reminded me of him, a little—they were all surprised to learn he had a sister. They'd thought he was an only child, that his mom was a single mom. Which she was, in a way. But they were glad to meet me. They were sorry it had to be on such a sad occasion. They were sorry for my loss. As if they had any idea what I'd lost!

There was one woman—an old girlfriend of Chris's—who kept staring at me in a funny, excessively curious way. The weird thing was that she looked a little like me.

I was sure that Chris's former girlfriend knew or sensed some-thing . . . off . . . about me and my brother. But the guilty always think that someone knows their secret.

None of them seemed aware, and I saw no reason to tell them, that my husband had died in the same wreck as Chris. I pretended that it was only Chris in the car when it hit the tree. It seemed easier that way—less explaining to do, less unwanted pity. There was enough of that already.

After the service, we went to a local bar. Everyone bought rounds and gave tearful toasts to Chris's memory. Everyone got roaring drunk. I stuck very close to Chris's friend Frank, clinging to the phrases and gestures that reminded me of my brother. We were the last ones left at the bar.

That night I did something I was later deeply ashamed of. I told Frank that I was too drunk to drive back to my motel, which was true. But I also invited him to my room where, I said, there was a minibar. We could have a nightcap. I knew *that* wasn't true. The motel was too cheap to have a minibar.

As soon as the door closed behind him I started kissing him. He knew that I wasn't in my right mind, and he was a decent guy. He kept saying, "Are you sure you want to do this?" I think he knew that it was all about Chris and not about sex—or about him. So maybe he was feeling a little used, the way we think only women do.

We lay down on the bed. He lifted my blouse and pulled aside my bra and began to suck on my nipple.

"Excuse me a minute," I said. I went to the bathroom and got violently sick.

Frank wasn't insulted or even upset. We were both grieving for Chris. He waited till I got into bed, and he tucked me in. He gave me his cell number and told me to call if I needed him. Or if I wanted to. We both knew I would never call.

I woke up with a blinding headache and a major case of self-loathing that hurt worse than the headache. Unconsciously, I realized, I had taken off my wedding ring and put it in my purse before Chris's funeral. And my guilt got even more intense when I realized that I'd been so drunk the previous night—and so busy doing the totally wrong thing—that I'd forgotten to call Davis's mom and make sure Miles was all right.

I made coffee in the pathetic in-room coffee machine with the chlorine-tasting water from the tap. I drank both cups of coffee, then made the decaf and drank that too. And then I threw up again.

I phoned Davis's mom. No one answered. I knew something must be terribly wrong.

I called a cab and somehow managed to find the bar where my rental car was still in the parking lot. I drove to the Madison airport. I tried Davis's mother again, and again no one picked up. I tried her landline. Nothing. It was all I could do to stave off my growing panic.

I have never been so sure that my plane was going to crash. I was positive that I would never see Miles again, and that this would be my punishment for what I had done the night before—my punishment for what I had done all those nights and days with Chris. I no longer knew what I believed in. But that day, as the plane took off, I prayed.

Please let me live to see my son, and I will never do anything like that again. Please let him be all right. I would exist only for Miles. I would swear off men. I would never again have risky, inappropriate sex with the wrong people. The only happiness that would matter to me was Miles's happiness. I would give up everything else. *Just let me make it home.*

I picked Miles up at his grandma's house in New Hampshire. I asked why she hadn't answered the phone, and she told me that, in her grief and distraction, she'd let her cell phone run out of power and had forgotten to recharge it. And her landline went out every time it rained heavily, which it had last night. She apologized for how worried I must have been. I wondered why she hadn't thought to call me. I'd always suspected that she never really liked me. And now that her son was dead she probably liked me even less.

Miles shrieked with joy when he saw me, and I hugged him so hard that he yelped. I was so relieved that my knees went weak, and I had to grab onto the arm of the sofa to keep from toppling over, or fainting. All the way back to our house in Connecticut, Miles stayed awake in his car seat, using the few words he knew to tell me (I think) that his grandma had taken him to see a pony.

I was so glad to be alive that it wasn't until we walked in the door of our house that I remembered: Chris and Davis were dead.

I kept my promise. No more men. No more bad choices. It was all about Miles.

Until Emily disappeared and I got to know Sean.

Maybe loss unhinges me. Maybe grief sets loose some demon that would otherwise stay hidden deep inside me.

20

STEPHANIE'S BLOG
AN UPDATE ON . . . VARIOUS AND
SUNDRY THINGS

Hi, moms!

I'm sure you moms must think I'm the world's worst blogger, not having posted for so long. But I'm back, with lots to tell you. So much has happened since you heard from me last.

I always believe that it's better to be honest and open, even if there are some moms in our community who might have a problem with what I'm about to say. I'm asking them to soften their hearts and broaden their minds and hear me out—to try to understand before they judge me.

Sean and I have moved in together. Who is to say there is anything wrong when kindness and cooperation turns into love? And as we know, the heart wants what the heart wants.

Nothing will bring Emily back. Sean and Nicky and I will never get over our loss. But we help each other become other, better people. Sean and I and the boys can be a family. The children can be brothers. Neither of us wants to give up our house and the memories it holds, so we have decided to divide our time between our two homes. The boys' school is closer to my house, so I do most of the dropping off and picking up.

The boys have their own rooms in both houses. They can bring what they want back and forth, and they have doubles of toothbrushes and socks and stuff. I know it seems wasteful, having two houses when so many people in the world don't have one. But anything else would mean making a decision we can't make right now. Though at some point, I will. *We* will.

Sometimes Sean and I spend nights apart. Sometimes alone, sometimes with both kids or just our own kid. I wasn't sure I would like this way of living, but I do. I like being with Sean—and I like being alone with Miles.

It's an unusual arrangement, but for now it feels right. We are doing our best to give two little boys the best childhoods they can have, under circumstances that no one would ever have chosen. Neither boy has to give up his own house or his alone time with his own parent.

Nicky's therapist has been very helpful. Still, Nicky is sad, which he has every right to be.

If any of you moms out there want to share your story or have advice about how to talk to a child about death, please post a comment below.

After I drop the boys off at school, I drive Sean to the train. He's gone back to the office part-time, which is great for everyone, especially Sean, though Nicky cried at first when he got home and his dad wasn't there. The company has promised Sean that they'll cut way back on the travel, and he's promised me that I won't often be left alone with Miles and Nicky.

After Sean leaves, I have to check the house for whatever act of mini-sabotage Nicky might have done. The toy fire truck thrown down the toilet. The TV remote at the bottom of the toy chest.

The dark looks that Nicky gives me now and then would turn anyone's blood to ice. And he's developed a series of finicky OCD-like habits. He'll eat only with certain forks, or else there will be an hour of tears. Or he'll only eat radishes. Or homemade french fries. He tells us what he wants, and he'll starve before he eats anything else. He counts the steps up to his room and the steps from the front door to Sean's car. His therapist has suggested that we put off medicating Nicky—Sean asked specifically—until he's had a chance to work through the stages of grief.

I'm glad Nicky is seeing a therapist, but we don't need a professional to remind us that the poor child's mother is dead. I've been spending my precious spare time searching the web for useful sites offering help with the job of being a stepmom to a newly bereaved five-year-old.

I keep thinking that Emily would have known what to do. But I can't even talk it over with Sean for fear of making him feel worse. He doesn't need to know how many hostile things his son does. I've been trying to spare him. Is that wrong?

Which is why I'm asking you moms: Have any of you been in this situation? What did you learn that helped? Can you recommend a book about this? I'll be grateful for advice in any form.

Thank you in advance, dear moms.

Love,

Stephanie

21

STEPHANIE

W hen you live in a family, it's easy to stop noticing things, to quit paying attention. That's one way you know it's a family. We take things for granted. Some people call that tolerance, or laziness, or being in denial. I call it getting through the day.

I soon got used to how difficult my (unofficial) stepson was being. His bad behavior was mostly directed at me. He was always nice to Miles. They loved each other as much as before. Like brothers. If their friendship had started unraveling, I might have been quicker to bring it to Sean's attention.

Sean was making up for lost time at work. He wasn't home all that much. He'd left Nicky to me for a while. And when Sean was around, Nicky wasn't going to waste what little time he had with his dad on a display of anger or unhappiness.

Dealing with that was my job, and I took it on gladly. For Sean, for Emily, for Nicky. But I couldn't help feeling that something was going to happen, that something awful was going to shatter the calm before the looming, dangerous, unpredictable storm.

Whenever people got on the subject of dogs and how smart they are, my brother Chris used to tell a story about visiting a friend in the

Southwest and going on a hike in the desert with his dogs. The dogs were barking; the birds were making bird noises; the breeze was blowing, and all of a sudden the noise just stopped. The dogs and the birds fell silent. Even the wind quit blowing.

Chris looked on the ground, and not twenty feet away was a coiled rattlesnake, hissing. I remember him saying that silence could also be a warning, louder than a siren.

I found the story compelling and sexy. Chris told it when we were with Davis, and Davis looked at him with such hatred and scorn that for a heartbeat I was sure that Davis knew about Chris and me.

All this is by way of saying that I got used to Nicky's mini-aggressions and never lost my sympathy for him—or my patience. It was when he *stopped* acting out that I got scared.

One afternoon Nicky came home from school and seemed to have become the best little boy in the world. Most days he hardly spoke to me and refused to answer when I asked what he'd done in class. But that afternoon he asked me how *my* day had been and what I'd been doing.

A child asks an adult what *she* did that day? *Really?* I didn't tell him I'd wasted hours trawling the internet for advice on how to deal with *him*. I said I'd spent part of the day straightening up the house, which was true.

At dinnertime, Nicky said he would eat whatever I cooked—even if it was vegetarian. He was totally unlike the angry kid he'd been just the day before. It made me happy. Time was working its healing magic. We were taking small steps forward, tiptoeing out of the darkness into the light.

And yet . . . and yet . . . I had an uncomfortable feeling. Something was wrong. I don't know why I felt that way, but I did. A mom's intuition.

It was as if the world had gone silent, and I'd heard the rattlesnake hiss.

The boys were hiding something. I knew it. I was always catching them whispering, like evil conspiratorial children in a horror film.

What weren't they telling me? Why was Nicky suddenly acting so thoughtful? When they were playing and I walked into the room, the boys looked up as if I'd interrupted a secret conversation.

One night, when both boys were staying at my house—Sean was working late in the city—Nicky padded into the living room and said he couldn't sleep. Would I read him a story? I took him back to the guest room that I'd turned into his room. I read him one book after another, as many as he wanted. I waited till he said he was tired, which kids hardly ever do. I turned off the light and tucked him in. I stroked his smooth, slightly damp forehead.

Many people (including children) will tell you things in the dark that they would never say with the lights on. I asked, "Has anything fun or special—or maybe upsetting—been happening in school?"

Nicky was silent for so long I wondered if he'd fallen asleep.

Then he said, "I . . . saw my mom today."

I got the chills. Nicky's therapist had warned us about how much trouble children have accepting the fact that a loved one has died. And now, without Sean here to help me, I was going to have to deal with it. I was going to have to tell this suffering child that however much he wanted to see his mom, he couldn't have seen her. She was gone. Gone for good.

I took a deep breath.

"I'm sure you *thought* you saw her, sweetie . . . We often think we see people we love even though it can't really—"

"I *saw* her," Nicky said. "I saw Mom."

The important thing was to keep him talking and encourage him to confide in me, to tell what he so desperately wanted to be true that he'd convinced himself it *was* true.

"Where?" I asked him. "Where did you see your mom?"

"She was just outside the school yard fence when we went outside for recess. They let us go outside to play today because it was warm. I wanted to run to her. But recess was almost over, so they were yelling at us to hurry up and get back inside."

"Are you sure it was your mom? Lots of people look like people they aren't really . . ."

"I'm sure," Nicky said. "I could read her lips. She was saying, 'See you tomorrow. Tell Stephanie hello.'"

"She said that? Tell Stephanie hello?"

"Yup. I saw her there before . . . a couple of days ago . . . the last time they let us play outside. I told Miles. He thought I was making it up. I made him swear not to tell."

Nicky believed every word he was saying.

It was hard for me to sort out my complicated feelings. Mostly, I was sad. I had so much sympathy for Nicky. But I was also frustrated. Nicky had made no progress toward accepting the loss—the permanent loss—of his mom. I couldn't bring myself to tell him that he'd imagined it, to try to explain (to a five-year-old!) the concept of hallucinations brought on by wishful thinking. Anyway, that was Sean's job. He was the dad.

I kissed Nicky's forehead and pulled up the covers.

When Sean got home from the city, I poured him a glass of scotch. A double. I snuggled against him on the couch.

I said, "Something disturbing happened this evening. When I was putting Nicky to bed, he told me that he saw Emily outside the school yard."

Sean sat up very straight. He stared at me. I saw so many warring emotions in his eyes: shock, disbelief, hope, fear, relief.

He said, "This *is* disturbing. It can't be good for him. It's unhealthy. He was with me when we scattered Emily's ashes. What am I supposed to do now? Teach him about DNA? Explain that his dad sent Mom's toothbrush and the coroner made a positive match?"

I'd never heard him sound so raw and out of control. "Stop," I said, "I can't stand it. Enough."

"Oh, that poor boy," said Sean. "My poor son."

I turned out the light, and we sat in the dark. I held him in my arms, and he leaned his head against my shoulder.

Finally Sean said, "Let's not break his heart so soon again. If he wants to live in that dream for one more day, let's not force him to wake up."

The next night, at bedtime, Nicky said, "I saw Mom again today." He said it very simply and calmly. As if he was stating a fact.

This time I explained to Nicky that people had dreams in which they thought they saw people who weren't there anymore—or ever. I said, "They seem so real, and they speak to us as if they're actually there. But they're not real. It's just a dream. A fantasy. And when we wake up it's always sad. We miss them more than ever. But we understand that they are still with us, if only in our dreams."

Nicky said, "No, you're wrong. My mom was there. I saw her. I ran over to her. I got as close as I could with the stupid fence between us. She touched me through the fence. She touched my hair and my face. Then she told me to run back and join the others. And . . ."

"And what?" My voice sounded strange to me. Anxious, strained . . . and scared. But what was I scared of, exactly?

"And she told me she would never leave me again. She told me to tell you and Dad that."

I leaned over to kiss Nicky's forehead.

I noticed something familiar. It took me a while to realize what it was, to identify a memory that was already beginning to fade.

I nuzzled Nicky's skin and hair. I smelled Emily's perfume.

Sean was spending that night at his house, working. I was supposed to keep the boys overnight, but I called and said I wanted to come over. Sean heard the urgency in my voice. Without asking what was wrong, he told me to put the boys in the car and text him when I was outside his house. I carried the boys, still in their pajamas, into my car. When I reached Sean's house, he came out and helped me carry them to their rooms.

I told him that I had smelled Emily's perfume on Nicky, and that this time Nicky had insisted that he'd seen his mom. That she'd touched him.

Sean looked weary. His face got dark, and his tone was curt and even angry as he said, "Stephanie, please cut the *Twilight Zone* crap." He had never talked to me that way before, and for the first time it occurred to me that Emily could win this one. Until then I hadn't even known that it was a contest. But it was. He would always love Emily—love her memory—more than he loved me. Like Nicky, Sean would never get over her loss.

He said, "Stephanie, you're losing it. Emily is dead. No one wants that to be true, but it is true. It wasn't supposed to happen. But it has."

I had a vague memory of him saying that before: It wasn't supposed to happen. And again I wondered, What *was* supposed to happen?

Sean said, "We need to help Nicky accept that, not indulge him in his painful, destructive fantasies."

I knew he was right. But the smell of Emily's perfume had unnerved me. Maybe *I* was wishful thinking, wanting to believe she was still alive. Though I did realize that, if she were, I'd have some serious explaining to do. I told myself: Get a grip. We're all grieving, and grief makes people imagine and do crazy things . . .

Sean sighed deeply. Then he got up and took my hand and led me upstairs to the back bathroom on the second floor where, in the linen closet, way up on a shelf, was an atomizer of Emily's perfume.

He sprayed it into the air.

It was eerie. Lilacs and lilies. Italian nuns. It brought Emily back to us, just for a moment. Emily was there with us in the room.

He said, "I keep a bottle back here. Somehow Nicky found out. And he got the stepladder and dragged it over to the shelf and reached the perfume bottle and sprayed it in his hair. Poor little guy. I suppose it made him feel closer to his mom."

Part of me knew that it didn't make sense. Nicky hadn't been home for two days, and it was only tonight that I smelled Emily's scent on his hair. But I wanted a logical explanation. I wanted to believe Sean. And besides, there *was* no other explanation. I'd seen the autopsy report and the urn that contained my friend's ashes.

With Emily's perfume, with her sweet scent of lilacs and lilies hanging thickly in the air, Sean and I made love. It was shameful, how turned on we were. But maybe it wasn't all that surprising. Maybe we were just trying to prove something to ourselves and to each other.

Our beloved Emily was dead.

But we were still alive.

One night, I was at my house with Miles eating dinner: pasta with fresh tomato sauce, the kind of delicious vegetarian meal we used to have when it was just the two of us. It was a relief, in a way. A relief and a pleasure.

I was feeling peaceful, so that it was doubly shocking when Miles said, "Hey, guess what, Mom. I saw Nicky's mother today. She was heading into the woods behind the school when we went outside for recess. It was like she was waiting till we came out. And then she ran away because she didn't want anyone else seeing her. She was moving fast. But it was her."

Is it possible for your heart to stop beating while the rest of you goes on living? It must be. My heart stalled in my chest.

"Are you sure?"

"Yes, Mom."

"Sure sure?" I asked, trying to stay calm.

"Sure sure," Miles said.

There was a book we used to read. One of the moms who follows my blog recommended it when I blogged about that time when Miles was always hiding. And scaring me senseless.

The book is called *Where Is Buster Bunny?* The bunny keeps hiding from his mom and frightening her, though the kids can find him in the illustrations. And the mother rabbit is very worried because she has no idea where he is. Anyway, at the end, the little bunny promises that he'll never hide again:

"Do you promise with your little pink nose?" his mother asked.

"Yes," said Buster Bunny.

"Do you promise with every one of your cute little toes?"

"Yes," said Buster Bunny, and he never hid from his mother again.

It had become a game that Miles and I played whenever I wanted him to promise me something. Now I asked him:

"Was it really Emily? Do you promise with your little pink nose?"

"Yes," said my son.

"Do you promise with every one of your cute little toes?"

"It was her. I promise," said Miles.

22

STEPHANIE'S BLOG
ANOTHER SIMPLE FAVOR

Hi, moms!

This is going to be a quick one. Can any of you moms remember the name of a French movie I'm pretty sure I saw in college about a sadistic high school principal and his sexy mistress (Simone Signoret?) who conspire to scare his rich, fragile wife to death by making her think she has murdered him and then making it seem like he's come back from the dead?

I can't believe I would have made this story up. Do let me know.

Thanks!

Love,

Stephanie

23

Diabolique!

Thanks, moms, for the answer, which came back within seconds! I cannot believe how attentive you are, how this proves that there are moms reading this right now, and that if I need help—just a memory jog, in this case—they don't hesitate for a second.

Diabolique.

I was able to stream the film within minutes of posting my question.

What an amazing moment this is! You want something, but you don't know exactly what you want, and you put it out there into cyberspace, and you figure out what you want. And you get it.

If only real life were like this blog.

I'm undecided about whether to recommend this film to you moms. The mom who emailed me the name said the reason she remembered the title is that the film scared her more than anything she has ever seen. She would *never* watch it again, and she strongly suggests that I not make other moms live with the memory of it, as she has.

If we're the type who thinks that Patricia Highsmith's (just typing the name makes me miss Emily!) novels are creepy, this might not be for us. But I was engrossed because the plot is so twisty and because Simone Signoret is so outrageous playing the hot high school teacher/sinister-babe mistress.

The film begins at the school where lots of gawky French boys in short pants are running around yelling. The principal is a control freak. Everyone is scared of him, and he messes with everyone just because he can.

Simone Signoret is wearing dark sunglasses to hide the bruises she got from the principal, her violent lover. He also abuses his wife but only psychologically, because the wife's money supports the school. The wife's got a heart condition, so the guy makes her so unhappy that she thinks she's going to die of misery and humiliation.

Films like this always make me realize how, despite the mistakes I've made and the bad things I've done, I've been lucky in my choice of men. Because (as so many moms have discovered) it's so easy to get involved with a person you think is a nice guy. You have a child with him. And one day he turns . . .

The wife and the mistress both hate the principal so much they decide to kill him. They feed him drugged whiskey. Then they put his body in a basket and dump it in the school swimming pool.

The plan is to make it look like an accident. It was never going to work, but that turns out not to matter. When they drain the pool, there's no body.

Enough spoilers, moms. In case you decide to see it . . . not that I'm suggesting you do.

So let me just say that the dead man keeps showing up in unexpected and terrifying places, not like a slasher film (the phone call is coming from inside the house!) or a gore fest, but something darker and more wicked.

The story turns and turns. No one is what he seems. Nothing is what you think.

I stayed with it. I got the shivers. I was surprised by the end. It got me through a few hours.

See the film or not. The choice is up to you brave, intelligent moms.

All my love and, as always, thanks to you,

Stephanie

24

STEPHANIE

What I've just written in my blog is—once again—not what happened. In fact the film drove me crazy. Even as the film was scaring me senseless, part of me was wondering: What if everyone is lying? Gaslighting me? What if Emily is alive? What if Emily and Sean conspired to put me through this? To do this to me. But why? What did I do to them? It was extremely depressing.

I watched the film in my own house—secretively, guiltily, as if it were a porn film. The minute it ended, I wished I was at Sean's house. I needed to hear Sean tell me that I was just being paranoid. I needed to believe him.

It was worth waking up the boys and driving over to see Sean. Miles and Nicky would fall back asleep on the way.

Papers covered Sean's dining room table. He'd been working. We put the boys back to bed. Sean poured me a glass of brandy. A fire roared in the fireplace. The couch was comfortable and warm.

I said, "Is there any chance—*any chance*—that Emily could be alive?"

"None," he said. "None at all."

I said, "Miles saw her. Miles has very good eyesight. He's my son. I believe him."

"Kids are always seeing things that aren't there," said Sean.

"Not Miles," I said. "Miles knows what's there and what isn't."

First Sean looked annoyed, then horrified, then scared, then . . .
I had no idea what he was feeling. His expression changed in slow
motion. He got up and left the room. He didn't return for a long time.
I sat there, confused and worried. Should I go after him? Should I get
Miles and go home? Should I wait?

I waited. It was the easiest thing to do.

Finally, Sean returned. He sat back down on the couch and put his
arm around me.

He said, "I'm sorry, Stephanie. I am."

"For what?" I said.

"For not realizing how hard this has been on you. All the time, I
thought Nicky and I were the only ones suffering. But you've been in
pain too."

I began to cry.

"I miss her," I said.

"We all do," said Sean. Then he said, "Move in with me. Let's try
and make this work. Emily's gone. She's dead."

I was crying harder now. Sean was weeping too.

"Nicky wants his mom to be alive. He wants it so much he's convinced
himself that she is. And somehow he's convinced Miles that he's seen her.
But she isn't alive. And she would have wanted Nicky to have a mom, for
us to have a stable household. Come live here. Full time. Please."

"All right," I said. Within moments, I felt the fear and doubts of the
last few days vanish, like an illness from which I'd suddenly, miracu-
lously recovered.

Sean said, "We can stick together and protect ourselves from ghosts
or whatever it is that the kids are imagining. Circle the wagons, as you
Americans say." And he laughed through his tears.

Miles is delighted. He likes Nicky's house. He's comfortable here.
Their TV is bigger than ours. I don't miss the nights that Sean and

I and the boys spent in our own houses. I don't miss my own house. Not really. Sometimes I do. Mostly I like being here with the boys and Sean.

Every day we spend here means that Emily is one day further away. For so long I wanted to keep her close, and now I want her gone. I want to be the one Sean loves and, eventually, the one Nicky loves. I have to be patient.

There's a lot I can't blog about. Not blogging gives me more time to think, to wonder about my friend.

How could you think you know someone and know so little? How could Emily have been the person who would leave her child and drive to Michigan to drink and take drugs? That wasn't the friend I knew.

I became obsessed with what remained of her in the house. It was a hard conversation, but I convinced Sean to put some of Emily's things in storage. I volunteered to find the place and arrange the transportation.

I considered asking the moms if they knew the best storage facility on the New York–Connecticut border. But I was afraid they'd see through it and know that I was getting rid of some of Emily's clothing and possessions. It was something we had to do, to make room for me and Miles, to make us feel as if we really lived there. Sean agreed.

We arranged for Sean to work with the movers on a Saturday afternoon. I'd take the boys out to a movie, and he'd tell a whole team of professional household organizers what things he wanted to go and what he wanted to stay.

I was interested in what remained, in what Sean couldn't bear to send away.

Until then, whenever I stayed at Sean's, I had been respectful, honoring Emily's privacy. It would have felt wrong to go through her drawers and closets. (Sean had thoughtfully cleaned out a dresser and a closet for me to use.) But once I moved in, I began to look around more freely.

If I found something of Emily's that interested me, or that seemed to offer some information, I would examine it for evidence about who she really was, and why she did what she did.

Around this time I stopped blogging. I sent a message to the moms community announcing that I was going on leave and would be back soon.

It was too hard to write about my life with anything like honesty. I could have blogged about Miles's diet and helping him grow up to be a good person. I could have blogged about forming a blended family and navigating around the huge hole in our lives.

Moms aren't stupid. They would have heard the hollow note; they would have figured out that my interests had begun to lie elsewhere. Maybe they would sense that I'd gotten myself into a slightly dark place that I was going to have to get myself out of.

I'd become obsessed with how much I could find out about Emily.

What if Miles and Nicky were telling the truth? What if she *was* out there? Could she be alive? Could she and Sean be conspiring against me? Was it the insurance money? It was starting to look as if, with the help of the crackerjack lawyers from his firm, Sean was going to succeed in having her death ruled an accident, so the two million would be his, minus the lawyers' fees.

When the boys were away at school and Sean was in the city, I began to play a game. I would look for, and find, one interesting thing about Emily each day. One object that would provide a clue about who she really was. Then I would make myself stop.

The first place I looked was the medicine chest. Not very creative! I found a full bottle of 10-mg Xanax. Prescribed for Emily by a doctor in Manhattan. Why hadn't she taken it with her? If I were going to ditch my husband and leave my kid with my best friend and go on a drug holiday with alcohol and pills and swimming, the pills would be *just* what I'd want.

Unless she had so many she didn't need these.

I couldn't remember what the police report said they found in the cabin. Were there empty pill and liquor bottles around?

The second day, in a hall closet, I found a purple alligator purse with the Dennis Nylon logo. The purse was filled with bills, small denominations, some euros but mostly various pesos and rubles and dinars, all bright and with flowers and the faces of national heroes. Souvenirs of travel for Dennis Nylon. I imagined poolside parties with lots of local boys and fashion models and drugs.

Meanwhile Emily was writing press releases and controlling information. My friend hadn't been a drug-addled mess but a responsible mother and a loving wife with an important job. Or maybe she was all those things. The currency was Emily's collection. Her travel diary.

Maybe there had been a crime. Maybe the Russian mob was moving into fashion, and Emily got in the way. My imagination was spinning out of control. I told myself to relax.

I found a box full of photos of Emily. It seemed weird that there were no pictures of her childhood or of her life before she married Sean. Had Sean gotten rid of those snapshots? Or was there something about her past she'd wanted to erase? Sean had said she was estranged from her parents, but she'd been vague about the reasons. Wasn't it strange that they could be married and he didn't know? I told Davis a lot about myself. About my parents. But I'd left out one big thing: my relationship with Chris.

The only pictures in the box were of Emily and Nicky together. I remembered that Sean gave the photographs of Emily alone to the police, and we hadn't gotten them back yet. I'd helped him edit out the pictures with Nicky because we decided that we didn't need our little boy's face all over the papers, or the internet.

In a back closet beside the place where the chimney ran up through the attic, I found a pale blue dress on a hanger and a pair of stylish pale blue high-heeled sandals placed neatly beneath it.

The dress swayed when I opened the door. Like a person hiding in the dark and waiting to jump out and scare me. Boo! I *was* scared, at first.

Was it Emily's wedding dress? I couldn't ask. I didn't want Sean knowing that I was rifling through the closets in the attic. He'd told me that he wanted me to feel as if this house was my own. But I didn't think he meant this.

I slipped the blue dress off the hanger and took it, together with the shoes, down to our bedroom. I put on Emily's clothes. The dress was too tight, and the sandals were a bit of a squeeze, but I loosened the straps. I felt like Cinderella's stepsister trying to stuff her feet into the glass slipper.

I looked in the mirror. I felt sinful. I felt sad.

I pretended I was Emily. I lay down on our bed with my legs draped over the end so I could watch myself in the mirror. I reached up under the filmy pale blue dress and began to masturbate. I pretended I was Emily and that Sean was watching me.

I came in about a minute. When I came, I laughed out loud. It was no surprise by now that I was a perverted person. Was I a lesbian too? I didn't want to have sex with Emily. I just liked pretending to be her. I took her clothes back upstairs and hung them neatly in the closet where I'd found them.

In the guest room, there was a deco vanity table with a big round mirror, the sort of thing that might seem irresistible at an auction but when you got it home you wondered why you thought you needed a vanity table that a 1930s movie star would sit at to powder her nose.

In one of the drawers, I found a manila envelope full of birthday cards. Drugstore greeting cards. They were still in their envelopes, addressed to Emily Nelson (she'd never taken Sean's name) at the addresses she'd lived in at different stages. Her college dorm at Syracuse. Her first apartment in Alphabet City in Manhattan. You could track Emily's progress up through Dennis Nylon Inc. as you watched the addresses get more upscale. Then the cards went to East Eighty-Sixth Street—where she'd lived with Sean after Nicky was born. But when had she lived in Tucson? She never told me about that. Or maybe she was just visiting for her birthday, and her mother's card caught up with her there.

The cards were standard stuff. Flowers. Balloons. HAPPY BIRTHDAY TO MY DEAR DAUGHTER. HAPPY BIRTHDAY TO OUR DEAREST DAUGHTER.

There was nothing more personal than that, no notes or endearments. Nothing handwritten but the salutation, *To Emily*, and the signature, *Love Mom*. The handwriting, always in brown ink and with a real fountain pen, belonged to another era, when girls were graded on their penmanship. The penmanship was stellar—spidery yet assured.

In the top left-hand corner of each envelope, in the same handwriting, it said, *Mr. and Mrs. Wendell Nelson*. And there was an address in Bloomfield Hills, Michigan.

Emily's parents' address.

I took the envelope and put it in my dresser. I felt it was important to have the address, though I couldn't have said why. If anyone could help me clear up the mystery of who my friend was, her mother might. I knew she suffered from dementia, but I remember hearing that she had her good days. Maybe I could visit on one of those. I would never have the nerve—or the time or freedom!—to go see her. But I liked having her address.

There was one more thing. An important thing. And that was completely by chance.

One afternoon Sean called from work and asked me to look in his top desk drawer for a piece of paper on which he'd scribbled a client's contact information. He'd forgotten to bring his phone to the meeting with the client, and then he'd forgotten to enter the information into his contact list. And he needed the guy's number. Right away.

I could tell he was embarrassed; he thought he'd screwed up. I kept reassuring him, saying it was nothing. People forget more important things. He'd been under a lot of stress. I didn't say, Give yourself a break. Your wife died. But we knew what I meant. I told him I'd look for the paper and call him when I found it.

The scrap—torn from a yellow legal pad—was where he'd said it would be, along with a lot of bills and receipts, old phone chargers, and a tangle of those ID badges people wear at meetings. I was surprised by the mess. Sean is such a neat person. But no one's perfect. And I'd seen how he could let things get out of hand when work was involved. When we first moved in together, I often had to (neatly!) clear files and stacks of paper off the dining room table so we could have dinner.

Just before I closed the drawer, I noticed a small box, covered in deep blue velvet that had gotten slightly dusty. A jewelry box. It was as if I heard a voice warning me not to open it, but that same voice made it irresistible.

I opened it. And there inside was Emily's ring: the sapphire surrounded by diamonds.

I held it between my fingers. And then I saw her. I saw Emily. I saw the diamonds flashing in the air as we sat on her sofa and she moved her hands, talking about the books and movies she loved, about Nicky and Sean, the things she cared about. As we laughed and joked and celebrated the gift of our wonderful friendship.

On impulse, I held the ring up to my face. And it seemed to me that I could smell the cold, dark waters of the lake in Michigan, and beneath that, a faint whiff of decomposition. Of death. It was impossible that a ring could smell like that. But I was sure of it all the same.

My friend was gone. This was all that was left—this ring and our memories. I put the ring back in the velvet box, put the box back in the drawer, and slammed the drawer shut. I began to cry—harder than I'd cried since we learned that Emily was dead.

I pulled myself together. I called Sean. It was all I could do to keep from falling apart again as I read him the client's number. Sean thanked me. I wanted to tell him I loved him, but this was not the moment. I wanted to tell him I'd found Emily's ring, but I knew I never would.

I stopped searching the house for clues. There was nothing else I wanted or needed to know.

We settled into a routine. The boys went to school and Sean went to work. Maricela came on Wednesdays, so I didn't have to clean. I kept busy, straightening up the boys' rooms and collecting art supplies for making projects when they got home. Baking muffins and making model airplanes.

I tried to forget about Emily unless I could remember her in a good way. A helpful and positive way. I decided that the boys saying that they'd seen her, and Nicky smelling like her, and my own doubts—that was just part of our grief. Our refusal to believe that she was gone.

But she *was* gone. Sean had seen the autopsy report. The DNA results. If that wasn't her body in the lake, whose was it? Even in a Michigan town, they didn't make mistakes like that.

I read cookbooks and learned to make dishes—eggplant parmesan, Korean tofu stews—that Sean and the boys resisted at first but came to like. Or maybe they ate them to humor me. They ate them, just the same. I didn't want us to eat meat every night. I started feeling good about being in Emily's kitchen. I was feeding the people she loved. Food was sustenance. Food was life. Emily had put together a kitchen and married a husband and found a best friend who could take care of her little boy after she was gone.

Everyone was making compromises. Nicky stopped acting out and was as nice to me—or almost—as he'd been before his mother vanished when the four of us did fun things on Fridays after school. I turned the guest room—the one with the vanity table—into a kind of office, and decided that soon I would go back to blogging. Enough time had passed for my readers to accept that Sean and I were a couple.

I would have a lot to say about the challenges and rewards of raising two boys instead of one. Easier in some ways, harder in others. So far they have still never fought. I was grateful, but I wondered if it would last.

Sex with Sean was as amazing as it had been at the start. Or almost as amazing. The heat dies down when you can have the person whenever you want. That's only natural. Unless you do it every night, which you do at first and then not so much. Some nights you lie there side by side like sister and brother. And you notice, though you try not to.

Maybe that was why the heat never died down between me and Chris. Because we couldn't have each other when we wanted. Not by a long shot.

The boys never again mentioned seeing Emily near school or anywhere else. I decided to pretend that it never happened. I remembered reading about cases of mass hysteria, where a group of people all have the same hallucination at once. It is especially common with school children. It had happened with Nicky and Miles, but they showed no signs of lasting damage.

We'd come through it, I thought.

We had a quiet Thanksgiving, just the four of us. The boys helped me cook the turkey. It was perfectly done, crispy skinned and moist, the stuffing was delicious. Sean sweetly pretended not to know what the holiday was about so the boys could tell him what they'd learned at school. How the pilgrims had come here and how the Native Americans had showed them how to plant corn and grow their first crops so they could survive the cold New England winters.

That night, after the boys were asleep, Sean and I sat on the couch, finishing up the wine. He put his arms around me and said that maybe we should all go away together somewhere for Christmas vacation, the four of us. Someplace warm. An island. Someplace that was only ours. He didn't have to say: somewhere he'd never been with Emily. Mexico maybe, or the Caribbean. A guy at work had gone to Vieques and loved it.

Rum drinks. Hammocks on the beach.

I said that sounded wonderful. And it did.

We stayed up and made love. I thought, Maybe this will work.

The next morning, I dropped the boys off at school and took Sean to the station. Then I came home. I had begun to think of it as home. No longer Emily's house, or Sean's house. But home.

I made myself a cup of coffee. I sat at the sunny kitchen table. Then I took my coffee into the living room and settled into the couch. For a second, I thought, Emily's couch, then I made myself stop thinking that way. My couch now.

I thought about my life so far and about the chance that things had settled and come to rest. With luck, we could go on this way. That would be fine with me.

The phone rang. The landline which no one ever used.

I scooted over to answer it.

The caller ID said OUT OF AREA. I picked up and was sorry. I heard the silence you hear just before the robocall recording comes on.

I was about to hang up when a voice said, "Stephanie. It's me."

It was Emily. I would have known her voice anywhere.

"Where are you?" I said. "You've got to tell me!"

"Outside. Watching you."

I rushed from window to window. There was no one out there.

"Go around to the kitchen," Emily said. "Hold up your hand. I'll tell you how many fingers you're holding up."

I held up my hand. I raised two fingers.

"Two," said Emily. "Try again."

This time I held up both hands. Seven fingers.

"Lucky number," said Emily. "You always were a clever girl. Okay, got to run. For now. Talk soon." That had been Emily's sign-off: talk soon.

"Wait!" I cried. There was so much I wanted to ask. But how would we begin that conversation, with me in her house, living with her husband?

"No. *You* wait." Was I imagining that it sounded like a threat? She hung up.

I looked around at Emily's things. Emily's furniture. Her house.

There was no way that could have happened. Within a few hours, I managed to convince myself that I'd imagined Emily's phone call.

I'd been lying on the couch. Maybe I'd fallen asleep and dreamed it. I'd been having vivid dreams ever since Emily died. Some of them had her in it. Maybe this was one of them.

I wasn't convinced. Part of me knew it had happened.

The next morning, after I came home from taking the boys to school, I dropped off the groceries in the house and took a couple of deep breaths and walked out into the woods.

I calculated where Emily must have stood to see me in the window.

I stood there and looked at the house.

Nothing moved. It was spooky.

I heard branches crack deep in the woods. I could hardly breathe.

Then I saw myself in the window. In the house. And that was the scariest thing.

It was me. And it wasn't me.

I was someone else. I was all alone. I was out in the woods.

Spying on myself.

PART
TWO

———

25

EMILY

Peeping. Something about the word makes me almost physically sick, and at the same time I adore it. *Peeping.* The word gives me a feeling that's like the tingly nausea jitters you get just before the roller coaster drops. Some people will do anything for that feeling. And, as the song goes, *God, I know I'm one.*

I've been *peeping* at Stephanie, Sean, and the boys. Just *thinking* the word is almost as nauseating and exciting as creeping up to my kitchen window and watching Stephanie pretend to be me. Sleeping with my husband, raising my child, overcooking disgusting hunks of dead cow in my kitchen. To be honest—I'm borrowing Stephanie's phrase here; she's always saying *to be honest,* maybe because she so rarely is—I'm more fascinated than furious.

Spying on Stephanie in my house is like playing with some weird 3-D live-action dollhouse. As if the people inside were all animated figurines that I can move around. I can make them do things. I can control them with my magic weapon: a burner phone.

Dial the magic number—and the Stephanie doll runs to the window.

Stephanie can have the house, but I want a few things back. She can have the husband, his hopeless stupidity proved forever by the fact that he's fucking her.

I just want Nicky. I want my son back.

Even as a little girl, I was always hiding and spying. Crouching under the windows, lying in the grass, I waited for the grown-ups to do something dirtier and more private than make coffee or look in the refrigerator or (in my dad's case) sneak a cigarette on the porch. I saw where Mother hid the liquor bottles and how often she *had* to get the big dictionary from the bookshelf. What was the word she needed to look up? Her bottle was behind the book. I saw my mother drink so much that it no longer seemed secret but just like something she did. I didn't blame her. The poor woman was married to Dad, a popular gynecologist and exotic orchid breeder who named his new bioengineered orchid strains after his "favorite patients."

Only rarely did I break the spy code of watchfulness and silence. Drunk Mother sounded so stupid! I put water in her gin bottle. I watched from the window as she drank straight from the bottle, though she would have killed me if she caught *me* drinking milk from the carton. After the first swallow, she looked puzzled, as if trying to remember how it was supposed to taste. Then she finished off the bottle and put it in a paper bag and took it outside to put in the trash at the end of the driveway.

When I was in junior high, I began to take sips of her gin, then larger and larger swallows. She never noticed, or never said. My parents could have been cardboard cutouts for all their lively interest in me. Working at Dennis Nylon, you hear a lot of people, after a few drinks, talking about how *unparented* they feel. Every time I hear that word, I think: You should meet *my* unparents. Though that would be unlikely now. Father's been dead eight years, and Mother is in no shape for a conversation about the mistakes she made as a parent.

Everyone has a hellish childhood, everyone still thinks it was supposed to have been heaven. That everyone else's childhood was pure paradise. That's the message we get from movies and TV. When you're little, you think your family is the only one that isn't as happy and cool as the ones in the sitcoms. The irony is that I would never let Nicky watch the modern versions of those mind-rotting television shows, yet his life (comfy upper-middle-class suburbs with a loving mom and dad) is closer to TV life than Sean's and mine were, and we actually did watch those shows.

I want Nicky to be happy. It's the one thing, the only thing, that I know I want.

When you grow up, you find out that you weren't the only unhappy child, which is nice. Nice if you're the kind of person who is cheered up to find out that someone had the same bad luck you did. Stephanie likes to think that everybody is walking the same rocky road. Even though she talks about how you can never know another person, she thinks you can. She likes thinking that another person is suffering exactly as much as (or worse than) she is. If you have a problem with your kid, it's supposed to help to know that other mothers have the same problem. If your best friend disappears, it's supposed to comfort you to learn about all the women out there whose best friends have vanished.

That's a pretty small demographic, waiting for the call from *Investigative Reports*, waiting to tell the reporter how sure they are that the husband did it.

During the day, Stephanie sits in her little office corner of the sunporch—*my* sunporch—where she's put an old-fashioned rolltop desk the size of a tank and a round braided rug. Very homey, very corny. Mommy blogger paradise. But she seems to have stopped blogging.

Total strangers felt sorry for Stephanie when she lost me. Her best friend. They posted love and hugs and emoticon hearts and frowny faces.

From the day I disappeared, I was high on the self-restraint it took not to completely mess with Stephanie's head. It was like having my brain in bondage. I've just dipped my toe into torturing Stephanie, and it's mildly entertaining. But it's painful too. At the end of the day, at any time of day, that's my house, my husband, my son.

It makes me think less of Sean that he could stand to be with a person like that. Even if he's using her to get over his grief about me.

In theory I could give him another chance. Let him know I'm not dead. See how fast he drops Stephanie. That would be entertaining to watch.

But he's already failed a test, two tests. I'm not going to give him a chance to retake the exam.

The point was that Stephanie isn't that smart. That was what we needed. That was why I chose her.

I never told Stephanie about Mother's drinking. It wasn't anything I wanted anyone knowing, though Sean knew because his mom liked her big glass of sweet disgusting sherry, so Sean and I had that in common.

That was pretty much all Sean knew about me. I was careful with information. Controlling information is what I do, what I *did*, for a living. That's why Dennis paid me. Before most people caught on to disinformation, I could make Dennis's court-ordered stint at a boot camp desert rehab in Tucson look and sound like a wild two-week sex and drugs orgy in Marrakesh. I could make something seem like something else. I could make the failing Batgirl look the hippest thing on the planet.

I only told Sean the things that made him feel the same as me, nothing that would have made him feel different from me. Which meant leaving out some fairly basic things. God, how Stephanie used to go on about secrets. I'd listen to her, or half listen to her, and I'd think: We *have* to have secrets. We need them to live in the world. I have plenty. More than my share. You have no idea.

Spying on my mother, I learned: We don't know we're being watched. We like to imagine we're alert. We fool ourselves into thinking we have something in common with creatures that can survive in the wild. But we've lost that instinct, that sixth sense. We couldn't survive for one day in the wild—if the wild was full of predators.

It only takes one predator. And for the moment, that's me.

Unless we see or hear something, the woods behind our house

could be crawling with snipers. A pervert could live across the court-yard behind our apartment, binoculars smashed into his eyes, praying to the pervert god that we'll take our clothes off.

There was a guy like that across the alley from my first New York City apartment, around the time I started working at Dennis Nylon.

I caught the guy. Big sloppy gut, wife-beater T-shirt. Superspy binocu-lars. Pants around his knees. I gave him the finger across the alley. He gave me the finger back. He put down his binoculars. His eyes never left my eyes.

I couldn't deal with it. I moved. I lost my security deposit.

I got a nicer apartment.

I asked Dennis for a raise, and I got it. He loved being so powerful that he could throw me a handful of spare change and rescue me from a pervert.

Now *I'm* the neighborhood pervert. Stephanie needs to be rescued. From me.

There's a movie I love. *Peeping Tom*. It's British. It's about a psycho-pathic serial killer who films himself in the act of killing women. He has a camera attached to the end of spear on which he impales pretty girls so he can film the terror on their faces. A real artist, a real obses-sive.

It's Dennis Nylon's favorite film. So we had that in common.

It was one of those movies that ruin a director's career. Everyone finds out how sick the guy is, and no one will work with him. Espe-cially when the film loses money. *Peeping Tom* was too far out for 1960. Even now, it would be. But not for me, not for Dennis.

I was surprised that Sean hadn't seen it, being British and for a while on the fringe of an arty crowd. Didn't his friends watch films like that? There was no one I could ask, no one he still knew from those days. His cool university friends hadn't gone into banking, and by the time we met, he no longer saw them. I knew I could have him, if I wanted, by making him think that he could still be the coolest kid if he was with me.

Sean could make deals, make money, do business, but he'd never had a real love affair. I showed him what passion was. I made him think he couldn't live without me. He was so easy to reprogram, to convince that *he* was in control. That was part of his appeal. It was a bonus thrown in that he was a good lover: patient, creative, and hot. That counted for more than it should have, or would have if it had been more common in the male population. So many men make love like there's a taxi with the meter running waiting outside in the street.

I could make Sean into whatever I wanted him to be. All I had to do was figure out what I wanted him to be.

Sean and I met at a particularly awful charity dinner at the Museum of Natural History. I was in tears half the night because everything was going wrong, starting with an important investor falling down the stairs, moving right along to the expensive celebrity chef slicing off his fingertip. I was working my ass off so no one noticed the major screwups, which would have infuriated Dennis, and we *all* could have lost our jobs.

Sean introduced himself and said he worked for the investment firm that was partnering with Dennis Nylon. I acted as if we'd already met, in case we had, but I was sure I would have remembered.

He said, "Could we have dinner sometime?"

Very sweet, very cool, very clear.

Soon after that, I invited Sean to my apartment to watch *Peeping Tom* on DVD. It was our third date. It was a test but also a risk, inviting an attractive, rich, basically decent, basically straight-arrow guy to watch your favorite film about a psycho serial killer. If I'd pretended that my favorite film was *The Sound of Music*, I might as well have given up before I started. Who would want to be with a guy who wanted a woman like that?

We watched *Peeping Tom* with his arm around me. We'd already had sex, good sex, maybe even great sex, so I guess he thought that it demonstrated his self-restraint and good manners to be doing anything other than having more great sex. I don't mean to sound cold-hearted or boastful when I say he thought the sex was even better than it was. I think he had limited experience, mostly lukewarm relation-ships with disgruntled British university students and frustrated in-terns at the bank.

Now he was indulging me, watching a movie I liked. I'd had enough boyfriends to know that this was the kind of thing guys do at the start of a relationship. Later, they leave the room or ask you to watch the *other* TV—or they just grab the remote and switch to the basketball game.

All through the film, Sean and I didn't speak. Afterward, he said, "Brilliant," in that annoying three-syllable way the British pronounce it. "But I thought it was a little much. Didn't you?"

Failed! He thought it was *a little much*. Was he one of those wussy guys who want to believe that people are *nice*? The kind who avoid books and movies that feature any kind of pain or suffering or vio-lence. There are guys like that out there—more than you might think.

But not Sean. He was just pretending to be a good boy. Or maybe he was a good boy pretending to be a bad boy. It turned him on; it excited him that I liked *Peeping Tom*. He thought it was sexy. Scary, but scary good. It was the kind of film that that a guy might like, unlike girls, who he thought (probably because of his boring former girlfriends) just want to come home from the office and curl up with a glass of pinot grigio and the latest BBC remake of Jane Austen.

I prefer tequila or, better yet, mezcal. But never around Sean.

Later it turned out that he was a big fan of dark TV series: *Breaking Bad, The Wire*. Shows I didn't like all that much, though all the kids at work did. I can't keep track of the characters.

We eloped to Las Vegas. We told no one. We got married in the Elvis Chapel and spent three days in bed in a suite at the Bellagio. It was a nice break: sex, room service, champagne, TV. Showing off for each other.

It wasn't the smartest thing for Sean to suggest we visit his "mum" in the north of England for our honeymoon. He kept telling me how green it was, how romantic the moors were. He knew that I loved *Wuthering Heights*. His town was only an hour from Haworth Parsonage, home of the Brontës.

Two weeks of bleakness and drizzle, hideous cold, leaky rain, clouds hanging so low I couldn't see the moors. I hate that sensation when the cold leaches through your skin to your bones. And for what? Just so Sean and I could trudge through a sad little house filled with weepy teenage girl tourists? And back to spend the night in the damp, under-heated, mildew-infested row house of a sour, shrunken apple core of a woman who didn't like her son and who liked me even less?

In general, I try not to feel sorry for people. I don't think it's good for the person being pitied, or for the person doing the pitying. But when I saw that house! The cracked linoleum, the stinky gas heaters, the thick dark drapes, and the furniture reeking of every lamb stew cooked there since the reign of Henry VIII. Poor Sean!

One day—when Sean was off doing the marketing—I offered his mother a sip from my flask. I made an introduction: Sean's mom, meet Jose Cuervo. Jose, meet Sean's mom. (Herradura, actually. Cheap tequila gives me a headache.) After a lifetime of sherry, it was a revelation. I told her I would kill her if she told Sean, and she laughed, a constipated *heh heh heh*, because she thought I was joking.

That night she went to bed early so Sean never suspected that she was drunk. And it gave me and his mum a conspiratorial alliance that made our stay there almost entertaining. Almost.

Oh, there *was* one fun thing that happened.

I'd suffered from a sort of suffocating boredom, on and off, all my life, and I knew when an attack was coming on, the way other people can sense the approach of a migraine or a dizzy spell. I knew I had to do something to keep myself from going under or acting out in a way I would regret. I'd had those feelings since I was a kid, and I had learned that something *had* to be done to make it go away. It was like an insect bite I had to scratch.

So I stole Sean's mother's ring.

It was very pretty, a sapphire surrounded by two large diamonds, set simply in gold. I complimented her on it soon after we arrived, and she blithered on about how the stones were cut and set, how her husband gave it to her before they were married, who had owned the ring before, its history all the way back to the Neanderthal era. I stopped listening. I don't remember if I decided to steal it right then, or if the idea occurred to me on impulse when the chance arose.

One night, I'd gotten Sean's mom a little tipsy, as usual. I was surprised that her son didn't notice when Mom got even more unpleasant and hypercritical than normal. I suppose he had low expectations. That night she nagged him into going into the "parlor" to watch the "telly" while "the girls" tidied up. She carefully set the ring down on the windowsill above the sink to keep it safe while she did the dishes, and she toddled off to the "loo."

I put the ring in my pocket. It was as simple as that. Now you see it, now you don't. Impulse? Premeditation? I don't know. I don't care. I am not, by nature, a klepto. This was something special.

She didn't miss the ring until she'd finished the washing up. Then she went instantly crazy. Moaning like a wounded animal. Her ring! Her beautiful ring! It wasn't there! It wasn't anywhere! Had it fallen down the sink? Why hadn't she been more careful? How could she live without it?

We turned the house upside down, and poor Sean, the obedient son, had to go down to the basement and take apart the disgusting plumbing to search for it in the pipes.

Guess what? The ring never turned up. When his mum said goodbye to us, she was still weepy—more upset about the ring than about the fact that her son and his new bride were leaving.

I pointed this out to Sean on the plane, going home to New York. Business class.

I said, "Your mum loved that ring more than you."

He said, "Don't be hard on her, Emily."

That's when I took the ring out of my purse and showed it to him. He was overjoyed.

"You found it!" he said. "You darling angel! Mum will be so thrilled."

"No," I said. "I took it. I have no intention of giving it back. She'd just take it with her into the grave. What a ridiculous waste."

Was this my weird American sense of humor? A practical joke? Sean smiled tentatively, as if to show me he got the joke.

I wasn't joking.

"You stole it?"

I raised my eyebrows and shrugged.

"I wanted it," I said. "And I took it."

"You have to give it back. I'll tell Mum that it dropped into your purse when you were in the kitchen, and that you didn't find it until now."

"Please keep your voice down, dear." The flight attendants were looking at us. Were the cute newlywed lovebirds (Sean had told them we were on our honeymoon) already having an itty-bitty honeymoon spat?

"I'm not giving it back," I said. "What's your mother going to do? Extradite her son's bride and have her arrested? And if you try and tell your mother that I found it, that it wound up in my possession by accident, I'll *tell* her that I stole it. That I *meant* to do it. And what do you think will be worse for her? Thinking she lost her ring—or knowing that her son has married a thief and a liar and a sadist who wants her and her son to suffer?"

Which is *not* why I did it, actually. I didn't want anyone to suffer. I just wanted the ring. I liked it. I didn't understand why it wasn't mine.

I said, "Maybe I should tell her that *you* stole the ring so you could give it to me."

Sean stared at me. He knew I was determined. I saw that he was afraid of me—of something about me that he'd never suspected. There was a lot about me that he didn't know, some things he *never* found out—and maybe never will.

What did he think I would do? That was never clear. But why would he proceed to raise a child with someone he distrusted and feared? I suppose because he loved me. And maybe he was in love with the fear.

"And now," I said, after I'd ordered more champagne, "you're going to put this ring on my finger. And you're going to tell me you'll love me forever. Say, 'With this ring I pledge my troth forever.'"

"You already have an engagement ring," he said.

"I like *this* one," I said. "I've already sold the other one you gave me. Did you really not notice?" In fact I'd worn it the day before. I'd sell it when I got home.

Sean took my hand. He slid his mother's ring on my finger. His voice shook as he said, "With this ring I pledge my troth forever."

"Forever," I said. "But for now . . . meet me in the bathroom in twenty seconds. Knock twice."

We had sex standing up, my ass pressed against the sink, in the cramped airplane bathroom. I had him. He was mine.

––––––

UNTIL NOW IT never occurred to me that Sean might be *really* stupid and weak. Stupid enough to have sex with the first woman who made it clear that he could have her if he wanted.

I know he thinks I'm dead—even though I specifically told him *not* to believe reports of my demise. Couldn't he follow instructions? Did I have to tell him not to believe the autopsy report? Did I have to say that even if he got back my ring—his mother's ring—it wouldn't mean that I was dead? Though to be fair to Sean, even I hadn't expected that the ring would get back to him. That was a bonus, an accident. Once more Sean's mother's ring was working its magic.

Sean's an honest guy. Too honest. Too trusting, as it turns out. And altogether too simple.

I told him: I will not be dead. No matter what you hear. I will not be dead. It was like a warning in a fairy tale. Don't turn around and look back at me on our way out of hell. And once again, the hero blew it.

Even if Sean believed that I'd taken a drunken, pill-addled fatal swim in the freezing lake, shouldn't there have been a decent mourning period? Time for him to grieve and begin to forget about me and recover? To resolve to "move on," to quote Stephanie again. Maybe after a suitable lapse Sean would find a woman whom he would never love or desire as much as me—but who would cook and clean for him and take care of Nicky.

But my "best friend" Stephanie? It's *embarrassing*! *Insulting* that he could *look* at her after he'd seen me! She's a wounded mess consumed by guilt and determined to repent for her sins by being the best mom in history. She's like a fuzzy bath mat pretending to be a person.

Sean's being with her is *maddening*. How could I have married a guy who hits on Stephanie the minute he thinks I'm dead?

Maybe revenge is in order.

Sean's stupidity is what I'm looking at as I stand behind a tree at the edge of the yard and watch Stephanie flap from window to window like a bird trapped in a house. Trying to see me, to see where I am. Holding up two fingers, then seven. Staring into the woods.

Thinking, Help me! Help!

I let Stephanie run around my house, skittering from window to window. She's afraid to go outside. I watch her for a while more, then leave. My car is parked just beyond the driveway.

I drive back to my room at the Danbury Hospitality Suites, where I am registered with a phony credit card and under an assumed name. I'm driving my mother's car, which I took from the lake house after I ditched the rental in the woods.

I'm betting that Stephanie won't tell Sean I called, or that I'm spying on them. She used to ramble on about being afraid that people might think she was paranoid and crazy. She'd say (I'm hearing her voice now), "Isn't it awful how people are always trying to convince moms"—(how I hated the way she said that word *moms*)—"that they're insane." *That* was what I had to listen to on those dreadful Friday afternoons as I tried to figure out how I was going to go to work on Monday and deal with Dennis's latest meltdown.

If Stephanie suggested that a dead woman is not only alive but also a Peeping Tom—well, that might make her seem cuckoo indeed. It would prove that she *is* crazy. I never worry that anyone will think that I—the flawlessly dressed and made-up public face of Dennis Nylon, the cool, competent mother and wife—am crazy. Though if anyone knew the truth, they might conclude that I am way loonier than Stephanie, who is just silly and not too bright and terribly insecure.

If Sean admits to anything, he will have to admit to everything: we had a plan to defraud his firm's insurance carrier of a (relatively) small fortune. Sean has learned from his work in finance not to show his hand. Poker players and bankers know. And thrill seekers, like yours truly.

––––––

OUR PLAN BEGAN with a little game I'm sure lots of couples play. What would we do if millions of dollars fell into our lap? We'd quit our jobs. We'd take Nicky to some beautiful place and live till the money ran out. That was the fantasy.

Sean was doing well at work. I had a good job. We had a nice house, a great kid.

You might think that we would have liked our lives. But we didn't. Maybe discontent isn't the greatest thing to share. Maybe restlessness isn't the strongest foundation for a marriage. But it's probably better if both people in the couple are restless and discontent, rather than just one. Sean despised the crooks he worked for. He resented the time and energy his company sucked out of him, which made it easier for me to persuade him that what I was planning was some righteous Robin Hood sort of thing. Bonnie and Clyde, that was us. Outlaw heroes.

Meanwhile I'd had it up to here with the fashion business, with everyone acting like the world was coming to an end if a runway model stubbed her toe. The models were temperamental. They lived on water and cigarettes.

Sean and I bought lottery tickets every week. If we won, we would quit our jobs and move to rural Italy or the south of France and live there for as long as the money lasted. Then we'd figure out the next step.

I was the one who thought of a different sort of . . . lottery. A lottery over which we had more control. The jackpot we needed to save ourselves. To live large, to have the lives we wanted. To have time for our son and not be tired and stressed all the time, even when we weren't working.

That's what I told him we wanted. Now it turns out that he wants Stephanie. Which is fine with me.

I always wanted Nicky. I wanted my kid. I still do.

I made Sean watch the films I liked, black-and-white thrillers from the thirties and forties. I streamed them every night. That was how we began to joke about insurance fraud. It *was* a joke, at first. Sean never imagined how far I would take it.

I explained the logical steps, and Sean went along, like the all those scammed, bewitched men in those movies. He was the Fred MacMurray, I was the Barbara Stanwyck.

We needed Stephanie—or someone like her. She was almost too perfect. Sometimes I had the scary feeling that I'd created her to be so exactly what we needed that we could skip a few steps on the way toward putting our plan in action.

She was so perfect that everything made more sense than it did before she came along and unknowingly became a part of it. It began to seem more possible than when we were daring each other, when our plan was just a fun idea.

Stephanie couldn't suspect. I was sure she wouldn't. She was so happy she'd found a friend. Whenever she used the phrase "a mom friend," I thought I was going to be sick.

I picked her out of a crowd. A gaggle of mothers waiting for their kids to get out of school.

When people talk about predators, what they mostly mean is sex and power and weakness. Criminality. Pedophiles prey on children. Rapists prey on women. In nature, predation is driven by hunger. The big sharks eat the smaller fish. The strong prey on the weak.

But this wasn't like that. Stephanie is an adult. It was perfect that her son was Nicky's friend. It was meant to be.

It was always about Nicky. Sean and I worked so hard—late nights, sometimes through the weekends—that we hardly saw him. He was growing up, and we never got to spend time with him. He was our only child. We were never going to have another.

Conceiving him had been easy, but giving birth to him had been very hard. Our doctor called us into his office (never a good sign) and told us that trying to have another child could prove fatal for me and the baby, even if I succeeded (small chance) in carrying it to term.

I'd gone on the low-dose birth control pill, and it seemed to work fine, with no side effects. Or none that the doctors would admit. If you ask me, I felt excessively irritable, even more restless and impatient. But maybe it wasn't the pill; maybe it was life. Everything and everyone annoyed me. Everyone but Nicky.

I wonder what sort of protection Sean is using with Stephanie, who has a disturbingly uneven record when it comes to contraception. She claims that Miles was unplanned, that she and her husband conceived him by accident after an expensive hipster wedding.

My scheme—and Sean's capitulation—was the result of a combination of things. Those old films and the new employment contract that I actually read. Twenty-some pages, clause after clause, dozens of bright plastic labels flagging blanks for Sean to initial. And then—what do you know?—page twenty-two was an application for life insurance for Sean and his spouse, a gigantic payoff in return for a teensy paycheck deduction.

I was relentless. Every morning I'd mention it, every time we were together. Sometimes I'd wake Sean in the middle of the night and pick up where I'd left off. He was reluctant, at first. He lacked the vision to see the beauty of what I was suggesting. He probably thought I was crazy. But he knew I meant it. And if he said no? The result of his refusal would be worse than whatever I wanted him to do. Maybe worse than he could imagine.

One night, after we had sex, always the best time to approach Sean or any man, I brought it up again. Maddening. You have the smartest, coolest idea in the world, but you have to fuck them first.

"Our lives aren't so bad," he said. "We're working our asses off, darling, but we won't be forever. Nicky seems happy."

I said, "Is this what you want, Sean? Working round the clock, hardly ever seeing our son—the only child we'll ever have. Do you want to wake up one day and realize he's in college? Gone? Do you want day after day of this sameness, this . . . boredom?"

I'd said too much. I'd come too close to revealing something about myself that I would just as soon keep hidden. Everyone has secrets, as Stephanie says, ad nauseam.

"Are you saying you're bored with me?" Sean asked.

I was. But I wasn't going to admit that.

"Sean, don't you want to take a risk? Put all our chips on the line. Gamble. Live recklessly. Live on the edge. *Do* you want to get to the point where we say, 'Is this all there is?'"

That stopped him. He could tell that what I meant was, Are *you* all there is? What would prevent me from finding a man with more money and time than Sean—and taking Nicky with me?

I would never do that. Sean was Nicky's dad. Nothing could change that, and no one could replace him.

I hammered away at him. If we wanted to keep leading the life we were living, the life that was leading *us*—the mortgage, the car, the art on our walls, the clothes that cost plenty even with my office discount but that I had to wear to work—we were trapped. There was no way out. Property values had flatlined since we moved to Connecticut, and if we sold the house, we would take a loss. We couldn't afford to move back to Manhattan unless we wanted to live in Bushwick or squeeze into a postwar one-bedroom in Midtown. Even with Sean's salary and mine we'd need a huge mortgage, or we could rent, which would be expensive and not ideal.

For the first time, I didn't object when Sean wanted to relax in front of the TV. But now I made him watch *House Hunters*, *House Hunters International*, and all the house-hunting shows. Every night a couple decided to start a new life in some exotic place. Antigua, Nice, Sardinia, Belize. Why? Because they wanted to get away from the rat race, to spend more time with their family.

"*They're* doing it," I'd tell Sean. "Those losers are doing what you're afraid to try."

"Where did they get the money?" he'd say. "They never tell you."

"I know where to get the money," I said. "Money is not the problem. You're having the balls to *do* something about it is the problem."

I hadn't forgotten the look on Sean's face when he put his mother's ring on my finger on the plane. It was just a matter of time until he did what I said.

Sean would take out the maximum life insurance that his company offered. I'd disappear. Lie low for a while. I'd have to fake my own death. This was the difficult part. But people did it in books and films all the time. And in real life. And they got away with it!

So it must be possible. That part needed some thought.

I'd stay out of sight for however long it took, depending on how hard the authorities seemed to be looking for me. Then I'd change my look. Get a fake passport.

Sean would collect the insurance money, and we would move to some paradise in Europe where no one would ask any questions about the attractive American expat couple and their adorable son. We'd pay the rent in cash.

When the money ran out, we'd take stock. But if we were careful that wouldn't happen for a while. And we'd have fun. We'd do what we wanted, all the time. We would never be bored again.

It wasn't the most sensible plan. It had a few wrinkles that needed to be ironed out. Maybe no sane person would have imagined that this was going to work. I liked that it was a long shot. The opposite of tedious and safe.

I've read about what's called *folie à deux*. Two people (here comes another sickening word) *enable* each other's mental illness. I reread *In Cold Blood*, and this time I paid attention to the evil chemistry ignited when those two guys met, and to those killings that wouldn't have happened if either had been on his own.

Could Sean and I be like that if we embraced this scheme and went for it? Could we enable each other to do things we would never do alone? And who were we harming, really? We weren't blowing away a decent, hardworking farmer, his wife, and their two beautiful children. We were helping ourselves to funds from a company that had stolen the money from decent, hardworking people like that farmer and his family.

Maybe it wasn't a good sign that we both found it sexy. Talking about it began to turn us on. Scheming was foreplay, and sex was almost as hot as it was when he'd put his mother's ring on my finger on the plane from the UK. Almost.

I told myself that it *was* a good sign. A hot marriage was good for us, good for our bodies and souls, good for Nicky.

On the outside, we looked like normal people. Better than normal. A successful upper-middle-class couple who could hold down two important jobs and have a fabulous house and raise a wonderful kid. And oh, yes. Make a best friend.

I needed someone to believe me and tell the world my version of the story. Most of all, I needed someone who would take care of Nicky during what was going to be a hard time for him until our little family was reunited. I had Alison, Nicky's terrific nanny. But she was determined to go back to school, and she'd never wanted to work more than part-time. I needed someone who would make Nicky her highest priority, maybe one place beneath her own son, but that was close enough.

It was a crazy plan. The kind of insane Hail Mary–pass scheme you read about in the papers and think: Who is going to fall for that? Who would imagine that anyone would buy it? But Sean and I couldn't manage to sit down and find a reasonable step-by-step exit strategy. *That* would have been bad for our marriage. Sean still needed to see me as the rebel girl who'd invited him, on our third date, to watch *Peeping Tom.* And he still needed to see himself as that rogue girl's husband.

I became a friendship predator, on the prowl for a new best friend. It wasn't about sex or power but about closeness and trust. About raising our kids. About motherhood.

Every Friday afternoon, I got off early from work. That had been something of a struggle, though Dennis Nylon Inc. made a lot of noise about being flexible and family friendly. I was the one who wrote the press releases about our flexible family friendliness, so it would have looked bad if Blanche—Dennis's second in command, his attack dog—told me I couldn't leave early on Fridays to pick up my son at school.

I stood under a tree near Nicky's school. I watched the other mothers. I was looking for Nicky and at the same time trolling for the right mother.

The best friend.

It was easy compared to what I had to do for work at fashion shows, promotional events, and meetings, scanning the rooms and arenas for the first flutter of disruption. A celebrity had gotten the wrong brand of vodka! Disaster!

Looking for a mother to befriend, I felt like a pervert trawling the mall for that insecure, overweight preteen girl chewing on her hair. I was looking for Captain Mom.

Captain Mom was what Sean and I called the ones with the

backpacks and front packs and harnesses and strollers, the portable cribs and high chairs, the baby harnesses strapped to their bodies, the quilted jackets like space suits in which they could rocket to Mars, if they had to. With Baby all warm and safe.

I was looking for the Captain Mom who wanted to be best friends. The Captain Mom who was looking for me.

Stephanie was right about the other mothers being unfriendly. But Sean and Nicky and I had lived on the Upper East Side, so frostiness was nothing new to us. Months later, we were still thawing out from that Manhattan cold shoulder.

For the first few weeks of school, I saw Captain Mom looking in my direction. But it wasn't until that rainy day, when she'd forgotten to bring her umbrella, that we made eye contact. Even from a distance I could see that flicker of panic. As if forgetting her umbrella was a catastrophe. It wasn't even cold, nor was it raining hard. I was accustomed to celebrities acting that way, but not normal people. Then I saw her looking anxiously at the school door, and I realized she wasn't worried about getting wet but about her *child* getting wet during the one-minute walk to her car.

I waved her over. I'd brought the company umbrella, which Dennis's licensing people designed to be extra sturdy, wide—and light.

They made a dozen of them and then canceled. Too goofy for the price. After that Dennis went traditional. The next prototype was a masterpiece. Practically a tent. Modeled on a British umbrella, a traditional banker's accessory. Sean was touched when I gave him one of those, as if I'd had it tailor-made for him. It wasn't till after we'd moved in together that he figured out that I'd gotten a half-dozen for free; they were extras from some celebrity event at which Dennis Nylon Inc. gave out top-of-the-line swag. Those parties were so much work. There was always some diva trying to make my assistant get her special shoes we didn't make. Dennis Nylon has sold a hundred thousand of those banker's umbrellas, mostly in Japan.

Anyhow, I invited the super-anxious mom—"Hi," she said, "I'm

Miles's mom, Stephanie"—to share my oversize designer umbrella decorated with swimming ducks. It was made for Stephanie; that's who it was made for. As usual, Dennis was correct about it not being right for the brand's demographic.

You would have thought that my cruise ship had picked up Stephanie's life raft bobbing on a shark-infested sea. Letting Stephanie share my umbrella was like asking an overexcitable puppy to share your bowl of kibble.

I gave her the umbrella because I wanted her to feel special, chosen. I told her it was the only one Dennis had made. Later, when we got to my house, I saw her eyeing all the other umbrellas like it, and a warning bell went off. Girl, I told myself, get your story—your *stories*—straight. And I have, from then on.

Nicky and Miles were friends. She'd assumed I knew that. Otherwise, this being snooty Connecticut, I would never have waved her over.

I knew that Nicky had a friend named Miles. But at that point Nicky and I didn't talk that much. We didn't have time. He was often asleep before I got home, fed and put to bed by Alison. Sometimes Sean didn't see Nicky all week.

That was the reason behind our plan. Or a part of it. Reason one: I wanted to see my son. Reason two: I needed to do something that was risky and not boring. Reason three: Who could pass up a chance to make two million dollars just for having a little fun?

I invited Stephanie and Miles back to our house. I knew Sean would be working late, even on Friday night. The two boys ran off to play, thrilled to be together.

I can't remember much about that first conversation. I probably agreed with everything Stephanie said. Yes, motherhood was demanding. Yes, it was all-involving. Yes, the emotions and the responsibilities had come as a total surprise. A shock. Rewarding. A nightmare. A joy.

I nodded and nodded.

Stephanie was ecstatic. She'd found a kindred spirit. And I'd found the magician's helper who runs the sword through the box from which the pretty assistant has mysteriously vanished.

Years ago Pam, the creative director at Dennis Nylon Inc., set up a fashion shoot. Professional poker players, guys who appeared on TV, were supposed to be photographed wearing the skinny suits Dennis was showing that year. Tropical, light, vaguely gangster, a slightly shiny charcoal.

Pam hadn't thought it through. The poker champs wore weird sizes. Fat cowboys, stocky guys from Hong Kong. Geeky mathematicians who would have looked like crap no matter what they wore.

Only one guy was hot, a famous player everyone called George Clooney though he wasn't George Clooney; he just looked like him. He had a girlfriend, Nelda, an eighties punk rock star, also a serious poker player who might win or lose thirty grand in one game and come back the next night.

The shoot had a lot of problems, and by the end it was clear that it had cost a fortune and likely couldn't be used. The idea was cool, but all the guys except George Clooney made the clothes look like garbage. It was embarrassing and expensive. It cost poor Pam her job.

After the shoot, I asked George Clooney and Nelda out for a drink. A drink on Dennis Nylon, just to apologize for how badly the day had gone. I was doing what I could, trying (unsuccessfully) to salvage the situation for Pam.

George Clooney and Nelda didn't want to go, especially when they found out that Dennis Nylon wouldn't be joining us. But they couldn't think of an excuse fast enough. There was a nice tequila bar nearby, which I knew my way around, and pretty soon George Clooney and Nelda were telling me about poker.

I wish I could remember the things they said because all the little tricks and techniques would be so helpful in daily life. What I remember is this:

There is always one person in a high-stakes game whom the others call "the fish." And by the end of the game, the fish will have lost all his money.

George Clooney said, "If you don't know who the fish is, chances are good that you *are* the fish."

Stephanie was the fish. Under no other circumstances would I have become friends with someone who had been blogging about how she wanted to reach out to like-minded moms.

At that first conversation, I talked about my job. Stephanie talked about her blog. I said I was eager to read it. That completed the circle for Stephanie. We weren't friends just because we had kids. We had minds and careers. We worked. We admired each other's professional life.

I knew that she had been widowed by a horrible accident. You couldn't live in our town without having heard about it. But it was better to pretend not to know, to wait for her to tell me.

The blog was what clinched it. The banality, those nerdy posts about being the perfect mom and reaching out to other moms, helping other moms, and maybe once in a while stepping back so you can reflect on the culture's efforts to turn you and the other moms into baby-making childcare machines with no life or identity of your own. Surprise, *moms*! It's already happened!

The blog was reassuring. I could leave my husband and son with Stephanie without being afraid that they would fall for her bullshit. Hilarious.

The joke is on me, as they say.

We all wish for what we don't have. Stephanie envied my career at Dennis Nylon, though she would never admit it. All I wanted—or *thought* I wanted—was to stay home with Nicky. With lots of money, in some gorgeous place. And without having to work. I wanted to risk getting caught—and not get caught. I'd deal with boredom later. If I got restless, Nicky and I could always figure it out.

Stephanie was deluding herself if she thought she could do my job. With her constant blabbing about Miles, she wouldn't have lasted five minutes at Dennis Nylon. No one there wanted to hear about kids. At first no one had families, either because they were gay, or if they were straight, because they were young and scared. Then the gay couples began having more kids than the straight scared ones. Occasionally someone at work would ask me how Nicky was, but not often, and Dennis didn't want to hear about Nicky. At all.

On paper we were child friendly. But that didn't mean *friendly* friendly. I didn't have Nicky when Dennis hired me. I'm not sure he would have hired me if I'd had a kid. Every time I mentioned Nicky's name, Dennis shut down, and I changed the subject to what Dennis was thinking of doing for his next collection. Dennis gets his power from being a genius and switching his attention on and off like a faucet.

If I needed someone to take care of Nicky when it was time to disappear, there was no one I could hire that would be as good as a Captain Mom. You can't pay for childcare like that. Who could have predicted that Stephanie would interpret her duties to include sleeping with my husband?

Really, I should have known. At first I thought that Stephanie's blog was just harmless, tree-hugging bullshit. But after I got to know her, it was interesting to observe the gap between the woman she pretended to be in her blog and the person she was. Reading the blog, you'd think she was the picture of respectability, the best and most honest mom who ever lived, when in fact she was a woman who had had a long passionate affair with her half brother and who may have been responsible for her husband's suicide.

I chose to see what I wanted to see. I should have taken her lies as a warning.

Of course she didn't tell me all her secrets right away. But she always hinted that there was something a little extra, something dark in her history that was maybe a bit kinky, something that would hold my interest if my attention chanced to stray from the fascinating question of how the boys were liking their teacher, and her efforts to get Miles to eat vegetarian.

Her secrets were her capital. In the beginning, our conversations were like a guessing game. She would hint at these secrets, and I would have to manipulate her into telling me what they were. Or at least what they were *about*. It was all fake. She *wanted* to tell me. She couldn't *wait*.

I knew how her husband and brother died, but I pretended not to. And it was such a sad story that I cried. Real tears. That meant a lot to her, because she'd thought I was reticent, even chilly, though I had been trying my best, working overtime to seem cozy and warm.

After we'd cried together, she said how great it was to have a friend, a best friend, like we did when we were teenagers.

It was hard for me to respond. Not that it mattered. She was so sure that she knew who I was and how I felt about her, she was never curious about the truth.

Stephanie was weak but pushy and forceful in her weakness. She willed us to be best friends forever. As if we *were* teenage girls. She studied me: my clothes, my style. How I talked to Nicky. It's flattering when someone wants to be you, even if it gives you the creeps. *Single White Female* is one of the scariest films ever made.

Sean and I reminded ourselves: It was all about Nicky.

I didn't want a best friend. I wanted a character witness and a temporary caretaker for my son.

Stephanie poured her heart out to me. I could have been a priest or a reverend or a rabbi or her therapist. It's hard to know what to say when your son's best friend's mom tells you that she had an affair with her half brother. An affair that lasted from when she met him at eighteen to not long before he was killed—and that may have caused her husband to kill himself and his wife's lover. His brother-in-law.

"Wow," was all I could say.

"Wow indeed," Stephanie said.

What did I have to trade her, secret for secret? Isn't that how a friendship is supposed to work? I complained about Sean and how stressful it was to visit his mom in the UK. I told her what a fabulous lover he was. I complained about how hard I worked. I complained about Sean thinking he was smarter than me and not giving me credit for how much I did. All of which was true, but I couldn't tell her the big secret, which was that all this—every conversation, every after-school glass of white wine and greasy burger and game of miniature golf—was part of a plan that Sean and I had put in motion.

I'm not sure she ever listened. She needed to talk, to hint that there was more, something else she had to tell me, something darker that she was holding back. The carrot at the end of the stick of my fake friendship with Stephanie.

She picked a strange place to tell me that last big secret, which, to tell the truth, I already intuited, and I'd been expecting.

It was a Saturday in August. Sean had to work in the city. Stephanie and I decided to take the kids to the county fair. I told myself it could be fun: the heirloom chickens and prize-winning pigs, the blue-ribbon bottles of pickles. The boys would like the farm animals and the cotton candy and the carousel.

But the day was extremely hot. The fairgrounds were dusty and airless. The roiling vats of frying onion blooms and (new this year) deep-fried Oreos hung in the air, an oily, sweaty mist. For a few minutes I thought I was going to faint or vomit.

As the boys ran ahead of us, never out of sight, Stephanie and I wondered: What mother in her right mind would let her kid ride that creaky, ancient roller coaster? I would have loved to ride it, but I didn't feel I could say that.

The one ride that the boys were old enough to go on by themselves, and that they didn't think was insultingly babyish, was a ring of little cars made to look like submarines. Attached to a central pole by rods, the mini-subs turned slowly, rising slightly in the air and gently dipping toward the pool of water beneath them. A toddler ride.

It looked completely safe, but still I was surprised that overprotective, neurotic Stephanie let Miles go on it. She and I leaned on the fence that encircled the ride and watched our boys turn and dip. I wondered if she remembered *Strangers on a Train*. I'd made her watch it with me. She'd been very disturbed by the carousel scene. I don't think she ever finished the book, though she pretended she did.

Stephanie said, "Look at Miles. Look when he comes closer."

"What about him?"

"Take a good look. Do you remember I showed you those pictures of my brother, Chris?"

"Of course." I recalled a dark, handsome, muscular guy in a white T-shirt and jeans. Shy in front of the camera, slightly shifty. I could see why she'd been drawn to him because I'd also seen photos of her husband, Davis, and the brother was way more attractive. I remember her showing me his picture along with her parents' wedding photo and pointing out the resemblance between her dad and her half brother. Between her mom and her.

Then Stephanie said, "I need to tell you something I've never told anyone ever."

She'd started a lot of conversations that way. Some of her stories had been intense—her affair with her brother—while other "secrets" seemed so insignificant that I instantly forgot them.

Miles and Nicky passed in their little submarines. They smiled and waved, and we smiled and waved back.

I was thinking about the scene in the Hitchcock film. The merry-go-round spins faster and faster, further and further out of control as Farley Granger and Robert Walker struggle to the death. The only person who knows how to stop it is a little old man who crawls under the carousel. Watching him put himself in danger is far scarier and more suspenseful than the fight.

What would *we* do if Miles and Nicky were spinning faster and faster? Who would crawl under the merry-go-round to save our boys? The girl who took tickets was texting someone. I realized that I was having the kind of thought that Stephanie would have. You're Emily, I reminded myself. Not her.

I went around to Stephanie's other side and switched on the fancy tape recorder I'd started carrying in my pocket for moments like the one that was about to happen.

The submarine ride was playing disco classics but not very loud. The ticket girl was keeping the music down in case she got a phone call.

Stephanie said, "I'm pretty sure that my half brother, Chris, was Miles's father."

"Hi, honey," she called out to Miles, and I waved at Nicky.

"Why do you think so?" I asked, trying to sound calm. "Stephanie, are you sure or not?"

"I'm sure. Davis was away for a while. On a site in Texas. Chris came over. Miles looks just like Chris. He doesn't look like Davis at all. Davis's mom says she can't see one single gene from her side of the family in her grandson."

I'd known she was going to say that. I'd been expecting it for a long time. Still, it was shocking to hear her admit it.

"Miles looks like you," I said.

"Do you think people suspect?"

"Of course not." No one was going to figure it out. Surely not Miles's teachers. Maybe Miles himself, later, when he asked to see pictures of his father and his uncle.

No one except your dead husband, I thought. But I wasn't going to say that.

"Emily, you know me so well. I love you so much. It feels so good to tell someone, not to have to keep it bottled up inside. Am I a terrible person?"

As their submarines came around again, Miles and Nicky seemed to have slipped into a trance.

"The boys are great," I said, as if in answer to Stephanie's question. She would think it was the answer.

The kids had two, maybe three more times around before the ride ended. Under pressure now, Stephanie spoke rapidly. "I can't bring

Miles to the doctor without feeling like a liar and a fraud. When they ask for the medical history of his father's side of the family, I pretend they're talking about Davis. Obviously, I don't mention that his dad is my half brother."

The ride slowed and stopped. The boys got off. They wanted to talk about the fun ride. It was hardly the moment to press Stephanie further on the subject of her son's father.

I couldn't believe that anyone would confess something like that. That kind of information gives someone so much power over you. Power to use however they want. Stephanie always said that you can never truly know anyone else. But she thought she knew me—and that I could be trusted. That was her mistake. She chose to forget that what I did for a living was to control information. To bend and use it in the most helpful way.

A few days later, in bed, I played Sean the recording of what Stephanie told me at the fair.

He said, "No wonder she always looks as if she's afraid of getting arrested."

Did a statement like that suggest that my husband found her attractive? I think not. I thought not. Another joke on me.

———

THERE WAS ONE thing I hadn't worked out: how to make it seem as if I was really dead so we didn't have to wait forever to collect the insurance money.

A solution presented itself. It landed in my lap—and I knew that it was time to move. At least Sean was smart enough not to ask what that solution was. He was better off not knowing.

Would everything have worked out differently if he'd trusted me when I said "Whatever happens, don't believe I'm really dead"? Maybe he wouldn't have slept with Stephanie. I wouldn't have wound up spying on them from the forest behind my own home.

Stephanie doesn't look at Sean as if she's scared of being arrested.

She should feel guilty—guiltier than she's ever felt about anything. She looks at my husband as if he's a god, the lord of the manor who sneaks down to the kitchen to make out with the besotted cook.

One thing that made me choose Stephanie as our fish was how obsessively she blogged about trying to feed her son healthy food. It was almost unendurable to hear her talk about it, but if I was going to leave Nicky with her, I liked it that she wouldn't be letting him live on candy-colored cereal and french fries and junk food burgers.

I didn't expect the rage that surges through me when I watch her in my kitchen. When I see how happy, how (Stephanie's word) *fulfilled* she looks.

Like a calming prayer, I repeat to myself: She is feeding my child. It would upset me more to dwell on what she is doing for my husband.

Does Stephanie know that Sean knows who Miles's father is? I doubt it. She believes that she's making Sean happier, making Nicky less miserable, filling in for her dead best friend. She's being a Good Samaritan. She imagines I would thank her if I knew. If I were alive.

Stephanie is as transparent as Sean turns out to be opaque. What is *he* doing with *her*? He's the one I never knew. Now I wonder: Who *is* this guy who creeps up behind my "friend" as she's doing the dishes and nuzzles the back of her neck and acts like they'd be having sex on the kitchen counter if the kids weren't in the next room? How could I not be enraged? Has Sean fallen in love with her? Lost his mind? In my opinion, that would amount to the same thing.

We'd agreed that for six months we'd stay out of touch. By then the interest in our case would have diminished. For six months, I would be dead. A suicide, some people would think. A drunken, pill-addled accident, Sean's lawyers would insist. And they would prevail.

But our separation wasn't supposed to be permanent. We weren't supposed to find someone else. That is a *serious* departure from our plan, and it changes everything.

One perk of working in the fashion industry is that everyone is about fifteen years old. They pride themselves on knowing how to use burner phones and open fake credit card accounts and set up phony email addresses and get bogus IDs—skills implying that being young and single in New York is the equivalent of being a criminal. A rebel. If they don't know how to do something illegal, they know someone who knows someone who does, usually in Bushwick.

We got a passport for Nicky. I got a fake passport, for when I would need it. I wore a wig and glasses, changed my appearance for the photo. I would use that look when we traveled. After I had my picture taken, it took me about ten seconds to lose the wig and glasses and go back to my "natural" look. What a relief—to look like myself again.

Sean and I each got a sworn affidavit giving the other permission to leave the country alone with Nicky. I was going be a stranger that Sean met in Europe and remarried after a suitable period of mourning for his wife—for me. And we would live on the insurance money from the accidental death of his first wife. Also me. Strangers would assume that we were an appealing, independently wealthy American expat couple.

I told the kids at work that I was having an affair and needed a fake identity for calling and renting hotel rooms. They loved it that the middle-aged head of publicity and bourgeois suburban supermom was cheating on her hunky Brit husband. They were delighted to help. They swore to keep their mouths shut. I was afraid they would tell, but they didn't. They liked the secrecy, the romance.

When my death was announced, they were genuinely sad. But they also liked knowing the inside gossip. They liked being privy to the fact that I was having an affair. They assumed my secret romance had something to do with the pills and booze, the suicide or accident. How tragic.

I figured out how to keep hidden. For a while I stayed in our family cabin, on the lake up in northern Michigan. Then I ditched the rental and took my mother's car. I moved to a house in the Adirondacks that belonged to friends of my parents. I'd gone there as a child. I knew it would be empty. I even knew where the key was. Neither the lake house nor the Adirondack cabin had a TV or internet connection. It was great to go off the grid. People find it hard, but I loved it. I didn't miss anything about my life—except Nicky.

It wasn't till later that I began to read Stephanie's blog and figure out what was going on. What she and Sean were doing. How Nicky was, or how another woman *thought* he was.

It is putting it mildly to say that I was appalled. It took a while for me to admit: I should have seen it coming.

It was all about Nicky. I couldn't stay away. I couldn't not see him. I missed him too much.

For once, I wasn't lying when I agreed with Stephanie: Motherhood had been a shock. The force of my love for the baby kicked in the first time I held him. I was lucky, I knew. It takes longer for some women. Even now, every time I see film footage of a birth, any birth, tears well in my eyes. And I am not a weeper—or a sentimental person.

Becoming a mother is like getting hit over the head, which I suppose is Stephanie's idiotic blog boiled down to one absurd sentence.

When I was hiding out, pretending to be dead, I dreamed about Nicky. I thought about him all the time. I wondered what he was doing.

I reached the point at which I felt that I couldn't live another day without seeing my son. I didn't know how I'd imagined that I could bear it. It had been insanity to try. Being without Nicky for six months was like being without an arm. Without a heart. I noted that I didn't feel anything like that about Sean—and that was even before I knew about him and Stephanie.

I stationed myself outside the school yard where the kids played during recess. I made sure Nicky saw me and the teachers didn't. Just seeing him was pure joy. I waved to him. I put my finger to my lips. The fact that I was alive was our little secret.

I decided to stay in the area. Mainly because I couldn't stand not to see Nicky.

I registered at the Hospitality Suites motel in Danbury. I was taking a risk, being so near home when I was supposed to be dead. But it was worth it if I could see my son. Besides, I liked taking risks. That was the part I liked best.

There was a chance, a small chance, that I was putting our plan in danger. Except that it was *my* plan now. That plan was all about Nicky.

I told the clerk that yes, I'd pay an additional fee to his cheapskate extortionist corporation for the use of the internet. I checked in and logged on and started reading Stephanie's blog: all the posts I'd missed since I left Nicky at her house.

When I read the posts that Stephanie started writing when I didn't show up to get Nicky, I thought, This is as real as Stephanie is ever going to be. The poor thing was terrified. It was touching to read her pleas to the stressed-out, isolated mothers. As if those overworked women had nothing to do but cruise the streets, searching for the missing friend Stephanie couldn't even describe. As if they weren't busy enough changing diapers, making grilled cheese, filling sippy cups with milk.

I was curious to see what Stephanie had to say about my disappearance. Her theories, her analyses of my character and my motives, her laments for our lost friendship. When all that time she was planning to seduce my husband and try to take my place. As if she could.

I will never forgive them.

I never would have predicted that Sean and Stephanie would do this. Now I have to watch them, keep them in my sights until I decide what to do.

During our friendship I read her blog and paid just enough attention to talk about the subjects (motherhood and herself, mostly herself) that she blogged about. But her drivel was nothing I would have chosen to read. The self-delusion, the posing. The madness of seeing your child as the epicenter of the universe.

It was after I read her posts about Sean that I became really enraged.

The self-serving, delusional lies! That was my husband! My son with whom she was trying to replace me, whom she wanted to forget me. I'd chosen her because I thought she was someone who could take care of Nicky, not someone who wanted another child. She was like those sad crazy women who steal newborns from the neonatal ward. You want a kid, you take someone else's. But Stephanie wasn't that crazy. And the child she was stealing was mine.

––––––––

I LIKE THE Hospitality Suites. My room is clean, and the bland beige decor is soothing. I've made my peace with the ineradicable stains on the carpet. The sheets and blankets are clean. Nothing smells bad, and everything is where it's supposed to be. It's quiet; it feels safe. It's got none of the downsides of motels. I don't have to improvise a bathtub stopper. I've stayed in worse when I traveled for Dennis Nylon.

I take a lot of baths. I bought halfway decent bath gel and shampoo at Target.

There's a pretty good Salvadoran pupusa restaurant around the corner and a well-stocked convenience store down the block, close enough to walk. It sells decent fresh fruit and ramen I can make in the coffeepot in my room. The owner liked me from the start. He could tell that I wasn't going to hate him for being Muslim, which he isn't. From the wall behind the counter, the Hindu elephant god blesses the lottery tickets.

My room has a refrigerator; there's an ice machine in the hall. I buy bottles of premium mezcal at the liquor store and mango nectar at the health food store. Every night I make a cocktail with mezcal and mango juice. I learned the recipe from Dennis Nylon. It was his drink of choice.

I bought one cocktail glass at the mall. I like to drink my cocktail and read. I order books on my iPad. I'd never read Beckett before. He's describing how it feels to be me at this moment in time.

I'm surprised by how little I miss my job. It was such a part of my life. I don't miss the nasty surprises that will be my fault unless I figure out how to fix them. I don't miss Dennis's drug binges, or Blanche's cyclonic rages. I don't even miss the perks, the buzz. What does it mean that I'm happier in a Hospitality Suites motel in Danbury than in Milan or Paris representing Dennis Nylon Inc.?

The motel TV works well enough, though they don't have the premium stations. There are some shows I like. Cooking contests. People looking for houses on beaches and building tiny rolling homes in which the couple will split up or kill each other. I used to watch those house-hunting shows with Sean. It's more fun watching them alone. I can just enjoy them and skip the boring conversations about how those people are starting new lives, so why can't we? What a joke! Now I'm supposed to be dead—and Sean has started his new life without me.

Will he get to keep the money if I stay an accidental death? A dead woman can't take care of Nicky, so something will have to be done.

The local news is mostly about traffic accidents and domestic and gang-related violence in Newburgh, Hartford, and further into New England depending on how many people got shot. Many reporters are black or Hispanic. The women have shiny salon-curled hair. Once a day I go online and read Stephanie's blog about living with Nicky and Miles and Sean. The happy, healthy blended Brady Bunch. That alone is infuriating. That I *want* to know what she writes. That I care.

When we were "friends," I only read it because she insisted.

Two nights after I phoned Stephanie just to scare her and let her know I was there, this post went up on her blog:

26

STEPHANIE'S BLOG

THE AFTERLIFE

Hi, moms!

Some of you are going to think that I have finally lost it completely. You'll think that the sad, life-changing events of the last months have driven Stephanie out of her mind.

All I can say is I'm still here. Despite everything, I'm still me. Stephanie. Miles's mom.

Today I want to write about something that no one discusses, except in Bible class or church. When a person says "thank heaven" or "go to hell," they're not thinking of heaven or hell as places where we might wind up. The subject doesn't arise at drinks or dinner parties or over coffee.

The afterlife.

Even if we never go near a church or a synagogue or a mosque, most of us have noticed how having a child can make a person more spiritual. Miles has told me that, after we die, we all get together on a big happy cloud. That's a nice way to see it. But grown-ups hardly ever ask, Where do *you* think our loved ones go? It's a more untouchable subject than sex or even money.

Are the dead near us? Can they hear us? Will they answer our prayers? Do they visit our dreams? I've been thinking about these questions a lot, wondering where Emily is now. I've been asking myself what I would say to her if I thought she could hear me.

So with this blog I'd like to get a little experimental, a little . . . further out than usual.

I'm going to write this as if I could communicate with my friend who has passed. As if she could read this. I hope that writing it will be healing for me. And I urge you moms out there to write your own letter to someone who has passed and you still want to talk to.

So here goes:

27

STEPHANIE'S BLOG
THE AFTERLIFE (PART TWO)
DEAR EMILY, WHEREVER YOU ARE

Dear Emily,

I don't know how to begin. What do people say in emails these days? Hope this finds you well!

I hope this finds you at peace.

I'm sure that, if you could read this, the first thing you would want to know is how Nicky is. He's thriving. Of course he misses his mom. We all miss you more than I can ever say. He knows that you'll always be his mom. That no one will ever replace you. But he no longer cries every night, like he used to. I know you wouldn't want that.

Would you?

Sometimes I hope the dead are with us, near us, that Davis and Chris and you—and my parents—are over my shoulder, watching out for me, helping and advising me, even if I don't know it. At other times I hope they're spared the pain of seeing life go on without them.

I know it would be painful for you, dear Emily, to see me cooking in your kitchen. But I want you to know that I am preparing the most delicious, nutritious food for your son. I can never take your place. All I can do is love the people you used to love and try to make their lives better.

Which is what I know you would want, if you loved them.

Rest in peace, my dear best friend.

Your friend forever,

Stephanie

What do you think, moms? Write in with letters of your own or with your comments and concerns. And thank you, as always, for your love and support.

Love,

Stephanie

28

EMILY

That blackmailing, lying bitch. I slammed down my laptop so hard I was afraid I broke it. I was relieved when I flipped it back up and my background—the selfie Nicky took of himself staring into my computer—came back on.

That mindless slut. She knows I'm not dead. She knows I'm watching her. And not from heaven. Even she isn't stupid enough to believe she's blogging to the dead. Maybe she's convinced herself that she imagined my phone call. Maybe she's tried to put it out of her mind. But she can't. She knows.

She can't tell *that* to her blogosphere moms. She's talking to *me*, in case I happen to be reading this. That Stephanie assumes I'm reading her blog is maddening, though not half as maddening as her moving in with my husband and son.

She got used to thinking I was dead. She got to like the idea. So much for friendship. For grief. So I'd called to let her know I'm not dead.

My number comes up as OUT OF AREA. There's no way for her to reach me, except through her blog. She thinks everybody reads her blog. I alone would have a good reason. She probably wishes I *were* dead. Someone who wants me dead is tucking my son into bed every night and sleeping with my husband.

And she has the nerve to write that this is what I would want? Maybe she is crazy, which means a crazy woman is raising my son.

It pains me to admit that Stephanie was right about how you can never really know anyone. If Stephanie wants to play cat and mouse . . . she can be the mouse. I'll be the cat. That cat is patient. The mouse is afraid. The mouse has reason to be afraid.

Because the cat always wins. The cat is the one who enjoys it.

29

STEPHANIE

I no longer know what's real. For a while I managed to convince myself that I'd hallucinated the phone call from Emily. It was like when you have a worrisome pain and the pain goes away. First you try to forget about it. Then you do forget it.

I always knew I would be punished for my affair with Chris and for deceiving my husband and having my half brother's child. I should never have told Emily who Miles's father is. No one could be trusted with that information. I had the foolish idea that telling someone would make my punishment lighter. I confessed to the wrong person. Now the punishment comes.

If she's alive, someone knows what I've done. Someone who wants to harm me.

I always knew that Emily was smarter than I am. I should never have let this happen. I should have died of loneliness and sexual frustration before I let myself sleep with Sean and move into Emily's house.

I'm no match for her. She's probably laughing about my pathetic attempt to contact her on my blog by pretending I thought she was dead. She is the only one who knows how much of my blog is a lie.

I wonder how much she told Sean. Not everything, I think. When I mention Chris, I never catch him looking at me nor studying Miles for signs that he's been damaged by incest and inbreeding.

Sean seems to love Miles. Miles is lovable. And I've grown to love Nicky. Do Sean and I love each other? I don't want to think about that.

Wouldn't Emily have wanted this?

Not if she's alive. Which she is. Maybe. Probably. And I'm being punished.

What have I done to deserve this? All I did was try to make a friend, to befriend the mother of my child's friend. Bad call, Stephanie!

What will Emily do now? Nothing. She's dead. Or is she out there? Watching.

I keep imagining someone—a police detective—asking me why I did this or that instead of this or that other thing. I keep saying I don't know. I no longer know what makes sense. I focus on what's best for Miles. But I'm no longer sure that the best thing for my son is living with my best friend's husband when, for all I know, she is watching.

I pull the curtains; it doesn't help. She's out there. Or maybe I'm imagining it. There is always that chance.

I don't know why I don't tell someone. Actually, I do know. What would I tell the police? Remember my friend who disappeared? And you guys did nothing? Well, now I'm living with her husband. And she might be back, and they might be collecting millions of dollars in insurance money from her apparent death. Who would believe me? Who am I? A mommy and a blogger. Women like me get locked up in psycho wards all the time. They see the dead; they hear voices; they can't accept the truth; they insist on their nutty stories until someone in protective services decides that their child would be better off in foster care.

I'm afraid that the story of my friendship with Emily and my relationship with Sean might lead the police to the truth about Miles's dad. They'd have a false missing persons report and maybe insurance fraud on their hands, and self-centered me, I'm sure they'll focus on a possible case of incest.

Whatever Emily is up to, she can count on me. I gave her that power at the county fair when we watched Miles and Nicky on the ride.

I didn't tell Sean that Emily called. Maybe I don't really trust him. I'm no longer sure whom to trust. I trust Miles. And most of the time I trust Nicky.

I'm almost sure that Sean believes she's dead. And if she's alive, she hasn't tried to contact him. Or maybe she has, and he hasn't told me. If she's angry about Sean and me, why is she blaming *me*? He was her husband. *Is* her husband.

I can't imagine how to tell him. I can't find the right time. I'm living with him, yet I can't say, I think your dead wife called on the phone.

I realize that the blog post addressed to my not-dead friend won't work. It might make things worse. But it was a welcome distraction, figuring out what to say.

My inbox filled with ghost stories, which have been helpful. Moms everywhere are seeing the dead. Some of the stories were very touching. One was about a dead mom whose spirit brings her daughter a book that's fallen open to a short story about a dead mother. The daughter felt her mother's reassuring presence in the room. I cried when I read that one, thinking about my own mother and the hell she went through.

In none of the moms' stories does the dead person turn out to be alive. That's a comfort, I guess!

I haven't heard any more from Emily. And I've convinced myself that she's dead. Some cruel joker must have imitated her voice and somehow gotten it right. Maybe someone at her job. It could have been a prank call. Why would someone do something like that? People do worse things all the time. And what about the caller knowing how many fingers I was holding up?

Lucky guesses, is all.

Don't think about it, Stephanie. I still love and miss my friend. But the truth is that her being dead may be better than her watching me from the woods. Watching me with her husband.

———

THE SECOND TIME Emily called, she again waited till I was alone. The caller ID said OUT OF AREA.

She said, "I'm still here."

I said, "Emily, where are you?"

She said, "The fact that I am not in heaven is proved by the fact that I can still read your ridiculous moronic blog. Blogging to me in the afterlife is really stupid, Stephanie. Even for you."

"*Mrrrr.*" I made an angry cat sound. "Harsh. That's unlike you."

She said, "How do you know what *like me* is? You don't get it, do you? You never got it."

"I do," I said. "I get it." Though I wasn't sure if I did. The caller had her voice down. This time I had to be sure.

I said, "How do I know it's really you?"

"Listen hard," Emily said. There was a silence. I heard static, then a clattering, like something banging against the phone. Then I heard carnival music . . .

I heard my own voice saying, "I'm going to tell you something I've never told anyone ever . . ." I heard myself confessing that Miles is Chris's son.

The tape recorder clicked off.

"They have marvelous voice-recognition technology these days," Emily said, "to authenticate this, if needed."

"Who would care?" I was bluffing.

"Everyone would," said Emily. "Miles would, for one. If not now, then later."

"I can't believe you would do this," I said. "What do you want?"

"I want Nicky," Emily said. "You can have everything else. But I want you to keep your mouth shut. For once."

"I will!" I said. "I promise."

"Talk soon." Emily hung up.

After that, some homing instinct kicked in. I wanted to be home, if only for an afternoon. In my own home. Not in Sean and Emily's home. In the home that Davis and I built, in which I'd lived with Davis and Miles, and then for three years with Miles after Davis's death. I must have been mad to think that I could move into a place vacated by a dead woman. My so-called best friend.

I'd told myself that the four of us living together would be better for the boys. But it was worse for me. As I drove to my house, I felt dizzy. The road I'd traveled so many times looked strangely unfamiliar. I reminded myself to concentrate.

Finally, there it was. My house. Completely real, but like a house in a dream. How I loved that house! I always had. I should never have left it.

I was home. The lawn was lightly dusted with snow. How good it felt to walk up the front stairs. My feet knew the height of each step, measurements that Davis had spent hours of his too-short life figuring out. My hand knew how to turn the key in the lock, my shoulder knew how to hold the door open so I could get through even if I was holding packages, which I wasn't. I'd come with nothing, like a refugee.

I walked into the kitchen. How I'd missed it and how I longed to be here, cooking for Miles and me. I would talk to Sean. We could work out another arrangement that would let us be home more often.

I drifted into the living room. It took me a moment to figure out what was different—what was so disturbing.

I smelled Emily's perfume. I should never have given her my keys.

30

STEPHANIE'S BLOG
WISE CHILDREN

Hi, moms!

Here's another story about how beautiful our kids are, how they know so much more than we give them credit for, sometimes more than we do.

I was never good about birthdays. The only birth dates I ever remembered were those of my parents, my half brother, my husband, and Miles.

So I was taken aback when, early in March, Nicky asked, "Are we going to celebrate my mom's birthday this year?"

I told Nicky, "Yes, of course." We got a cake with a single candle.

I let Nicky choose the cake. Chocolate with bright frosting flowers.

We lit the candle and said a silent prayer. We didn't sing "Happy Birthday." I think Nicky was happy about it. It was one of those things kids do to help us heal.

If you can read this, my dear friend Emily, wherever you are, happy birthday!

We love you.

Stephanie

31

STEPHANIE

Someone remembered Emily's birthday. A card arrived for her at Sean's.

That afternoon, in the mailbox, along with the bills and junk mail and fashion magazines that—now that Emily was gone—no one ever read, was an envelope addressed to Emily Nelson. Same handwriting, same brown ink as the ones in the manila folder I'd found in the vanity table.

It was one of cards that Emily got from her mother every year. The sight of it gave me chills.

Did Emily's mother still think she was alive? Had her caretaker not gotten around to giving her the bad news? Had she decided that Emily's mom wasn't strong enough? Or was there something else? Did some lingering mom intuition tell the old woman that her daughter *was* still alive?

That same night, I showed the card to Sean. He stared at it, clearly unnerved and upset, trying to look as if he had no idea what it was. He knew what it was.

He said, "The poor old thing is so demented she forgot Em is dead. And Bernice can't bring herself to keep reminding her. I think she's letting Mrs. Nelson believe that her daughter is alive . . ."

For just a moment, I wondered if he could be lying. He'd never

called Emily "Em" before. Besides, Emily wasn't dead. Did Sean know
that? Were they playing some cruel joke on me? Was I the pawn in
some evil plan they'd dreamed up together?

That I didn't know and couldn't ask made me conscious of how
little trust there was between Sean and me, though that didn't seem to
interfere with there being heat. Not every night, but often enough so
that we were both willing to stick around for it. Sean wasn't the cud-
dliest guy on the planet. I didn't expect him to be. He was British. He
was right with me when we were having sex, but afterward he'd grunt
and turn away, as if he wanted me gone.

Finally I said, "You have to tell me if this isn't working out for you.
If you're having second thoughts. Tell me. Do you want me to leave?"

He said, "What are you talking about, Stephanie?"

It was worse than his saying yes.

The postmark on the envelope was illegible, but I could make out the
letters *MI*. Michigan. Could Emily have sent the card to herself? Was
it part of her scheme to mess with my head? Was she somewhere outside, watching us celebrate her birthday with our candle and cake?
Without her. What was she looking for? What was she planning?

I asked Sean, "Can I open the card?"

He said, "Sure. Go ahead."

In that same spidery brown ink, it said, as always, *To Emily*, and
From Mother.

Unless Emily had done a terrific job of forging her mother's handwriting, she hadn't sent it. And why would she send a birthday card to
herself from Michigan and make it look as if it came from her mother?

The only explanation was that her mother didn't know that she was
dead. That she was supposed to be dead. Or her mother knew something I didn't.

I couldn't get the birthday card out of my mind. It became another
obsession.

Call it sixth sense or whatever, but I became convinced that I would understand everything if I could only meet Emily's mother and ask her a few questions. It was more than the usual curiosity about where a person came from. I was sure that Emily's mother could solve the mystery of where Emily had gone and why, of how she'd disappeared and why she seemed to have returned from the dead. Even if her mother didn't know what happened, she might say something useful that would make everything clear. Was she as ill as Sean said? She, or someone, had remembered Emily's birthday.

I found the phone number on the internet. I felt a little breathless when it came up on my screen: Mr. and Mrs. Wendell Nelson in Bloomfield Hills.

I called the number. Twice. The first time it rang and rang. The second time an old woman with a reedy voice answered.

"Hello?" she said. I couldn't speak. She said, "Is this those damn kids next door fooling around again? I told you I'm not home."

I hung up.

The third time I said, "Mrs. Nelson, I'm Stephanie. I'm a friend of your daughter's. A friend of Emily's." Under normal circumstances, I would have told her how sorry I was about Emily. But the circumstances were anything but normal.

"She never mentioned a Stephanie," the woman said. "I never heard anything about a Stephanie. Who did you say you were?"

I said, "A friend of Emily's. Your grandson Nicky is my son's best friend."

"Oh," she said wistfully. "That's right. Nicky."

So this was one of her good days.

"How old is he now?"

"Five."

"Oh," she said. "Dear God."

My heart went out to her. How long it had been since she'd seen him?

I don't know what possessed me to ask, "Do you think I could come visit you?"

My whole body tensed as I waited for her to hang up or say no.

"When," she said.

"Next weekend," I said.

"What day?" she said. "What time? Let me check my schedule."

I knew Sean wouldn't want me to go. I invented an Aunt Kate, desperately ill in Chicago. I asked Sean if he could watch the boys, and he said yes. Neither of us had to mention how much time *I'd* spent alone with the kids.

That I couldn't tell Sean the truth reminded me that there was no one I could rely on. I was all alone. Still, I trusted him in the most important way—to take care of my son when I was away overnight.

I was still sleeping with Sean. But I couldn't tell him that Emily was calling me and taunting me with secrets only she knew. He would say I was making things worse. That I couldn't face the truth. Maybe I'd lost touch . . .

Was I losing my mind? Imagining things? Maybe I was still in shock from my friend's disappearance and death. Maybe Sean was right. Maybe I was refusing to acknowledge the reality of Emily's death and making things worse for everyone.

Especially me.

I flew to Detroit and rented a car. I found Emily's mother's house, a mansion with pillars and a portico, like the house from *Gone with the Wind* transplanted to the Midwest. There was a circular driveway and hummocks of overgrown shrubbery hiding a lawn covered with dead brown weeds.

The old woman who answered was small and bent over, dressed in a cashmere sweater, stylish pleated pants, and expensive shoes with higher heels than I expected. Her white hair was pulled back neatly, her bright red lipstick expertly applied. She looked a little like Emily, but more like Grace Kelly if Grace Kelly had lived to be eighty.

The air smelled of rose potpourri as she showed me into a large,

grandmotherly living room full of good old furniture and dark paintings of shadowy figures in heavy frames.

"Remind me who you are," she said. "I've gotten a bit forgetful, I'm
afraid."

"Stephanie," I said. "Emily's friend. My son is Nicky's best friend."

"I see," said Emily's mother. "Do you need to use the bathroom?"

"That's all right," I said. "I'm fine, really. I'm fine . . ." I was bab-
bling.

Mrs. Nelson perched on a chair covered in rose-colored velvet, and
I sat on the edge of the couch. It was an uncomfortable couch but
remarkable, in a way. Old-fashioned, faux French antique, with shiny
silk embroidery. Deep pink-and-white candy striped. It was so unlike
anything that Emily would ever have allowed in *her* house.

"My husband is dead," her mother said.

At least she knew her husband was dead. This must be one of her
really good days.

"He worked in public relations for an auto company. Who would
think Emily would also go into PR after having seen what the '88 recall
did to her father?"

She pushed her glasses down her nose, leaned forward like a bird
pecking at grain, and for the first time actually looked at me.

She said, "You don't have any idea what the '88 recall was, do you?"

It was better to be honest. I shook my head no.

She said, "You really are stupid, aren't you?"

Already I could understand why Emily might have chosen to keep
her distance. I felt so sorry for her, having a mother who would say
something like that! Then I remembered that Emily had called me
stupid that last time she'd called on the phone. Passing along the
damage she'd sustained from her toxic mother. I'd so often blogged
about people trying to make moms feel stupid. I was really sick and
tired of being called stupid. Of being made to feel stupid. But I couldn't
afford to react.

If Emily's mom thought I was stupid, if she doubted that I was really Emily's friend, she would never tell me what I wanted to know. I had no idea what that was. I would know when I heard it.

I said, "Would you like to see pictures of Nicky?"

"Nicky?"

"Your grandson," I said.

"Of course," she said politely. "Where?"

I brought my phone over to her and stood beside her chair, flipping through my photos of Miles and Nicky. She seemed attentive. I couldn't tell if she wanted me to stop.

Then she said, "Which one is . . . ?"

"Nicky," I reminded her.

"Of course. Nicky."

I pointed to her grandson.

"Adorable," she said uncertainly.

I was relieved when she said, "That's enough. He's very cute."

She looked at me and sat back and said, "I've seen this in a movie. You and I were in a movie I saw on TV. You wanted to look at childhood photos of Emily. That's why you're here, isn't it?"

"Yes. I'd like that."

Even as I said it, I realized it was true. That was *exactly* why I was there.

"Would you like some tea?" she said.

"No, thank you," I said.

"Good," she said. "I don't think there is any. I'll be right back."

She rose and slowly shuffled out of the room. I heard murmuring. Mrs. Nelson and another woman. Her caretaker, I assumed.

I had a few minutes to look around. A grand piano draped with an embroidered Spanish shawl. Soft lighting. A mirrored credenza and a formal portrait of Emily's mother in an evening gown, decades ago. Probably before Emily was born. It made no sense that this was where Emily grew up, though I realized I had no idea what kind of place that would be. She'd never talked about her childhood home.

There was a funny anger in the way Mrs. Nelson moved her head and thrust the album at me, or maybe she was just in a hurry to sit back down in her chair.

The album was like the albums in which people keep CDs. Each photo had its own clear slipcase that gave off a faint plasticky smell.

I turned several pages before I understood what I was seeing.

In every picture there were two Emilys. Identical little girls.

Two identical Emilys in a garden, on a beach, in the woods in front of a sign that said Yosemite National Park. Two girls with blond hair and dark eyes, two Emilys aging as I flipped the pages.

"What's the matter?" said her mother. "You look terrible, dear. Are you all right?"

I thought of the Diane Arbus photo over Emily's fireplace and remembered her telling me that it was the thing she loved most in her house.

Mrs. Nelson said, "Remind me which one is Emily. Was she the one with that odious birthmark under her eye? Lord, I positively begged her to have it removed. Though it was sometimes the only way I could tell them apart. Of course, later, when Evelyn was always drunk or high, that made it easier."

I said, "I hadn't known that Emily was a twin."

She frowned. "How is that possible? Are you sure you're a friend of my daughter's? What do you really want here? I'm warning you. I've got security cameras everywhere."

I looked around. There were no security cameras.

"It's just strange," I said. "She never mentioned—"

"Evelyn. Her sister."

"Evelyn?" I said. "Where does *she* live?"

"Good question," her mother said. "I never know. Evelyn has problems. She's spent time in some extremely expensive rehab facilities that guess-who paid for. From time to time, I've lost track of her, and it turns out she's been on the street. Emily tried to save her sister. Tried and tried. I think she gave up."

How could Emily not have mentioned the fact that she was a twin? Why did she keep it a secret? For a moment, I couldn't remember her face. Which of the twins was she?

Through my shut eyelids I heard Mrs. Nelson ask if I needed water.

"I'm fine. It's a lot to take in."

She said, "Emily blamed me for Evelyn's problems. But I'm telling you—do you have children, by any chance?"

"My son is Nicky's friend," I reminded her.

"Then you understand. It wasn't my fault. They're born the way they are. There's not much you can do to change that. Every parent knows that. I loved the girls the same. Mental health problems run in my family, though no one was ever allowed to say so. We weren't supposed to notice that half our aunts and uncles were in the loony bin.

"Yes, the girls were identical. They have the same DNA! But I never mixed them up. Emily had the mole underneath her eye, and there was something funny about the top of Evelyn's ear."

I was listening hard and at the same time my attention was drifting. Mrs. Nelson was a mother. I didn't know if she knew that one of her daughters was dead.

One of her daughters. It hit me again. *They have the same DNA.* The coroner might not have been able to tell the difference. The mole under the eye and the funny ear no longer mattered by the time they found the body in the lake.

My brain was working overtime, cranking out theories. Did Emily kill her sister and dump her body in the lake? Had she planned that all along? What a perfect way to fake her own death . . .

"Please get yourself some water," Emily's mother said. "You don't look at all well."

"That's all right," I told her. "I'm fine."

She leaned forward and touched my knee, and in a suddenly conspiratorial tone said, "Want to hear something ridiculous? When my husband was alive and the girls were younger, I felt I had to hide my drinking. As if *I* were the child. And now I can relax at cocktail hour with a glass of gin, and there is nobody around to tell me I can't do this perfectly appropriate thing that every adult should have the right to do. No one can tell me not to! Care to join me?"

It was two in the afternoon. "No, thank you," I said. "It's kind of you to offer."

Only now did I notice a tray with a decanter and two glasses on the table beside her chair. She poured herself a full glass of clear liquid and drank it in steady, grateful sips.

"There. Much better. Where was I? Oh yes, the twins. Emily and Evelyn were absolutely just as bizarre as people say twins can be. For one thing, they were telepathic. Even as children, they just had to look at each other and they could communicate. Can you imagine raising children like that?

"Emily was the dominant one. She was born first. She was six ounces heavier. She gained weight faster and walked first. Evelyn was always . . . smaller and sadder. Less confident.

"They went through their teenage wild years at the exact same time. A double picnic for their mother, believe me! Their adolescent rebellion continued well into their twenties. I think they played dirty tricks on men, on their boyfriends. They were pretty and popular. Decorative. Which meant there was drinking and drugs. Are you sure you wouldn't like a sip of this?" She offered me her glass of gin.

"Thank you, no. I'd love to, but I have to drive back to the airport."

"All right, then. One thing I remember. They got into a terrible fight in front of me and their father. It was a holiday. Christmas? Thanksgiving? I can't recall. We'd somehow managed to get all of us in the same room. This was a little before Evelyn *really* started to go down and Emily to go up.

"It was a vicious fight. I think about a boy. I can't remember. I'm not sure I knew at the time. They slapped each other. That stopped the fight. Stopped it cold. They went off to their rooms.

"The next day they went into Detroit and got those horrendous tattoos. Those vulgar barbed-wire bracelets. To remind them that this was the hand that slapped her sister. Or some baloney like that. It was a promise they'd never fight like that again. I don't think they ever have. Not to this day."

Not to this day. She thought they were both alive.

Unless Emily had told her sister what I'd told her at the county fair, it was Emily who had called. And it was Evelyn's body that had washed up on shore.

"Where did you say Emily's sister lived?"

"Last I heard, Seattle."

"Anything more exact than that?" I asked. "Do you have an address?"

"I wish I knew. Bernice helps me with the birthday cards. I just sent one to Emily in Connecticut. But the last address we have for Evelyn is an awfully seedy motel in Seattle. Bernice googled it, and we saw."

She leaned forward. "What business is this of yours? Remind me, dear."

She'd said *dear* like a witch in a fairy tale. Threatening and insulting.

"I don't know," I said. "I'm sorry . . ."

All through my visit, it seemed as if she could turn the lights on and off behind her eyes. Now they'd clouded over again. Night, night. Nobody home.

"I'm tired," she said.

"I'm sorry, I didn't meant to . . . thank you." I stood up from the pink and white couch, looking behind me to see if I'd dirtied or messed it up. "It was kind of you to let me visit."

"Remind me why you wanted to meet me?"

"Curiosity," I said.

"Killed the cat," she said. I heard a note in her voice—like Emily's. I felt another chill. I shivered. The old woman noticed. She liked it. She tilted her chin and laughed almost girlishly. She was present again, for the moment.

"I'll be leaving now," I said. "Do you want me to . . . call someone?"

"She's leaving!" said Mrs. Nelson.

I heard footsteps. A tall and still beautiful woman in her fifties wearing dark blue nursing scrubs and a tangle of gray dreads tied behind her neck appeared in the doorway.

"This is Bernice," said Mrs. Nelson. "And this is—?"

"Stephanie," I said. "Nice to meet you, Bernice."

Bernice gave me a neutral, forgiving look. I sensed that she had been monitoring her employer's conversation and approved of, or at least hadn't minded, our talk. First Mrs. Nelson, then Bernice held out their hands for me to shake. I shook their hands and thanked them.

Bernice walked me to the door then closed it softly behind her, and we stood on the front porch.

I said, "I understand the police spoke with you. I'm so sorry about Emily."

"If it *is* Emily," Bernice said. "They never could tell those girls apart, maybe not even in death."

All this new information, these new theories and new suspicions were a lot to process at once. I thought of Miles, which always calms me.

I asked Bernice, "Did you mention your suspicions to the police? Did you tell them about Evelyn?"

"I let them think what they want to. This is Detroit, baby. Rich white Detroit, but still . . . Best not to contradict or come up with anything new. The less you mess with the police, the better off you are. I tried to call Emily and figure out what was what, but she never picked up her cell. Her mama's better not knowing. I don't want the poor thing to suffer any more than she already has. Sometimes she thinks she has two daughters, sometimes none, sometimes one . . . I can never predict what will stick with her and what will slide right off. Lots of times she surprises me with what she remembers . . . Did she mention the car?"

"What car?"

"She remembers *that*. Evelyn stole her car a while back. Both the girls had car keys. And one of them got into the garage and drove the car away in the middle of the night. My bet, it was Evelyn. Emily can rent any car she wants. Am I right?"

I nodded. That sounded right, and yet it made everything even more confusing. I wanted to stay here and ask Bernice questions all day. At the same time I wanted to hurry back to my hotel room and think about what I'd heard.

"Mrs. Nelson was hysterical. She kept asking me how she would get around. I couldn't bring myself to tell her that she hadn't driven for years. I said we'd take taxis, like we always did. I told her not to worry. I helped her send Emily's birthday card, just like I have for years."

"She's lucky to have you, Bernice," I said.

Bernice made a face. I was afraid that I'd insulted her. But she wasn't thinking about me.

"She deserves some good luck," she said. "She's had such bad luck with those girls. In the islands, we're careful around twins. You watch yourself." She listened for sounds from inside the house. "I've got to get back in there . . . There's no telling what she'll . . . You have a safe trip back."

There was no time to ask her what she meant by being careful and watching myself.

Once I left the suburbs, it was a bumpy ride. Considering that Detroit was the home of the auto, I was surprised that the roads were so bad. Steering around the potholes made me focus and kept me from freaking out over what I'd just heard.

Emily was a twin.

I was so jumpy that when I pulled into the rental place and the guys in uniform swarmed all over the car, one of them asked if I was okay.

I said, "I'm fine! Why is everyone asking?"

I got rid of the car and took the shuttle to the Detroit Metro airport hotel. I was glad I hadn't gone for the cheapest option, glad there was a minibar, glad I could drink two little bottles of bourbon, one right after the other. I was glad the bed was nice and clean so I could get under the covers with all my clothes on. Glad I was together enough to call down and ask the desk clerk to phone my room in plenty of time for an early flight.

I pulled the blanket over my head and closed my eyes. The Diane Arbus photo of the twins swam up from the darkness. I saw it more clearly, I remembered it better than Emily's mother's snapshots. I could still see their party dresses, but I couldn't recall what Emily and her sister were wearing in the family photos. They weren't dressed identically. Was that something their mother told me? She never dressed them alike. Or was that something I'd figured out? What difference did it make?

The last picture seemed to have been taken at their high school graduation. They were wearing caps and gowns. They both looked young and hopeful.

What happened after that? Mrs. Nelson thought Evelyn was in Seattle. But she had no address. How long before the old woman forgot them both? Was this something Emily knew and counted on to help her do what she was doing?

Whatever that was.

I could have reacted in all sorts of ways. I got angry. As if *I* was the one who'd been wronged. I knew some people might fault me for sleeping with Emily's husband. But I felt as if she'd done something to me first, tricked me, used me . . . not telling me she was a twin. Letting me and Sean—or maybe only me—think that she was dead.

And then deciding to let me know that she was alive.

The dominant twin. She had all the power.

Did Sean know she had a twin? He'd never mentioned it. Had she managed to keep that secret even from her husband?

I lay there thinking of how to let Emily know that I knew.

After a while it came to me. Emily had slipped up. She shouldn't have let me know that she read my blog. That was how I could get in touch with her. It gave me a little control, a way to be heard. And I didn't have to worry about Sean, who didn't read my blog.

I lay awake working out the wording to my blog post. How could I let Emily know that I'd been to her mother's and I knew her secret— but without revealing what it was?

32

STEPHANIE'S BLOG
ON CLOSURE

Hi, moms!

I could write a whole blog about closure. Or I could tell you a story about closure around the tragic accidental death of my best friend.

It's a complicated story, but here are the basics:

I visited Emily's mother at Emily's childhood home in a suburb of Detroit. I met her thoughtful and lovely caretaker, Bernice. I sat on the old-fashioned pink-and-white-striped silk sofa, and Emily's mother showed me a photo album full of pictures of Emily when she was a little girl.

It's hard to explain. But as we looked at the childhood photos together, I felt that I was being given a moment of understanding, a clear window into my friend's childhood. As Emily's mother and I remembered and celebrated Emily's life, I felt I understood everything. And I realized that Emily's story was *twice* as interesting as I could possibly have imagined.

And I could finally let my beloved friend Emily go.

Moms, please feel free to post about your own most moving and satisfying moments of closure.

Love,

Stephanie

33

———

EMILY

always knew that something bad would happen in the cabin. Maybe that was why I was so afraid of being there alone. I often dreamed of some evil . . . *presence* waiting for me on the screened-in sleeping porch where my sister and I spent so many childhood nights whispering in the dark, telling stories, inventing the fantasy kingdom (population: two) where we could live together forever without any grown-ups to ruin our fun or tell us what to do.

Our favorite song was "Octopus's Garden." We sang it over and over, faster and faster until our throats hurt and we couldn't stop laughing. It makes me cry now. What if one of us met the octopus first?

The night before I disappeared, the phone rang. Sean and I were asleep.

"Who is it?" Sean mumbled.

"Dennis," I said. It was not uncommon for Dennis Nylon to call at odd hours. It meant he was on another binge, spiraling toward another stint in rehab. He dialed through all the names on his work-contacts list till someone answered. I always answered because I knew that if no one else picked up, he'd move on to his next list: press and media people. I was the one who would have to deal with the ensuing shit storm. It was easier to talk Dennis down, to let him ramble until I heard him snoring on the other end of the phone. Then I could go back to sleep.

"I'll take it in the hall," I told Sean.

I practically sprinted down the stairs. I knew it wasn't Dennis.

"Will you accept a collect call from Eve?"

I always did.

Eve and Em were the not-so-secret names that my sister and I had for each other. No one else—*no one*—was allowed to call us that. Once, early in our relationship, Sean called me Em, and I told him I would kill him if he ever called me that again. I think he believed I meant it. And maybe I did.

I had to leave the room to accept a phone call from my sister. Sean didn't know I had a sister. No one did. No one but Mother, if she still remembered, and Bernice and people who'd known us in high school. But who cared about them? I'd had to get rid of a lot of old snapshots. At that point, I was still talking to Mother, so I sent them back to her with the excuse that I was moving a lot and I didn't want to lose them.

"Hi, Eve," I said.

"Hi, Em," she said. And we both began to cry.

I don't remember exactly when I stopped telling people that I had a sister. More or less around the time I moved to New York. I was sick of saying that I was a twin and having strangers pry or think they knew something about me. Didn't they see how it bored me when everyone asked the same questions? Fraternal or identical? Did you dress alike? Are you close? Did you have a secret language? Was it weird, being a twin?

It was weird, and it's still weird. But not in any way I could—or wanted to—explain. Sometimes, after I'd started pretending that I didn't have a sister, I could almost forget I had one. Out of sight, out of mind. It was easier. Less pain, less guilt, less grief, less worry.

No one at work knew I had a twin. The first time Sean and I played our "Who had the unhappier childhood?" game, he told me that he was an only child, and I said, "Oh, poor you! Me, too!" After that, it became too complicated to explain how I could have forgotten I have a sister. It was easier, in every way, to keep Evelyn's existence a secret. If she showed up at my house, I would have some serious explaining to do. That never happened. By then, my job had made me an expert at explaining the inexplicable—controlling information.

Every so often, I tested myself, my luck, and the people around me, daring them to guess the truth. Was Sean curious about why I spent a fortune on that Diane Arbus photo of the twins? Why I loved it so much? Of course not. It was a work of art. A good investment, he probably thought. The truth would have made him wonder what kind of person he married. That is, he would have wondered more than he did.

The first time Stephanie came to visit, I made a point of showing her the photo and saying that I cared about it more than anything in my house. But she just thought it proved that I had very good— very expensive—taste. Millions of people admire that picture, normal people who don't look at the image and wonder which of the twins they are.

I was the dominant twin. I pushed my way out first. I walked and talked first. I grabbed Evelyn's toys. I made her cry. I protected her. I put her at risk. I was the one who showed her where to find Mother's gin bottles and replace the gin with water. I lit her first joint and invited her to smoke weed with me and my friends. I was the one who split our first tab of acid, who gave Evelyn her first Ecstasy pill, who took her to her first rave in Detroit.

How was I supposed to know that she would like getting high even more than I did? Or that she would find it harder to stay sober? Or that the terror of boredom that I felt would also torment her but in a different and more harmful way? She was the weaker twin.

I took the phone into the kitchen and turned on the light. It was cold, but I was afraid to put the phone down long enough to put on a sweater. I was afraid she'd hang up or disappear. Again.

"Where are you?" I said.

"I don't know. Somewhere in Michigan. Guess what? I stole Mother's car."

"Nice," I said. "We can all rest easy knowing the world is a safer place."

She laughed. "I guess Mother hasn't been driving it all that much."

"Thank God for that," I said. "Remember that time she backed off our driveway and fell into a ditch, and we had to call a tow truck with chains to pull her out?"

"I don't remember much," said Evelyn, "but I do remember that." I was thinking, and my sister was too, that we were the only people who remembered that. I looked at my hand, holding the phone, and focused on the tattoo I hardly see anymore. Now I could see Evelyn, her wrist, her tattoo.

We got the tattoos after our worst fight ever. I'd found her kit in her bureau drawer—a hypodermic, cotton wool, a spoon, rubber tubing. Oh, and a packet of white powder.

We were seventeen.

I'd been suspicious for a while. She'd started wearing long sleeves, and she'd always had beautiful arms, nicer than mine; I get freckles in the sun. I'd known what I was going to find before I found it. But I was shocked when I did. This was real. My sister wasn't joking.

I began to shout at her, yelling that she couldn't do this to herself. To me. She said it was none of my business. We weren't the same.

By then we were yelling so loud I was afraid that Mother might hear. But Mother was floating on a warm, cottony substance cloud of her own.

I slapped my sister. She slapped me back. We stepped away from each other, horrified. We hadn't hit one another since we were little girls.

The next day we got our tattoos. We stole a handful of Mother's painkillers to make it hurt less. Neither of us was promising to stop getting high. That would have been too much to ask—and we would only have lied to each other. We were promising that we would never fight like that again. And we never did. We never have.

Mother always thought the argument was about a boy. But no boy would have been worth it.

What was happening to my sister began to seem like something I'd done wrong. A mistake I'd made. When we left home—Evelyn for the West Coast, me for the East—and I outgrew the drugs and she didn't, distance made it easier to believe that her problems weren't my fault. I missed her—and I made myself stop missing her.

We can control how we think and feel.

I was good at not missing people. Mother, for example. The last time I saw Mother was at Dad's funeral. Evelyn didn't make it home. Mother got extremely drunk (even for her) and blew up at me, saying that my sister's problem was the result of my heartless, selfish dominance. I said it wasn't fair to blame me for something that started before I was born. It was a fight I could never win. I stopped speaking to Mother. I didn't need to hear her say what I feared.

It wasn't as if I hadn't tried to help Evelyn—to save her. I happen to know a great deal about the pros and cons of various rehab facilities. Working at Dennis Nylon has been an education. I've lost count of how many times I flew out west, faking some business trip to fool Sean, faking some family emergency to deceive the people at work. It *was* a family emergency.

I'd find Evelyn wherever she was. Luckily, she always wanted to be found—that's why she'd called me, in the middle of the night, always scared. Those plane trips lasted forever. I'd find her in some crappy motel, usually shacked up with a halfway-hot guy she hardly knew. I'd check her into rehab. Mother paid for that. It was the least she could do. After Evelyn got out, she'd call regularly. She'd tell me how amazing it felt to be sober, how much better food tasted, how she could enjoy a sunny day without her eyes hurting.

Then the calls would stop.

Everyone who has ever loved an addict or had one in the family knows how it goes, the hopes and disappointments, the plot turns always circling back to the same story. People get tired.

The last I heard from Evelyn was a postcard from Seattle with nothing written on it but my Connecticut address and, on the front, a brightly colored tourist photo of fish, beautifully arranged on ice in the Pike Place market. Dead fish: Evelyn's sense of humor.

"Are you still there?" I asked, unnecessarily. I could hear my sister sniffling on the other end of the phone.

"More or less," she said.

"Don't hang up," I said. "Please."

"I won't," she said.

"Are you high?"

"Does it sound like I'm high?"

It did.

"Where are you going?" I said. "In Mother's car?"

"I thought I'd go to the cabin. Up to the lake."

My spirits lifted slightly. Maybe Evelyn was going to try and get clean. Leave her old life, make a fresh start. The lake house was our retreat, our place of safety. Our own private mental asylum.

"You going there to chill?" I said.

"You could say that." She laughed bitterly. "I'm going there to kill myself."

"Are you joking?"

"No," she said. "I'm dead serious." I could tell she meant it.

"Please, no," I said. "Wait for me. Don't do anything crazy. I'll meet you there. I'll get there as soon as I can. Promise me. No, *swear* to me."

"I promise," she said. "I promise I won't do anything till you get here. But I'm going to do it. I've made up my mind."

"Wait for me," I repeated.

"Okay," she said. "But make it fast."

I stayed awake all night. By morning I knew what I was going to do and what was going to happen. I knew, and I didn't know.

My sister possessed the key that unlocked the door to the prison, the magic spell that would slay our dragons. She was the secret player with the power to help Sean and me win our little game. I didn't want my sister to die. I wasn't going to help or encourage her to kill herself. I loved her. But I was going to do what she needed me to do, even if it meant losing her. Even if it meant admitting that I already had.

I had no time to lose. The next morning I got up early and packed. I booked a flight to San Francisco, which I had no intention of taking but which I hoped might briefly throw anyone who was looking for me off my trail.

I called Stephanie and asked if she'd do me a favor. A simple favor. Could Nicky spend the evening at her house? I'd pick him up when I got back from work. Of course I could have told her that I was planning to be away for a few days. But I wanted her to go into full panic mode as soon as possible. It would make my disappearance seem more credible, more alarming, more urgent. And when the insurance company looked into the case, there would have been a police investigation.

Perhaps there would be a body. A woman who had looked just like me and who had my DNA.

That morning I dropped Nicky off at school five minutes late so I wouldn't run into Stephanie, who was always early. I didn't want nosy Stephanie wondering why I was crying when I kissed Nicky goodbye.

I knew that I wouldn't be seeing him for a long time, and my heart was breaking. I hugged him so hard he said, "Careful, Mom, that hurts!"

"Sorry," I said. "I love you."

"Love you too," he said, not even looking back as he ran into school.

"See you later," I said, so the last thing I said to him (for a while) wouldn't be a lie.

I kept telling myself that Nicky would thank us later. Who wouldn't want a childhood in the most beautiful spots in Europe? He would have a better childhood than his parents, who'd grown up in the boring suburbs of Detroit and the bleak north of England. Connecticut should have been good enough; I don't know why it wasn't. I guess it's never enough.

I wanted to do something exciting. I wanted to feel alive.

I drove home and picked up Sean. We drove to the Metro-North station and took the train into the city. Then we took a taxi from Grand Central to the airport. We needed him to be on the plane to London before I went missing. I made a big production of standing on the side-walk in front of the international departure entrance and kissing him goodbye in case the police located the driver who took us to JFK. But they never even tried—more proof that they weren't looking for me all that hard. I asked the cab to wait while we said our loving goodbyes. We'd be on CCTV: a devoted couple, sorry to be leaving each other, even for a few days.

"This is it," I whispered to Sean. "You know what to do." In London, he would set up a few meetings with clients with whom he'd failed to get something going before, the ones who liked him and were genu-inely sorry they couldn't invest millions of their company's money in Sean's company's real estate projects. They'd agree to have a drink with him—and give him an alibi.

"Where are you going?" he said. "What if I need to get in touch with you? What if there's an emergency?" He sounded scared, like a kid. It was embarrassing.

"Don't worry," I said. "*This* is the emergency. No matter what you hear . . . I'm not dead. I'll be back. Trust me. *I won't be dead.*" I needed him to believe that.

"Okay," he said dubiously.

"See you soon," I said, very loudly in case anyone was listening. No one was.

"See you soon, darling," he said.

I got back in the cab and went to the rental car agency.

I was on my way. I had that heady, bad-girl, wind-in-my-hair feeling about a scheme that might work, a plan that seemed like more fun than my current life, more fun than a job that many people would have seen as fun enough. I wanted something else.

I wouldn't mind a break from Sean. I could use a time-out beside the lake. Wasn't the whole point to step back from our overcommitted lives and disconnect and figure out what was important? Lots of people have that idea. But not everyone acts on it. Civilization would collapse if they did.

I was right to be uneasy about being separated from Nicky and—as it turned out—to be concerned about Sean's sticking to our plan. I certainly never expected Sean to fuck the fish. I didn't think that Stephanie would stalk me all the way to my mother's.

Life is full of surprises.

I'd brought books. The complete works of Charles Dickens, James M. Cain's *Serenade*. A Highsmith novel I couldn't remember reading, or maybe I'd forgotten. I bought enough food to last for a while—and a new CD player. I could play the music I liked without having to listen to Sean's awful screaming British bands from his youth.

I made an effort to cover my tracks, stopping at convenience stores where I thought they might not have state-of-the-art surveillance cameras. Still, when they started looking for me, it should have been easier to find me. I assumed they weren't looking that hard, whatever they might have been pretending and telling Sean.

I didn't know that till later. The lake house had no internet and no TV.

————

I NEVER IMAGINED that our plan would involve my twin. Now, thinking back, I realize I needed my sister for it to work. I needed her, just as I'd always needed her, even when I tried to escape or deny or ignore it. I must have known all along that Evelyn would be part of it. But I didn't want things to happen the way they did.

I must have known. My sister and I had always known things about the other without being able to explain or understand *how* we knew.

On the way to Michigan, I had a lot of time to think. Sometimes

I thought like the decent human being I wanted to be. Sometimes I thought like the scheming maniac I really am. I spent the night in a motel in Sandusky. A Motel 6 where I could pay cash.

I reached the lake house the next day. Mother's 1988 Buick was parked in the driveway. I wished it was just a car, any old car, but it was the car in which Mother had nearly killed us countless times during our childhood. After she'd had her license suspended for DWI, the car had remained in the garage. Bernice took it out every so often, to keep it running, but its forced retirement had preserved it with Mother's nicks and dents. I told myself that the car was Evelyn's now, but that only made me feel worse. Because I realized that pretty soon—too soon—the car might be mine. But what would I do with it? My sister would be dead, and I would be in another country, a multimillionaire with no use for Mother's beat-up Buick.

The cabin door was locked. I knocked. No answer. No one had fixed the torn screen on the porch, and I climbed through it. The house smelled like something had died in the walls. When that happened when Evelyn and I were kids, we'd scare each other by saying that a dead person was walled up in the cabin. Edgar Allan Poe was our favorite writer.

Usually it was a dead bat in the walls. All the bats were dying now. Dennis Nylon gave a benefit for a bat-disease research foundation to launch our Batgirl look. That was my idea. And, it occurred to me now, that was what I'd worked for: saving the lives of dead bats.

God, I hated being alone in the cabin. Had Evelyn changed her mind? She'd *better* be here. Don't let her be dead.

On the kitchen counter, I saw the bottles of orange energy drink and the packages of the marshmallow cookies and potato chips that Evelyn ate when she was high, when she ate at all.

"Evelyn?"

"In here."

I ran to the room where she slept when it got too cold to sleep on the porch. For years we'd shared the same room because it was so much fun to talk and tell stories and scare each other. Then for years we'd argued over which room was ours. Finally we settled on who would sleep where—the first of our separations.

I opened the door.

It's always a shock, seeing your double. Like looking in the mirror but much, *much* more bizarre. The strangest thing now was that we looked so similar and so different. Evelyn's hair was ratted as if a small animal was nesting inside. Her face was unevenly puffy, and her skin was a bluish skim milk pale. When she smiled at me, I saw that she was missing a front tooth. She wore several sweaters, one on top of the other. She'd crawled under the blankets, and still she was shivering.

She looked awful. I loved her. I always had and always would.

The strength of that love erased everything. The years of fights and worry. The crazed middle-of-the-night phone calls, the not knowing where she was, the dragging her into rehab, the disappointments and scares. All the resentments, frustrations, and fears were burned away by the happiness of being in the same room. Of her being alive. How could I have forgotten the most important person in my life? I had never loved anyone as I loved my twin. Anyone but Nicky. It was almost unbearably painful that my sister didn't know him. That he didn't know her. And maybe he never would.

I ran over and hugged Evelyn. I said, "You need a bath."

"Bossy, bossy," Evelyn said. She dragged herself up in bed. "What I need is a shot of bourbon, a beer, and two Vicodins."

I sat on the edge of the bed. "You're high."

"You know me so well," Evelyn said flatly.

Then she said, "I want to die."

"You don't," I said. "You can't." I was crazy to have thought that it would help Sean and me if she died. I had forgotten how much I loved her, how much I wanted her to live. I'd think of something else. I'd bring her home with me, I'd tell Sean and Nicky the truth—

She said, "This is not going to be like that play where the girl spends the whole play telling her mom she's going to kill herself. And then she does. Or doesn't. I can't remember. This is not going to be like that."

"Tell me you're not serious," I said.

"*This* serious." She pointed at the dresser behind my head where a dozen pill bottles were lined up like clear cylindrical bombs awaiting detonation. "I am not going about this like some amateur. This will not be messy, I promise."

"I need you to stick around," I said.

She said, "We've fallen out of touch, in case you haven't noticed."

"That can change. Starting now."

"Everything can change. For example, I've gotten quite neat. I plan to clean up the kitchen. Make the bed. I won't kill myself in the house, where you'd have to deal with my body. I plan to do it outside and let Mother Nature do the heavy lifting."

I said, "You still think this is about whose turn it is to clean up the cabin?"

"Wait," said Evelyn. "Here's an idea: Join me. One last swim in the lake. Two dead twins gone back to the element we came from. We won't have to worry about each other. Or think about each other. Or dread getting old and dying. No more terrors in the middle of the night. Do you know how sweet that would be? No more worry, no anger, no boredom, no wanting, no sadness, no more—"

"That sounds tempting," I said. And for a moment, it did. Dying with Evelyn would be the final big adventure, the ultimate "fuck you" to tedium and boredom. Deal with that, Sean and Stephanie and Dennis! But Nicky would need to deal with it too.

"Thanks, but I can't. I've got Nicky."

I was sorry as soon as I said it.

"And I don't," she said. "I don't have the cute little person who needs me. The nephew you never let me meet."

"I couldn't . . . you were so . . . I never knew . . ."

"Don't worry about it, Em. It's a little late. So without the cute little person, all I have is the big ugly death wish."

She put her wrist beside mine. The two barbed-wire bracelet tattoos made a squashed figure eight. My sister was always fond of theatrical gestures.

"No more fights," she said.

"No more fights," I said.

"Listen," I said. "There's something I need to tell you."

"You don't love Sean anymore," she said. "Big surprise."

"It's not about him. Or maybe it is. A little. Listen. I've disappeared. I'm faking my death to collect insurance money."

"Very Barbara Stanwyck and Fred MacMurray," Evelyn said. "I like it."

No one else would have said that. Not Sean, certainly not Stephanie. Maybe Nicky would, some day. But not for many years.

She said, "You're totally insane. But wait, wait a second. I think I'm getting the picture. The signal's coming in . . . It helps you, if I die. You can pretend you're the dead one. A win-win situation. We both win. Right?"

"How can you even think that?" She was the only person who knew me.

"Because I know what you're thinking." She laughed. "I love that I'd be dying for you."

"That's not true," I said.

"Joking," Evelyn said. "Why were you always the one supposed to have the sense of humor? This is really rich. Perfect. Now we both get what we want. For the first time ever, maybe."

I said, "Do you know that fifty percent of twins die in a few years after the death of their twin?"

"I do know that," she said. "We read that on the internet together in your college dorm. And I'm sorry. You'll survive. One of us is enough."

"I always found you," I said. "I always tried to help. You could find the right group and get sober and—"

She said, "Fuck you. *You* make amends. For crowding me. Since before we were born."

"My God, you sound like Mother. Blaming me for what happened before we were born."

"Don't play dumb," Evelyn said.

A silence fell. Evelyn wanted to say something else. She flexed her wrists and put her palms outward, as if pressing against something, and rocked back slightly. It was a signal we'd had as girls. We could send an SOS from across the room. Rescue me from this parent, this party guest, this guy.

She said, "If I had some horrible cancer or ALS and I asked you to help me die, I know—I *know*—you would. Well, the pain is as bad. It's just not visible on the MRI."

I said, "Okay. Enough. I'm tired. Will you promise me not to do anything crazy tonight?"

"Crazy?" she said. "I won't drown myself, if that's what you're asking."

"I love you," I said. "But I need sleep." I pushed Evelyn over and climbed into bed beside her. She smelled a little like a horse stable and a little like how she smelled as a kid.

I didn't sleep. Or maybe I slept a little. I kept waking up and putting my hand on her chest, the way I put my hand on newborn Nicky's chest to make sure he was breathing.

I missed my child. If Evelyn had a child, she wouldn't talk like this. But plenty of mothers kill themselves.

Evelyn was snoring lightly, a semi-peaceful alcohol-soaked snore. Her breathing was regular and shallow, broken by occasional hiccups.

For years all my feelings about my sister had tracked toward dread. It was as if I'd been preparing with endless rehearsals. I couldn't stop thinking about our childhood, and about her saying that I would help her if she had a fatal illness. I tried not to dwell on the fact that her death was what Sean and I needed for our crazy plan.

It was morning when I woke. It took a while to remember where I was. I reached my arm out for Evelyn. I slapped the bed. She wasn't there.

I ran into the kitchen. Evelyn was awake, sitting in the living room, nibbling a cookie.

She said, "Do you have any *idea* how loud you snore? You always were the loudest. Okay, good news, bad news. The strange thing is, it's both. Good news: I've changed my mind. I've decided to live. Bad news: I've changed my mind and decided to live."

My first response was pure joy. My sister would survive! I could put her into rehab, the right one this time. I could fix things so they would stay fixed. I'd introduce her to Sean and Nicky. Meet your sister-in-law. Meet your aunt.

"I'm so happy." I hugged her.

She held on longer than I did.

That's when I had a feeling I still can't explain. It was as if, *almost* as if, I felt disappointed. Cheated. The most upset I've ever seen Nicky be, the closest he's come to a tantrum, is when he expects something to happen, it's all planned out in his head. He's imagined the whole scenario. He's practically lived it. And then it doesn't happen.

That was how I felt about my sister's death. I had imagined the whole thing, what I would do and say, up to and including the feelings I would have. I had it all worked out.

And now it wasn't going to happen.

I should never have told her about the insurance scheme. We were sisters, after all. She could be doing this just to mess with me, because she could. She knew how. She was my sister.

"I've got a suggestion," I said.

"You always do," she said.

It was as if I heard someone else talking. Someone who wanted what I wanted but wasn't afraid to say it. That person said, "Let's have one last total blowout before we get clean forever. You and me. Sisters. Like the old days."

Evelyn gave me a quizzical smile. I still loved her, but the missing tooth was a bad look, and if she lived, I was going to have to fix that too.

"One last time," I said. "Let's get totally blasted. Let's get that demon out of our systems forever."

"Now *that's* a suggestion," my sister said.

When I thought that my sister was calling on me for comfort in her last hours instead of discovering (partly thanks to me) a reason to live, I'd brought along three bottles of designer mezcal.

I found two shot glasses, lacy with white cobwebs and speckled with mouse shit. I hadn't thought about it last night, but I was struck—as I had been last summer when I came here with Sean—by the fact that the water was running and the electricity on. Did Mother—that is, Bernice—pay the bills and hire someone to keep the pipes from freezing? I washed out the glasses.

I said, "Let's sit at the kitchen table."

The kitchen was full of ghosts. I was right about the cabin being haunted. Grandma and Grandpa, Dad and Mother were all there in the kitchen, watching Evelyn and me pour shots and drink at eight o'clock in the morning. If this wasn't bad behavior, what was? Evelyn was so happy to get her hands on a glass of something—anything—that she hardly noticed I was pouring only a fraction of that amount for myself. Or maybe she was thinking like a twin: less for her, more for me!

After four, maybe five shots, Evelyn said, "Do you have any memories from before we were born?"

That was how I knew that she was on her way to being drunk. She often asked me that when she drank. She would forget she'd asked before.

I said I didn't. She said she remembered being kicked.

"Oops." She made a screeching-tires sound. "Let's talk about something more friendly."

I said, "What kind of pills have you got?"

She said, "Yellow and orange and white ones."

"Let's do one," I said. "One apiece. That's all. No more."

"You're twisting my arm," she said. "Doctor, it's not my fault! My twin sister is an enabler."

I followed her into the bedroom. There was already a slight pitch and stutter to her walk. She dithered over the pill bottles on the dresser like a pharmacist, or like a bartender with mixological ambitions. At last she decided and dispensed two pale yellow pills, one of which she gave me and one of which she kept.

"I'm saving mine for a minute," I said.

"I'm taking mine now," she said. "If you don't mind."

"Go for it," I said.

"Actually, I think I'll bring Mother's Little Helper into the kitchen. Less trekking back and forth. Save on the wear and tear."

Evelyn took the pill bottles. I could have stopped her, but I didn't. And finally that's all that matters: I didn't kill her, but I didn't stop her.

She lined the bottles up on the kitchen table. She said, "I really shouldn't," and then was silent for a while, as if to give that thought time to wash over her and leave. "My medication regimen." She opened the first bottle and took a candy-blue pill shaped like a tiny heart.

My sister grew more mellow, even sentimental. After a while I had the sense that she wasn't really talking to me. She was passing the time, waiting. She was already on her way.

"First memory?" I said.

"A pillowcase with horses," she said.

"Wallpaper," I said. "Pineapples on the wallpaper by our playpen."

"What about me?" my sister said. "Do you remember me?"

"I remember that my name was your first word."

"Typical," she said. She refilled her glass and took another pill.

She said, "I have a pretty high tolerance."

I said, "I used to. As you know."

"Good for you," my sister said, with a little toasting gesture and the angry head twitch she got from Mother. "Here's to my sister, the cheap date."

"I love you," I said. I needed to get that information across to her, the sooner the better.

She didn't say she loved me. She shut her eyes. She sat there at the kitchen table with her eyes shut for a very long time.

Then she said, "Can I change my mind again? I actually *do* want to die."

I could have said, "It's the alcohol and the pills talking. Wait until you come down." Would my sister have believed me?

But what I said was "Sometimes you have to follow your heart. You know what's best for you. Do what you need to. Don't worry about me. I'll miss you, but I'll survive."

My sister's pale little face blanched with shock. She stared at me. Was I giving her permission? Did I *want* her to die? I wasn't telling her to live. I wasn't offering to protect her.

She buried her face in her hands. Then she turned away from me and looked toward the porch and said, "You know what? I think I'll go for a little swim . . . The cold water will wake me up . . . I'll be back in five minutes."

"Don't go," I said.

"Don't worry," my sister said.

Was I supposed to tackle her and keep her in the room?

I wanted to believe that the shock of the water would sober her up and make her realize she didn't want to die. She'd come back inside and ask me for help. I'd wrap her in towels and hug her and we'd start over. There was time to get her somewhere where they would pump her stomach. All I had to do was get her in dry clothes and into the car.

Forget the insurance money. I'd live a better life. I'd make my sister live with us. She and Nicky would love each other. Sean would get used to it. I'd get her a job at Dennis Nylon. We'd commute to work. Dennis could be her sponsor. He would love how crazy that was.

Evelyn took another pill and drained another shot.

She stood and stumbled once before she reached the door.

"Wait," I said. "There's something I want you to have."

I took off Sean's mother's diamond and sapphire ring and put it on her finger. Her hand was swollen from drink, so it took some doing.

"Ouch," she said. "What's this?"

"I want you to have it."

What I really meant was that I wanted someone to find it. Later. Evelyn knew it too. Mind reading up until the end. The very end.

"Brilliant," she said. "Thank you."

"Take care," I said, as my sister went out to die, and I didn't stop her.

I really believed she'd come back. Or maybe I half believed it. Or wanted to believe it. Meanwhile I was sleepy. I'd drunk more than I realized, keeping up. I'd hardly slept. I hadn't eaten. I'd gotten out of practice. I'd forgotten how to maintain my old bad habits.

I lay down on the couch and passed out for half an hour.

When I awoke, I went outside and looked for Evelyn. I ran along the edge of the water. I shouted her name. There was no one around. There was nothing I could do.

I went back into the cabin. I took two of my sister's pills and washed them down with mezcal and slept for thirty-six hours.

I woke up sober, knowing that I had killed my sister, still trying to convince myself that I hadn't. She wanted to die. To force her to live would have been selfish. Maybe for the first time, I had helped her— really helped her—get what she wanted.

I'd lost all my fear of being alone in the cabin—maybe because the worst had happened. I was glad to have time alone there, time to get used to Evelyn's death. Time to remember our lives. Time to think about who I was and who she'd been and who I was without her. I should have called the police right away, but I told myself that my sister wouldn't have wanted that. She would have wanted me to stay at the cabin and clear my head and let some time pass.

I lived on bologna sandwiches on white bread with mayonnaise. The diet of a ten-year-old. I wouldn't let Nicky live that way, but it was what I wanted. I wanted to pretend, while I was eating, that Evelyn and I were ten and spending the summer at the lake house.

I paced the cabin. I was afraid to go out to the lake, afraid of what I might see. Early in the evenings I fell exhausted onto the bed and slept until morning. I'd been something of an insomniac when I lived with Sean and took care of Nicky and worked for Dennis, but now I fell asleep at once.

A week passed, then another. I lost track of time.

I straightened up the cabin, cleaned up Evelyn's mess one last time. Or some of it. I left the pill and alcohol bottles. I left the rental car in the woods, hiked back to the cabin, and drove off in Mother's car.

I drove to the Adirondacks and stayed there awhile.

Maybe that wasn't the best place for me to be. I didn't have enough to do. I wanted to sleep in my own bed. I couldn't stop thinking about Nicky. I longed to hear his voice, his beautiful silly conversation. I wanted to smell the milky smell of his hair. I wanted to walk down the street holding his hand. I wanted to see his face when he spotted me waiting for him after school. Soon I was missing him so much that I felt frantic. And grief stricken, as if it were Nicky and not my sister who was dead.

I left the mountains and went to Danbury, which seemed safe, like a city where no one knew anyone else. I checked into a motel. That's when I plugged back in, reconnected. That's when I went on the internet and found out that Stephanie had helped herself to my husband.

I'd honored my sister's wish to die. But now I wondered if I would have fought harder to keep her if I'd known that Sean was a weakling and a traitor and that our plan was a joke. He was living with Stephanie. And I was alone.

Now Stephanie was harassing my mother, involving everyone I knew in her sick plan to become me. What Stephanie edited out of her blog is *what* she saw when she sat on that pink-and-white-striped couch and looked at Mother's pictures of me as a child.

At two of me. At Emily times two.

Big surprise: I was a twin!

I can imagine her dismay at this heinous violation of her best-girlfriend faith that we told each other everything. How could I forget to mention that detail about myself?

Sean believed I was dead. But that only meant he hadn't believed me when I said goodbye at the airport. I needed to talk to Sean, to see him, to find out what was in his mind. As if his mind was the part of him that had decided to sleep with Stephanie.

I called Stephanie one more time. As usual, I waited till she was alone.

I said, "If you tell Sean what you found out from my mother, I will kill you. I'll kill you and Miles both. Or maybe I'll kill Miles and let you live."

"I swear I won't." She sounded terrified. "I swear it."

That's how stupid Stephanie was. Even knowing how often I'd lied to her, she believed me.

Sean and I had agreed on code words we'd use in an emergency, and I texted them to him, and he texted me back.

The code words were "Peeping Tom."

I told him to meet me for dinner at a restaurant where we used to go when we first got together, an Italian restaurant in Greenwich Village where you paid to have space between you and the next table. You didn't go for the food but for the quiet. People went there to make business deals, to get engaged—and to break up.

Sean was there when I arrived. I wasn't sure how I'd feel when I saw him again. Now I knew. He had an open, stupid face. I felt annoyance, then rage. Whatever love I'd had for him was dead—colder than my sister.

When Sean saw me walk into the restaurant, you'd think he was seeing a dead woman walking. Who did he think had texted him? My ghost?

He rose, as if to embrace me.

"Don't get up," I said.

I sat down. I was glad that the volcanic flower arrangement half hid my view of my husband. I couldn't look at him. I wanted to stab him with a steak knife. I had killed the wrong person. I told myself: Be patient. Hear him out. You don't know what he's thinking.

"I thought you were dead," he said. "I really thought you were dead."

"Apparently, you were wrong," I said coldly. "What part of my telling you not to believe that I was dead did you not understand?"

"But the body," Sean said. "The ring."

"You don't need to know the details," I said. "You're better off not knowing. You'd probably just tell Stephanie."

I heard the fury in my voice. That was a mistake. I needed to stay calm—*seem* calm.

"I've been reading her blog," I said. "She's been blogging about your happy home. You idiot."

"Stephanie means nothing to me." *Did he hear himself?* Did he know that sounded like a line in the cheesiest afternoon soap?

"Prove it," I said.

"How?" he said, looking even more alarmed than he had when he first saw me.

"Break her heart. Torture her. Kill her." I wasn't suggesting that he kill Stephanie. I hated her, but murdering her wouldn't help. I just wanted to see how he reacted.

He said, "Come on, Emily. Be sensible. She's been good to Nicky. She's been helpful. Nicky likes having her around the house. And you were right. She's the perfect nanny. We'll dump her as soon as the money comes through."

He was telling *me* to be sensible?

Wanting to see him had been a huge mistake. I needed to leave, and yet I said, "We should eat." I was hungry. After this, I had to drive back to Danbury.

Sean ordered a veal chop, well done. I couldn't help giving his charred crematorium-smelling chop a dirty look. Stephanie cooked his food the way he liked it. I felt sick with rage and disgust.

I ordered pasta, something soft. I couldn't trust myself with a knife.

"Come on, Em," said Sean. He never called me Em. I'd told him never to call me that. It was Evelyn's name for me. And now my sister was dead. And this idiot—my husband—didn't even know that I'd had a sister. Stephanie knew, but I was pretty sure I'd scared her into keeping Evelyn a secret.

He said, "Our plan is working . . . it could still work . . . we'll get the money before too long." Even as he said it, I knew I didn't want the money if it meant spending the rest of my life with Sean. It wasn't worth it.

I said, "Your fucking Stephanie was never part of our plan."

"I'll tell her to leave. I'll tell her it's not working. You and I will get back together, and it'll be like it was, you and me and Nicky—"

"It can never be like it was," I said. "You made sure of that."

"But we were so happy," Sean said.

"Were we?" My sister was dead. And though I knew, logically, that Evelyn's death wasn't Sean's fault, I couldn't stop feeling that Sean was to blame.

I said, "I'll never forgive you for this. You'll be *very* sorry."

"Is that a threat?" Sean said.

"Possibly," I said. "Speaking of which, don't you dare tell Stephanie that I am alive, that you saw me. The last thing I want is the two of you talking about me and trying to second-guess my intentions. You and Stephanie put together aren't smart enough."

I got up and walked out.

I hated him more than I hated Stephanie. Despite all the pride she took in her dark secrets, and in her stupid blog, Stephanie was such a simple creature that I couldn't blame her for what happened. She reminded me of a spaniel swimming against the current. Or a not very bright child just wanting to make friends and have people like her.

Sean was different. He was the only person except my twin I'd ever let get even slightly close to me. The only person I'd trusted. Except Nicky.

Sean had betrayed me. I meant it when I said that he would be sorry.

PART THREE

———

34

_____

SEAN

I was afraid of my wife. It wasn't something that a man in my business, a guy in any business—or any man—should admit. I knew that Emily was trouble. It was part of her appeal. What do you do when on the third date a woman invites you to watch *Peeping Tom*? What are you to think when after five years of marriage she has never once let you meet her mother? When you've never seen one picture of her when she was little, when she refuses to tell you one thing about her childhood except that her mother drank and used to say she was stupid?

You give in; you give up. You surrender something. You lose your power, and you don't get it back. Samson and Delilah, David and Bathsheba. The Bible is full of such stories. What they don't say in the Bible is that the sex was great.

I fell in love with Emily and married her without knowing much about her. I had my illusions about who she was. She'd cried in front of the crowd at the Dennis Nylon benefit. It was hard to believe that the person who wept at the *thought* of women without clean water was the same person who stole my mother's ring. Much later, Emily confessed that she hadn't been crying for the poor women but because she'd had to deal with so many disasters at the charity gala and was facing another of Dennis's inevitable shit fits. The beautiful woman who'd wept out of sympathy and compassion—that woman never existed.

I should have left her as soon as the plane from the UK landed. It was so early in the marriage; we were returning from our honeymoon. We could have had the marriage annulled. I should have acted on what I saw when I told her we'd have to give the ring back to Mum and Emily threatened to ruin my life. I should have told her I'd made a mistake. Instead we had sex in the airplane bathroom—and that sealed the deal. I was hers. I loved her. I loved her wildness, her determination, her rebellious streak. It was part of what fascinated me, what I didn't want to lose.

She would stop at nothing to get what she wanted. And I suppose I was addicted to the uneasy feeling I got whenever I gave in and agreed to do what she said.

When we learned that she was pregnant, I was delighted. But I couldn't shake the superstitious fear that there might be something wrong—if not physically, then psychologically—with a baby conceived in the Virgin Atlantic upper-class loo.

Nicky was perfect. But Emily almost died having him. I don't know if she even knew that. The doctors didn't say as much, not directly. But I could tell from the looks on their faces when they came into the room where she was in labor, the room that was decorated like a comfy living room as if that would lessen her pain.

Something changed in her after that. She adored Nicky, but she grew more distant from me. It was as if she'd fallen in love with her child and fallen out of love (if she ever *was* in love) with her husband. I'd heard the guys at work complain about something similar; mostly they were grumbling about the lack of sex after their kids were born. But with Emily it was different. We still had sex, good sex. The missing element was something else: warmth, affection, respect.

I was always a little surprised to come home from work and find her still there. Maybe she only stayed with me because I was Nicky's father. Not that I seemed to have had much genetic input. He looked like her; he had Emily's beauty. But he did resemble me in one way: he was nicer than Emily, more like me. I loved him. The three of us were a family, a little family. I would have done anything to protect us, to make our lives better. Anything Emily wanted.

I told myself that I liked the fact that she wasn't one of those women who blather on about their feelings and want to know all about yours. She let me have my private thoughts. But something about Emily was . . . too private, I'd say. Even on the really good days, when I wasn't working and Emily and Nicky and I would be going to some fun place in the car, enjoying ourselves, I'd glance at her, and I'd see something in her eyes, something restless, something worse than restless: the panic of a bird trapped in a house. Which is not exactly the look you most want to see on your wife's face.

When Emily and I met, I had gone from being with the cool kids at university to being with my colleagues on Wall Street, definitely not the cool kids, though they thought they were. They were idiot savants who could do one thing and one thing only. They knew how to make money. But being with Emily proved that I still had something cool about me. I was married to the prettiest, coolest girl. She was always daring me, taking risks, inviting me to be her partner in crime.

I was afraid to not join in, to resist Emily's wild ideas. All leading up to the preposterous insurance-fraud scheme. I never thought it would work. I'm a practical person. I'm grounded in reality and have an important job on Wall Street. But I let her convince me because she would have thought that I was a coward if I pointed out the obvious flaws in her plan. I told her that two million dollars wasn't worth it. I made plenty of money. I could ask for a raise. But she kept saying that it wasn't about the money. It was about the danger, the risk. It was about feeling alive. And God knows I wanted my wife to feel alive.

It was supposed to be so simple. So brilliant. She'd fake her accidental death. I didn't ask about this part, and she appreciated my not asking. I could sign up for spousal life insurance from my company, and after the big payout, Emily, Nicky, and I would reconvene in some European paradise with enough to live on for a few years. After that we'd see where we were.

I wanted to believe that our plan could work. But I didn't. The one thing I *did* know was that our marriage wasn't going to last if I refused. Emily was blackmailing me, though we would never have called it that. She had a maddening way of making blackmail seem like consensus.

She was never supposed to die. I was blindsided. I couldn't understand how it happened. She'd told me not to believe she was dead, but the autopsy report—the DNA result—was convincing. Better-laid plans than ours went disastrously wrong.

The one thing she did say about herself was that she'd had a bit of a drug problem when she was very young. She told me that she'd gotten the tattoo on her wrist to remind herself of how bad things used to be when she was using. And she'd stopped using, early on.

I didn't believe for a moment that Emily meant to kill herself. She would never have left Nicky without a mother. I was certain it was an accident. She'd gotten high, had a few drinks, gone for a swim—and drowned. She was wearing Mum's ring. That item on the autopsy about liver damage and long-term drug use—that made no sense at all. They must have gotten that wrong. Doctors make mistakes all the time. They operate on the wrong patient, remove the wrong kidney.

I mourned Emily. I was numb with grief. Or, more accurately, I veered between numbness and excruciating pain. But I had to stay strong for Nicky even if I dreaded getting up every morning. At first I didn't want to go on living. I blamed myself for having gone along with my wife's greedy, impossible, illegal—stupid—game.

I believed—I truly believed—that my wife was dead. Maybe the autopsy report contained some mistakes, but I had to believe the evidence: my wife's DNA, my mother's ring.

That was the only reason why I let myself get close to Stephanie. I would never have done that if I'd thought Emily was alive.

Stephanie does everything I want, and for better or worse, she never scares me. Never challenges me. Stephanie plays the music I like. She cooks my dinner the way I like it, without Emily's friendly teasing, which I knew was barely disguised contempt for the boring British carnivore preferring his hunks of meat well done.

I don't love Stephanie. I never have and never will. But I don't mind having her around. I always know she's going to be there when I get home. She doesn't ask too many questions; she never seems distant. She lives to please Miles and Nicky and me. She is as eager to please in bed as she is everywhere else.

Living with her has kept me calm as I've discovered the negatives of Emily's plan: one, Nicky's misery; two, being questioned by the police; three, Stephanie's suspicions.

And of course the major negative: Emily's death.

Stephanie is right to be suspicious. She's what Emily said that poker players call "the fish." Stephanie is always hinting about dark things in her past, saying she wants to be an extra good person to make up for what she did earlier in her life. An extra good person? What does that *even mean?* I feel disloyal to Emily for not rolling my eyes so obviously that Stephanie notices when she says things like that.

She has no idea I know that her brother is Miles's father. And what if I do? What do I care? She imagines that her secret puts her at the dark center of the world. But she's the only one who cares.

She and my wife are both insane. They might actually have become friends if Emily hadn't been looking for a fish, if Emily was capable of friendship.

Not for one moment did I imagine that Stephanie and I would stay together. But she was comforting and obliging as I struggled to recover from the loss of my wife, who as it turned out, was never lost.

I was at my desk at work when the text came in: PEEPING TOM.

I shut my eyes and opened them. The two words were still on the screen. Two words that seemed too dangerous—too explosive—to read in my office. I jammed my phone in my pocket and took the elevator down. The smokers from my office all stood—just as the sign instructed them—at least twenty-five feet from the door. I waved to them as I rushed around the corner. I needed privacy. I needed air. I checked my messages again.

The two words were still there. It wasn't possible. It just wasn't possible. Either my wife was alive, or someone had found her phone. Her real phone.

I texted back: PEEPING TOM.

I waited.

A message came back: DINNER?

I kept hitting the wrong keys as I typed in: WHERE?

DORSODURO.

It was the restaurant where I'd proposed to Emily.

My wife was alive.

Dorsoduro was Emily's choice.

I chose to see it as a statement. A romantic gesture. She still loved me. We were still together. Man and wife. Things could still work out.

The minute I saw her walking toward me across the restaurant, I knew that I would never love anyone else, not as long as I lived. She was so bright, so sleek, so elegant. So sexy. Everyone turned to watch her. She had that kind of energy. Something in the atmosphere changed when she walked into a room. Alone, or with any man lucky enough to be with her. Whereas—I couldn't help thinking—when Stephanie walked into a room, you assumed that she must have come with some pitiful guy who was late or couldn't find a parking space. Or maybe she was meeting a date who was going to stand her up.

I didn't want to think about Stephanie. She was the last person I wanted to think about.

Seeing Emily again was like a dream, a beautiful happy dream, the dream that everyone most wants to have, the dream we so long to come true. The dream in which the dead beloved isn't really dead.

Emily looked terrific. How had she managed, all this time, to keep her black Dennis Nylon suit in perfect condition? If anything, she was more beautiful in life than she was in my memory, or when we kissed goodbye at the airport.

She was the greyhound beside Stephanie's yippy spaniel. The Mercedes beside Stephanie's Hyundai. Stephanie cooked the steaks the way I liked them, but Emily had never bored me.

I rose to embrace her, but Emily's stare froze me in an awkward position, half sitting, half standing. And all at once I knew that this wasn't the happy dream of the resurrected beloved. I could tell that this was going to be a very special kind of nightmare.

"Don't get up," Emily said.

The maitre d' pulled out a chair for her, and we waited until there was no one within eavesdropping distance before we spoke.

"I thought you were dead" was all I could think of to say.

"Obviously, you were wrong."

"I'm sorry. I'm really sorry."

"You didn't believe me," she said. "You didn't trust me."

"Then who *is* dead? Whose body was it? Who was wearing Mum's ring?"

"You don't need to know," Emily said. "If I told you, you would probably just tell Stephanie."

"That's a low blow, Emily. That's unfair."

"Don't you read her silly blog?" asked my wife. "All about your happy, healthy, perfect blended family, about her consoling poor little Nicky for the tragic loss of his mom."

"I never read her blog. I didn't . . . I wouldn't . . ."

"Well, you should have," Emily said. "It's been very informative, I can tell you."

"I'm so sorry," I said. "I can't tell you how sorry I am."

"Don't," said Emily. "Please don't."

That was when we should have gotten up and left. There was nowhere for this to go but down. And yet I kept on hoping.

Emily said she was hungry. We ordered food.

I told Emily that I didn't care about Stephanie. I never had. She was like a nanny we didn't have to pay. And she'd been helpful. Maybe I shouldn't have said *helpful*.

Emily recoiled, then sat up very straight. I recognized her head shake. Her merciless implacable *no*. I tried to tell Emily that she was the only one, that she had always been the only one, that I was sorry. She yawned.

It was too late. I was a fool. Just as my wife had always secretly, or not so secretly, thought. She told me that she would never forgive me. She said that I would be very sorry.

Very sorry.

She was threatening me. But what could she do? Another foolish question. Emily could do anything. She'd accused me of underestimating her. But she couldn't have been more wrong.

She got up and left.

The waiter came over and stood beside me as we watched her go.

"Hell hath no fury," he said. "Shakespeare got that one right."

"Fuck you," I said. "It wasn't Shakespeare who said that."

The waiter shrugged. What did *he* do? A while later he sent another waiter over with the bill. I actually finished my veal chop. It was half raw and awful, but I was starving. I left the waiter a big apology tip. Why not? I'd been apologizing all evening.

I caught the last train out of Grand Central.

I went straight to Nicky's room and hugged him, even though he was asleep. I didn't wake him. I don't know what I would have done if Stephanie had come into the room and tried to tell me how to put my own son back to sleep. If she'd *instructed* me in that annoying, cloying Captain Mom voice.

I went into my room and lay down next to Stephanie and rolled onto my side. I couldn't touch her, nor did I want her touching me.

"Rough day?"

"You don't know the half of it," I said.

I didn't move till I heard Stephanie snoring softly and making that gummy click at the back of her throat that had started driving me mad.

I got up and lay on the living room couch. I was awake all night.

The worst aspects of Stephanie's personality seemed to have rubbed off on me. Her anxiety. Her cow-in-the-slaughterhouse-chute paranoia. Who would have dreamed that such things were contagious?

I couldn't get over the feeling that Emily was out there in the darkness. Watching our house. She knew that Stephanie was here.

How long had it been since Stephanie asked me if I was sure that Emily was dead? Of course I'd been sure she was dead. Stephanie had said she was afraid that Emily was alive. And I didn't believe her.

I no longer knew who or what to believe.

After that, I stopped sleeping. I tried Stephanie's useless homeopathic remedies. Herbs and foul-tasting teas and whatever. Nothing worked. She said I didn't give them a chance. I ignored her. Her voice got even more irritating when she felt she was being ignored.

My doctor gave me sleeping pills along with a warning that two of his patients had had unpleasant side effects, in one case a psychotic episode. I said that *I* would be psychotic if I didn't sleep. I would take my chances with the meds.

When Stephanie asked why I seemed jumpy, I blamed the sleeping pills. I said that my bad mood was worth it. Insomnia was worse. Nervousness was a side effect. Some people got psychotic.

I didn't mention meeting Emily. I didn't ask if she'd contacted Stephanie. To say that my wife was still alive would have felt like another betrayal. When Stephanie had suggested that Emily might be alive, I'd thought Stephanie was deluded. But I'd been the delusional one.

I have no excuse. I'm trying to keep it together. I am living with the wrong woman, and I am being threatened by my wife. I'm under a lot of pressure. I'm not thinking clearly.

That is my excuse. That was always my excuse. I have no excuse.

One Saturday afternoon, a car came down our driveway and stopped in front of the house. A light-skinned, middle-aged African American man got out and, checking our address against a sheaf of papers in his hand, walked up to our door. I watched him from the window. He reminded me of someone . . .

The blue blazer, the white shirt, and the dark bow tie snapped the memory into place. He reminded me of a man I used to know as a child, a Mr. Reginald Butler. Mr. Butler was the pastor of a local church, a kind of religious group, maybe a beneficent sort of cult, the Manchester Brethren. His parishioners were all immigrants and local people of color. He came to Mum's door—much as this stranger was coming to our door now—seeking donations, warm winter coats to distribute to his flock. Mum invited him in, and they became friendly. Until Mum had a bit too much sherry and said something—I never found out what, and Mum never told me—at which Mr. Butler took offense. And we never saw him again.

Here he was in Connecticut. I opened the door. Of course it wasn't Mr. Butler.

The man said, "Mr. Sean Townsend?"

I admitted that I was.

"I'm Isaac Prager. From the Allied Insurance Company. I'm working on the claim payable on the accidental death of your late wife. For which I am deeply sorry."

Was he saying he was sorry that Emily was dead? Or sorry that he was working on the case? Or sorry that the claim was payable? Was it a coincidence that I'd *just* learned that Emily wasn't dead? I hadn't really had the time, or the peace of mind, to figure out my next step. Should I have notified the insurance company as soon as I came home from having dinner with my supposedly dead wife? It was way too confusing to explain what had happened and what hadn't happened and what I thought had happened. And especially what we'd *planned* to happen. Everything I could think of to say made us look guilty, which, I suppose, we were. It had been easier to put my head in the sand and pretend that nothing had happened. And to hope for the best.

This was the moment I'd dreaded, even though—until quite recently—I hadn't known exactly why. This was the moment when our game became real. Maybe I'd thought that Emily would give up our little charade before it came to this. I don't know what I was thinking.

Prager said, "I thought about trying to reach you at work, but I decided that this might be the sort of conversation you would prefer to have at home. I tried to call you here, but—"

"I'm sorry," I said. "I only rarely pick up when I don't recognize the number."

"No worries. I understand completely," said Prager. "Many people are that way."

We were still standing in the doorway.

"I'm sorry," I said. "Please come in and sit down."

"Thank you," said Prager. "I'll try not to take up too much of your time. This is just a formality."

A formality! I took that as a good sign. Surely, if he'd come here to suggest that my wife and I had cooked up a scheme to defraud his company, the conversation would take quite some time and be more than a formality.

I willed Stephanie not to appear, to keep on doing whatever Captain Mom activities she was doing in the kitchen. But minding her own business was way beyond Stephanie's capabilities. She appeared in the doorway wearing jeans and an old sweatshirt and fat socks that made an unattractive swish-swish sound as she walked into the living room. I wished I could have said, "Mr. Prager, this is Stephanie, our babysitter." God knows what would have happened then.

Instead I said the next worst thing.

"Mr. Prager, this is Stephanie. A friend of my late wife's."

"I see." Prager looked her up and down. "Pleased to meet you." They shook hands.

"Mr. Prager works for the insurance company."

"*What* insurance company?" said Stephanie. Brilliantly, I thought. Maybe Stephanie was a few IQ points smarter than I'd given her credit for.

"Emily and I had a policy," I said.

"Really?" said Stephanie. "I had no idea."

"A two-million-dollar policy, to be exact," said Mr. Prager.

"Oh, wait, that's right," said Stephanie. "I blogged about it." She was covering for herself, just in case Mr. Prager read her blog. As I should have, all along.

Stephanie plopped herself down on the couch, and I sat next to her, not too close. The couch was enormous. There was plenty of room. Prager sat on the edge of the club chair.

Stephanie offered him coffee, water, tea. Mr. Prager politely declined.

He said, "As I'm sure you folks realize, everyone is different. People have different ways of doing things, different reasons for doing them. Only rarely do we understand what anyone does or why they do it. Though you could say that's my job. To understand people. So there we have it."

"Mr. Prager . . ." I said.

"Oh, yes," he said. "Your late wife, Emily. I have been trying to think how I could phrase this in the least upsetting way. But there's really nothing to be done but say this as simply as I can."

"Say what?" I couldn't mute my impatience.

"Right," said Mr. Prager. "We have begun to think that your wife may still be alive."

It took all my strength of will not to flinch. "Why in the world would you think that?"

From the corner of my eye, I caught Stephanie giving me an "I told you so" look. Stephanie was an idiot. She had *no idea* how catastrophic this was.

Prager shook his head. It was hard to tell if he was mournful or amused.

I said, "But I saw the autopsy report."

Prager said, "Of course you did . . . Well, then . . . I'm afraid there are some very unpleasant parts to this that you might not wish to hear. Some people prefer *not* to have certain images lodged forever in their minds. That would be your choice. As I said, everyone is different."

"I don't know," Stephanie said. "I might be one of those people who doesn't want certain images stuck in her head."

"Then you can leave the room," I said.

Prager shrank back, almost involuntarily, as some well-behaved people do in the presence of domestic tension.

"I'll go check on the boys. Then I'll be back," she said. Warningly, it seemed to me.

When she left the room, Mr. Prager said, "Let me say what I mean. I'm talking about the autopsy report."

"I read it," I said.

"Once again . . . everyone will read something like that a different way. When *I* read it, for example, I was struck by certain things that might not have occurred to someone else. Someone not in my line of work. For example, there was the fact that the dead woman had been missing a front tooth for quite a long time. Long enough for there to have been bone growth over the gap. Mr. Townsend, I assume you would have known if your wife was missing a front tooth."

"I think I would have known something like that," I said.

I was frightened now, really frightened. If the dead woman wasn't Emily, who was it? Obviously, this was a question I should have asked myself as soon as I saw Emily at the restaurant in Manhattan. But somehow I'd managed to put it out of my mind. It was as if I'd persuaded myself that the dead woman—the body with my wife's DNA—wasn't merely dead but had never existed.

"I agree," said Prager. "You would likely have known that. And being that your wife worked in the fashion industry, we assume that, if she *were* missing a tooth, a dental implant would have been part, one might say, of her culture."

"I would assume so." My head felt suddenly heavy.

"Well, the woman in the lake had never had an implant. Just the missing tooth."

"Then it wasn't my wife," I said. "Except that it was. The DNA was a match."

"We think it might have been her sister," said Mr. Prager.

"Sister? Emily was an only child. What sister?"

Mr. Prager massaged his balding head and looked at me with what was clearly amazement.

"Mr. Townsend," he said, "Did you really not know that your wife was a twin?"

"Are you making this up? Are you *sure* you have the right woman?"

"Mr. Townsend, how is this even possible? Do you mind my asking how a person can live with someone, be *married* to someone, and not know that she has a sibling? Not just a sibling, but a twin."

"I don't know. I can't explain. She always said that she was an only child. I didn't think she—I didn't think *anyone*—would lie about something like that." Prager could tell I was telling the truth, at least about this. Knowing when someone was lying was what he did for a living.

Prager said, "May I say that your wife sounds like a very unusual woman."

Stephanie said, "What's going on?"

I hadn't heard her come in.

I said, "Stephanie, did *you* know that Emily was a twin?"

"Are you joking? You're joking." Stephanie was a terrible liar. She'd known. How could she not have told me? How could this not have come up? I suppose there was a lot that Stephanie and I didn't say to each other. I'd seen no reason to mention the fact that Miles was her brother's son. Maybe Stephanie and I got along better that way. Maybe the only way to get along with another person is to tell huge lies of omission. Emily had certainly told some gigantic lies. When did Stephanie find out that Emily was a twin? Had she always known? Was that information on her blog too?

I wondered, as Mr. Prager had said, how could I not have known? It made me question everything, and my entire past suddenly seemed foggy and unclear. In what way had my marriage been a marriage?

Stephanie and Mr. Prager and I stared at the Diane Arbus photo above the mantel. It was as if we all noticed it at the same time. No one spoke for a while.

"Well, there you are," said Mr. Prager. "There are some outstanding questions, and of course the larger question about when and what we plan to tell the legal authorities, who will doubtless turn it into another sort of investigation. Or maybe they won't. Maybe they will do less than I am doing now, which is what's happened so far. But the matter will have to be cleared up, of course, before there's any question of payment."

"Of course. When do you think that will happen? By when?" I tried unsuccessfully to keep the pleading note from strangling my voice.

"Soon enough," said Mr. Prager. "Meanwhile, though it's not in my legal authority, I would like to ask you both, as a courtesy, not to travel very far from here for any length of time."

"Absolutely not!" I said because I thought it sounded as if I was innocent.

"Our kids are in school," said Captain Mom, a bit self-righteously, I thought. But I couldn't blame Stephanie for playing the mother card.

"Naturally," said Mr. Prager. "I'm a great fan of your blog."

He got up and dusted himself off. He shook our hands and thanked us. He gave us each one of his cards. He told us to please feel free to call him at any hour of the day or night if we had any thoughts about this or any other subject, or needless to say, if we heard from my wife . . . He told us to stay in touch.

He said he could let himself out, and we let him. We had no

choice. We watched him go. Stephanie and I couldn't get up off the couch.

"Did you know?" I said. "How did you know about Emily's twin? How could you not tell me?"

"There are things you don't tell *me*," she said. "Everyone has secrets."

35

STEPHANIE'S BLOG

FOR REAL: WHEN A FRIEND ASKS FOR HELP

Hi, moms!

How do we moms know when something is real? How can we tell when our child is sick or when he is only pretending in order to stay home from school? The first few times, we get it wrong, but we learn. How do we know when our friend so desperately needs our help that we must forget the mixed feelings and awkward times we may have experienced in the past and we do what she needs, because it's real, and we *have* to help?

It's a gift that mothers develop, a built-in you-know-what detector, an instinct for the truth that can help us in our non-mom lives, in the many kinds of careers and artistic pursuits that we engage in at the same time as being moms. It is why women are so expert in the so-called caring professions and in ordinary family caring. It's why we make such good friends.

We know when our friend is asking us, really asking, for a simple favor. It's the way a friend says *please.* And we do what she needs, no matter what.

I'll have more to say about this, for sure. For now, I've got to run. I'm meeting a friend, and I think I may have important things to take care of that may keep me from blogging for a while.

More soon, or as soon as I can.

Love, in haste,

Stephanie

36

STEPHANIE

Mr. Prager's visit was extremely upsetting. Sean and I stopped communicating. We didn't trust each other, that much was clear. Maybe we never had.

I was intrigued to learn that Mr. Prager read my blog—another sign of how far my message in a bottle has traveled, how distant a shore it's washed up on. I was tempted to read back as far as I could to see if I'd posted anything incriminating. But whom would I have incriminated?

After Mr. Prager left, I asked Sean what was going on. Could he please—*finally*—tell me the truth? Had he and Emily pretended she was dead in order to collect an insurance payout? Had they played me? Was I the sucker in their scheme? Was I still?

He insisted that nothing like that had happened. He claimed that he was as confused as I was. He'd really believed that Emily had died. Otherwise . . . He didn't have to explain. I knew what he meant. *Otherwise* he wouldn't have invited me to share his life.

He was understandably fixated on the fact that Emily was a twin. And I had to admit: That was a very strange thing to learn about your wife of six years. *I'd* been shocked to find that out—and she'd only been my friend for a relatively short time.

Had Emily *ever* told me the truth? Was Sean being truthful now?

Not knowing should have made me hate them both. It was weird that it didn't.

I was going to have to make some changes. Though perhaps they'd be made *for* me. What if Sean and Emily both went to jail? Had I been chosen and groomed to take care of Nicky in case the worst happened? Emily hadn't been thinking of the worst that could happen. She wasn't even thinking of Nicky. Or the two million dollars. The lying and the game were what had gotten her high. The lying to everyone. Especially me.

I had a momentary fantasy: What if Emily and Sean *were* sent to jail and I got custody of Nicky? I'd always wanted to have a second child. Allowing myself to let that thought cross my mind, even for a split second, made me feel so guilty that I pinched myself to make the fantasy go away.

There were so many questions that Sean hadn't asked Mr. Prager. If the dead woman was Emily's twin sister, how did Emily's sister die? They already knew that. She'd drowned, her system overloaded with alcohol and pills.

———

A WEEK OR so after Mr. Prager's visit, OUT OF AREA came up on caller ID.

I knew I should despise Emily. She'd lied to me. She'd mistreated me. She'd betrayed our friendship. She'd terrorized me. She'd stalked me from the woods behind her house and entered my house when I wasn't there. So I cannot explain how happy it made me just to hear my friend's voice. I can't pretend, even to myself, that my emotions make sense.

Emily said, "Stephanie. It's me. I *desperately* need you to help me. *Please.*"

The way she said *please* made me want to blog about it—about helping a friend in need. About how we know when a friend really and truly needs us. I could never write the whole truth. But I wanted to write about why I couldn't say no. Maybe if I blogged about it, I would understand myself and why I did what I did, why I was willing to forget, or at least overlook, all the awful things that Emily had done to me.

All I knew now was that Emily needed my help. She'd gotten herself into a dangerous situation.

She said, "A man is following me. He's been following me for a couple of weeks. He's not making a big effort to stay hidden. I don't know what he wants."

"What does he look like?" I said.

"Middle-aged. Light-skinned black guy. Always in a suit and a bow tie. He looks a little like that hit man on *The Wire*."

"I never saw *The Wire*." I was stalling for time.

"Jesus, Stephanie, no one cares if you saw *The Wire*." In all the time we'd been friends, she'd never spoken to me in that tone. Why not tell her the truth? Especially when everyone else was lying.

"There was a man here who sounds like the guy you're describing," I said. "He's an investigator from the insurance company. He's looking into the claim that you and Sean took out. Your accidental death."

"I knew it," Emily said. "I don't know why. But I knew it. That's the vibe I got off the guy. This is *bad*. Did Sean tell him where I was?"

"Emily," I said, "Calm down. Sean doesn't know where you are. *I* don't know where you are. Remember? The last I knew, you were in the woods, watching me." It was the most critical (and the nerviest) thing I'd ever said to her, and I was holding my breath. But Emily wasn't thinking about my tone—or about our friendship.

"I don't know how he found me, then. Maybe Mother's license plate turned up on some CCTV footage."

"Be careful," I said. "He's not a stupid guy. He gives the impression of being a little bumbling, but I think he notices and registers every little thing."

"Stephanie, I need to see you." Emily's voice had tears in it. I'd never heard her sound like that, either. "I need to talk to you. I need your advice. I need a friend."

I knew that I was speaking to someone who had lied about some very important things. She'd lied to her husband, to me. She probably lied to herself. But I was also a liar. And she was my friend. I believed her.

This might be my only chance to get an explanation, to find out what she really thinks. Who she really is. There was so much she'd kept to herself. Emily's secrets were as dark as mine. Maybe darker.

You could say we were *meant* to be friends. We could still help each other.

"All right," I said. "I'll come see you. But you have to promise that you'll tell me the truth this time. No more lies, no more secrets."

"I promise," Emily said.

———

EMILY ASKED ME to meet her in the bar of a Sheraton Hotel beside the interstate, about thirty miles from our town, on a weekday in the middle of the day. Neither of us had to say that the boys would be in school and that Sean would be in the city. We didn't need to mention their names.

She said that she needed to meet me in a public place. Public, but private. Anonymous. "No one who knows me can see us. We should probably meet in an underground parking garage."

I didn't know what she meant, but I laughed. I could tell that I was supposed to laugh.

"Do you understand, Stephanie?"

Once more I said I understood, though I didn't. But maybe I would soon.

She said, "Could I ask you one more favor? Well . . . maybe two."

"What is it?" I said guardedly. Hadn't I done Emily enough favors?

"Could you bring my ring?" she said. "My engagement ring from Sean."

"I know where he keeps it," I said, then wished I hadn't. What a ridiculous thing to say. It would only remind her of my intimate knowledge of Sean and his habits.

"I know you do," she said.

"How do you know that?"

She didn't answer. Could she have seen me through the window when I looked through Sean's desk? Or was she bluffing, trying to unsettle me more than she already had?

"And another thing . . . this sounds a little weird. Could you bring me Sean's hairbrush? And don't, you know, feel that you have to clean it."

I sensed trouble. Real trouble. Had I learned nothing during this terrible time? Hadn't my trust in my fellow humans been damaged beyond repair? Did I still believe in friendship? In the natural bonds between moms?

My brain was no longer in control, if it had ever been. My heart was calling the shots. My heart was speaking to my friend. My heart said, Yes. What day? What time? What place? I'll be there.

I arrived first, on purpose. Emily had picked a strange place. A bar from another decade. A throwback. It was decorated like a fake library with fake books, which were actually part of the wallpaper, and a fake fire burning in a fake fireplace. Like an English gentleman's club, except that it was in a hotel on a small rise just above the interstate. In the middle of nowhere.

All that fake decor—was Emily saying something about the fake nature of our friendship?

The bar was comfortable, and I didn't mind nibbling on microwaved baked potato skins while I waited for her to arrive. There were only two other customers, an elderly tourist couple already on their dessert and coffee. The husband went to the men's room and took forever. Then it was the wife's turn. She took so long that her husband went to the bathroom again after she got back to the table. They weren't much fun to watch. I missed Davis. We would never grow old together like that couple.

I went through two orders of potato skins with cheese. I was hungry and nervous. I didn't know what to expect or what I was about to encounter. Was Emily setting me up to betray me again? Would this be another trick, another deception? Another chapter in her plan to punish me for sleeping with her husband?

I told the waiter I was expecting a friend. I don't know what he imagined. Boyfriend, maybe, or girlfriend. Who else would arrange to meet here except adulterous lovers on the down low?

This was nothing like that. It was my friend. It was Emily. Right there.

I searched her face for any signs of anger or lingering resentment, for any indications that she meant to hurt me—again. But I saw nothing like that. All I saw was the familiar face of the friend whom, despite everything that had happened, I still loved. And who still loved me.

I jumped up from the table. The elderly tourists watched us hug. Emily smelled like she always had. I pulled back and looked at her. She looked like Emily. Radiant. Beautiful. As if nothing had happened.

But something was different. She looked . . . I don't know. Sad. As if half of her was missing.

She was dressed for work. The way she would have been dressed that evening, months ago, when she came to pick up Nicky on her way home from Dennis Nylon.

But she hadn't come home. She owed me an explanation.

I ordered a gin and tonic, though I never drank in the middle of the day. Certainly never before I was supposed to pick the boys up from school. Emily drank one margarita, then another. All the time we didn't speak, until I finally couldn't stand it.

I said, "The man who's following you . . ."

She said, "Stephanie, please, can we talk about that later? First I need to know that you trust me. I'm sure you have some questions. Ask me whatever you want to know."

Her laying herself open like that made it hard to ask anything at all. It all seemed like such an intrusion. I didn't know where to begin. Why did you pretend to be dead? Why did you involve me? Are you still angry at me for what happened with Sean? What were you thinking? *Who are you?*

But all I said was, "Why didn't I know you had a sister? Why didn't you tell me you had a twin?"

I don't know why I led with that, out of all the questions I could have asked, the accusations I could have made, the mysteries I wanted explained. I suppose because it was the first question that popped into my mind.

"I don't know. I really don't." Emily opened her palms and closed them. A familiar gesture, but something was different. She wasn't wearing her ring. I had the ring, in my purse. The ring that had turned up on a corpse in a lake in Michigan.

"I compartmentalized," Emily said. "You understand how that can happen. You know exactly how someone can not talk or even think about things she doesn't want to think or talk about. How she can have secrets even from herself. That's one of the reasons we're friends."

I'd never thought about that before. But Emily was right.

"What was your sister's name?" I said.

Tears popped into Emily's eyes.

"Evelyn."

"What happened to her?"

"She killed herself at the lake house in Michigan. I rushed out there to try to save her. That's why I didn't get in touch with you. I'm so sorry for what I put you through. But I was frantic about Evelyn, and I had no time to explain to people who didn't even know I had a sister. Can you understand that?"

"Yes," I said, though once more I wasn't sure that I did.

"I tried every way I knew to help her. At first I thought I'd won. I'd thought I'd convinced her to live. She swore to me that she wouldn't kill herself." Tears slipped down Emily's cheeks. "She did it when I was asleep. And I'll never get over it. Never. Sometimes I feel as if I'm dead too. I knew that you and Sean thought I was dead. It was easier for me that way. I didn't want to see anyone. I didn't want to talk. I couldn't explain. I didn't want to exist.

"But finally I missed Nicky too much. And I missed you."

I said, "Do you think that was fair to us?"

"*Us?*" said Emily. "You're joking."

"I'm sorry," I said. "Sean *believed* you."

"Actually," she said, "he didn't. I was right to think I couldn't trust him. That's why I never told Sean about Evelyn. About how my love and fear for my sister controlled my life. I couldn't trust him with that information. I controlled information, that was my job. But I couldn't control something so . . . personal. So painful."

I looked at my friend and saw a whole new person. A more tormented person than the strong, glamorous, have-it-all mom with the personal assistant and the fashion-industry job. A more complicated and more human person.

She said, "Sean couldn't have understood. He was an only child. My love and fear for my sister was part of why I'd had problems with alcohol and pills. She and I were keeping each other company in our self-destructive addictions. And then I turned off that particular path, and she went on ahead, on her own."

Emily was finally being honest about her brushes with substance abuse—and about her sister. And about her husband. Our friendship would never be the same. There would always be that little hiccup now. That edge of . . . discomfort. We could thank Sean for that.

I felt as if she was reading my mind when she asked, "Did you bring the ring?"

I took it out of the zippered pocket in my purse where I'd put it for safekeeping.

"How did you know that Sean had it?" I said. "How did you know that I knew where it was?"

A silence fell. I held my breath.

"I didn't know," she said. "I hoped. I gave it to Evelyn before she died. I wanted her to have it. It was the only thing I had with me that I could give her that I thought might last. And I knew that it was important to Sean. He gave me the ring early in our courtship. It was his love gift to me. A memento of those happy early days. It had been his mother's, and she had given it to him so he could give it to me."

I braced myself against the pain I expected to feel when I heard about Emily's happiness with Sean—another reminder that Sean would never love me as much as he loved her. But the fact was, I felt nothing. Being with my friend was so wonderful. I was over Sean already. Sean was history.

Emily slipped the ring on and spun it around her finger.

"Look," she said. "It's loose. I must have lost a little weight during my . . . time-out."

"I don't know," I said. "You look gorgeous." And she did.

With the ring on her finger, it was like magic. Emily . . . transformed, is all I can say. She changed from a sad woman grieving for her sister into the force of nature she'd been when I knew her. Something—determination?—reanimated her features, or maybe it was just that she started moving her hands in front of her face, like the old Emily, and the jewels in the ring caught the light—what little light there was in the hotel bar.

Emily was back.

With tears streaming down her face, she finally told me the horrible truth: Sean had begun abusing her a few months after their marriage.

"He knew how to hit me without leaving a mark. But he only rarely did that. Mostly he threatened me. Whenever I made him mad, he told me how easy it would be to get his company mega-lawyers to do him a favor. The city's sharkiest custody lawyers would prove that I was an unfit mother. They would demolish me in court, citing my history with alcohol and pills. They would use my working in the fashion business against me. They would make my job sound like I was doing PR for Sodom and Gomorrah."

How terrified my friend must have been, to keep these things to herself, even after I'd confided so much and made it clear that she could trust me. We'd always assumed that I was the neurotic person in the friendship. But really, she was the paranoid one. Paranoid and skittish. Imagine recording my confession by the submarine ride in case she would ever have to use it against me! Why would she ever have had to use *anything* against me? Being friends meant that we were on the same side. How sad that she hadn't trusted me. But I knew what it was like, having problems with trust.

Did Emily think that she was the only woman with an abusive husband? I knew that such illusions were often part of the pattern of abuse. The husband makes the wife feel as if she's alone in the world. But Emily was never alone. She had Nicky. She had work. She had me.

I said, "The guy that's been following you . . ."

"Right. In a minute." Emily held up her hand. "There are some things I need to say first. Stephanie, I don't blame you. You thought that I was dead. I don't even blame Sean, but I can't forgive him for the things he did that gave me no choice but to leave Nicky. And you. I couldn't tell anyone, not even you. I'm only glad that he didn't turn his rage against you."

It was a lot to process at once. Sean had never seemed like an angry person. Even after Mr. Prager's visit, I did not see signs of the fury that so frightened Emily. Sean had always just seemed sad. But according to Emily, he was a skillful actor—and an evil one. It's amazing how convincingly we can pretend to be something we're not.

Sitting in the hotel bar, she told me how she'd had to work through her shock and sorrow. She'd been forced to survive the loss of her sister without being able to see Nicky, who would have been so helpful, so comforting with his love and warmth and sweetness. But she'd had to leave Nicky behind and go into hiding because she was so afraid of Sean and of what he might do to her.

I wanted another gin and tonic, but I had to drive all the way back and pick up Nicky and Miles.

"Sean will say I abandoned Nicky. He'll claim that everything was my idea. He'll make you testify for him. What choice will you have? He'll blame it all on me, when he was the one who came up with the insurance scam. He was the one failing at work. His company was only too glad to put him on half-time, especially when they knew that it wouldn't be great PR to fire a guy whose wife was missing and who had a little son. He believed he was doing it for me, because I wanted to do it. But that was a lie he told himself. Two million dollars wasn't a fortune, but it was an attractive golden parachute for a guy who might lose his job.

"There wasn't a single day when I wasn't afraid that Sean would turn on me and take Nicky and ruin my life. You have to believe me, Stephanie."

Suddenly, everything made sense: why Emily vanished and why I was the only one she had the courage to reach out to, why she appeared to Nicky before she tried to contact me.

It explained why Sean had so stubbornly refused to consider my suggestion that Emily might be alive. He *knew* that she was alive, which is why he'd tried to convince me that it was all in my imagination. He knew she was pretending to be dead. He wanted her to disappear and me kept in the dark. It was all part of his evil plan.

How could Sean do that to Nicky? His own son. Even when I had doubts about Sean, I never doubted that he was a loving father. My God, I'd left Miles with him when I went to Detroit. It scared me to think about that now.

I understood why Emily hid the fact that she was a twin. How excruciating it must have been, losing and finding and losing a sister. And now she'd lost her forever, just as she'd feared she would.

I'd believed that Emily was my best friend, but I hadn't known her at all. Now I had to help her. She still seemed so lost, so damaged. For once, I had to take charge.

"The man who's been following you," I said. "Let's talk about him."

"Right," she said. "I confronted him. I agreed to meet with him. Today, actually." She looked at her watch. "How perfect. Stephanie, would you come with me to talk to him? Would you be there for support? I guess I should have asked you before . . ."

I considered it for a minute. Maybe it was a good idea to see Mr. Prager again, this time as a friend of Emily's, this time to demonstrate that I was the trusted friend of a decent, loving family that had been having problems. They weren't criminals! I wouldn't have been friends with people who could commit criminal fraud. I would insist that things were going to work out, that everything had a simple and innocent explanation, that Mr. Prager's investigation would turn up nothing illegal or even shady.

"Exactly when are you meeting him?" I asked Emily.

She checked her watch again, even though she just did. She was obviously nervous.

"In half an hour."

"Where?" I said.

"Out in the parking lot. Trust me. Let's have another drink."

"In the parking lot?"

"You *need* to trust me. Can you trust me, Stephanie?"

I couldn't even trust myself to speak. I nodded.

With half an hour to kill until our meeting with Mr. Prager, we sat in the bar and strategized. What should we do about Sean? Emily had some ideas. Some sounded—well, I guess you could call them vengeful. But others seemed reasonable. Let the punishment fit the crime. We had to be careful. But should we rule out the shock element in dealing with a liar and a bully like Sean?

I was the one who should have been in shock. The man I had lived with and fallen in love with—or *almost* fallen in love with—was a monster.

Now all the complicated and confusing things that Sean had done turned out to have simple and clear explanations. He'd wanted me on his side so he could enlist me as a character witness in the event that Emily resurfaced and wanted to tell the truth. You can never know anyone. People keep secrets. I'd let myself forget that all-important fact.

I trusted Emily. I believed her. I was so sorry for what she had been through. But she and I would survive. We and our beautiful sons would get through this and make a wonderful life for our kids and not dwell on the past. Together we would move on.

"All right," she said. "Show time! Let's go meet our friend Mr. Prager and have this delicate conversation."

Emily paid the bill in cash, and we went outside. It was damp and chilly but bracing. Emily put on her gloves and a woolen hat that covered the top half of her face. As we crossed the parking lot, I felt as if we were two powerful cartoon characters—superheroines, superfriends—on our way to get justice, to speak the truth, to explain ourselves to a man investigating my friend for a crime she didn't commit.

I recognized the car from across the lot, the car that had parked near our house. I felt strange and self-conscious as we approached it, almost as if I was performing. But for whom?

Mr. Prager was in the passenger seat.

"Look," I said. "He's sleeping."

"He's not sleeping," said Emily.

"What do you mean?" I said.

"He's dead," she said. "Our friend is not waking up."

"How do you know?" I said, a slight nausea creeping up on me.

"I killed him," she said.

"This isn't happening," I said.

Nothing made any sense. If Emily was innocent, as she'd said in the bar, why had she killed him? All we had to do was *talk* to him. Explain things.

"Technically, it *is* happening," she said. "This is as real as it gets."

"Why?" I said.

"Because I couldn't risk it. Because I didn't think he would believe me. Because I was pretty sure that he wouldn't believe me. I had one conversation with him, and I knew. Because I didn't want to go to jail. Because I didn't want to lose Nicky. What happens to him if Sean and I go to jail, Stephanie? Did you think that Nicky would be yours if Sean and I got sent away?"

I couldn't look at her. How did she know that the thought had crossed my mind?

"Are those enough reasons for you, Stephanie? Or do you need more?"

I didn't want to look, but I couldn't stop myself from peering into the car. There was no blood, no indication of violence. Even though I knew he was dead, Mr. Prager really did look as if he was asleep.

"How did you do it?"

"In my other life," she said, "I got quite good with a hypodermic. I always knew where to get one, and I knew what to put in it. And I'm proud to say I still do. Our man OD'd. Who knew that Mr. Insurance Geek had a costly and unpleasant drug habit?"

There was an unsettling note in Emily's voice—almost as if she was boasting. I thought of Miles, of Davis, of the life I loved. I was putting all that at risk. Implicating myself in a crime. A serious crime. A murder.

But what were my choices? Either I could run back to the hotel and turn Emily in, or I could get in my car and drive off. Or I could wait to see what happened. Or I could trust her, no matter what. I knew that I wasn't thinking clearly, that I could hardly think at all. I was in no shape to make a major life decision. But I opted for believing in my friend, for taking things one step at a time and seeing what happened next.

Emily moved so that she was standing between me and the car, blocking my view of the dead Mr. Prager. That was considerate of her, I thought.

She said, "This is where I really need your help. A simple favor, okay?"

"Okay," I whispered.

"We're going for a little drive. You're going to follow me in your car. And I'm going to drive Mr. Prager in his car to a secluded pull-off I found, just up the way, on a back road that has hardly any traffic. Not too far. When you see me turn off the road and head up a slight ridge—I'm going to be driving very fast so it looks as if Mr. Prager was driving and lost control and veered off the road—you need to stop and park. Park directly over my tire tracks. In case anyone drives by, which probably no one will, they won't notice the tracks veering off the road and think something is wrong."

Emily's breathing had sped up, and she looked flushed, excited. If I saw her from a distance and didn't know what she was talking about, I'd think, What a happy woman!

She said, "I'll have stopped on top of the ridge. On the other side is a steep cliff. A chasm, really. The incline goes more or less straight down. No residents for miles around. No chance of collateral damage, no one watching us when we push Mr. Prager's car over the ridge. Best case, explosion, flames, everything incinerated, burnt clean. Just enough forensic evidence to ID Mr. Prager. Worst case, the car sits there until someone finds it on the other side of the ridge. Which reminds me . . . please tell me you brought Sean's hairbrush."

I pulled the brush out of my bag and gave it to Emily. The feel and sight of Sean's hair gave me first the shivers, then the creeps.

"I almost forgot," Emily said. "What kind of criminal mastermind am I?"

She plucked a few hairs from the brush and scattered them around the car interior.

"Worst, worst case, someone finds the car. Runs the forensics. And guess what? It was Sean. Motive. Opportunity. Hair."

I said, "I don't know . . . I have to get home in time to pick up the boys after school." What a ridiculous excuse. How lame and weak I sounded.

"Guaranteed," Emily said. "You'll be amazed how little time this takes. How little time and effort."

It was so horrible that it was almost fun. I once heard someone talk about "the second kind of fun." Something so terrible that it's fun. Driving behind my friend with a dead man in her passenger seat just did not seem real. It seemed like a horror movie that I was being tricked into believing was real life.

Luckily, the road was empty. In any case, no one passing us would have noticed anything suspicious. Emily must have tipped Mr. Prager over so that it looked, from the outside, as if she were alone in the car. If only she were! If only what had just happened could still turn out to be a bad dream.

I kept checking the clock. Reality was knowing when I had to get the boys at school. But it was still confusing. How could the responsible mom who was never a minute late to get her child be the same person who was helping her friend cover up a murder?

Suddenly, Emily pulled off the road and went bouncing up the rise. I stopped my car and parked on the shoulder. As I began to climb up the hill, I saw Emily getting out of the driver's seat of Mr. Prager's car.

This was the worst thing I'd ever done. By far. Looking back, my affair with Chris and having Chris's child and deceiving Davis into thinking that Miles was his and sleeping with my dead best friend's husband—that was nothing compared to this. That was child's play. And the weird thing was: it felt so liberating. As if I were being absolved for all the bad things I'd done by doing something so much worse. And doing it with someone else—my friend! I was so not alone!

The hill got steeper. How had Emily driven Mr. Prager's old car all the way up the hill without getting stuck? Had she practiced somewhere else? Sheer strength of will, I guessed. I was panting slightly, taking in oxygen; the wind was blowing through my hair. I felt such a sense of excitement, of adventure. Of happiness.

I had never felt so alive.

Emily was waving me on. "Hurry up," she said.

She hugged me when I reached the top. "Thelma and Louise," she said.

In the past, I'd often missed Emily's film references, though I'd always pretended that I understood. But now I totally got this one. *Thelma and Louise* was one of my all-time favorite films.

"That's us," I said. "Here we go. Girl power. Bad girls on the run."

Emily reached in the car and put it in neutral.

"Like this." She put one hand under the rear bumper and another flat against the trunk. I joined her and did what she did.

"One, two, three," she said, and we pushed. "Again!"

"One, two, three," I said. I was amazed that I could count to three, that's how giddy I was.

"Concentrate," said Emily. "Lean into it."

Grunting and swearing, Emily and I pushed. I tried not to think about how much it felt like giving birth. Because there was a similar feeling of . . . lightness, a familiar rush of pure joy when we finally succeeded.

The car went over the ridge. It flipped over, rolled, flipped again, then burst into flames. We cheered and whooped, like kids.

"Bingo," Emily said. "We got lucky."

"Luck had nothing to do with it," I said. "That was mom power in action."

Emily and I hugged from sheer exhilaration.

"Look at us," she said. Our gloves and boots were wet and slick with caked mud. Emily stripped off her gloves and threw them in the back of my car, and I did the same.

The explosion and fire were thrilling. Like fireworks, when you're a child. We stood on the ridge and watched. I tried not to think about Mr. Prager burning.

I drove Emily back to her car, and we hugged goodbye in the parking lot.

"We'll be in touch soon," she said. "I'm sorry for whatever came between us. Nothing like that will ever happen again. I promise."

"Why should I trust you this time?" I smiled, so she'd know that I wasn't serious.

Emily wasn't smiling.

"Because we're in this together," she said.

37

STEPHANIE'S BLOG

WE CAN WIN THIS

Hi, moms!

Usually, except in cases of emergency, I've tried to keep the tone of this blog as sunny and bright as I can. We moms have enough stress without my adding to it by bringing up things that we would rather not dwell on. But I've been thinking about a problem that needs to be addressed because it affects so many moms—so many women—everywhere. And it's one of those things that must be taken out of the shadows and looked at without secrecy or shame.

It's the problem of domestic abuse. Every day the statistics get worse—the percentage of women abused by their husbands and boyfriends, the chances that any one of us will find herself the victim when the man who seemed so nice suddenly turns out to be a monster. When the person we thought we could trust turns out to be our enemy.

Sometimes it comes as a shock. Sometimes, looking back, we see the signs we chose to ignore. Looking back on my earlier blog posts, I have to

wonder why I was so drawn to that French film about a wife, a mistress—
and an abusive husband.

Sometimes we deceive ourselves into thinking that a man who abused a
former wife or girlfriend will be an angel with us. Moms! Don't be fooled! If
a man does something once, he'll do it again. And it's not always easy to
identify the serial abuser. It's not always the guy with the tattoos and the
motorcycle jacket. It's just as likely the guy in the expensive haircut and
the elegant business suit.

That is to say: any man.

Sometimes it starts early, but more often it takes a while—until we're in so
deep that we can no longer remember life without him. Or until we have
kids. And we keep thinking that he'll never do it again. He's sorry; he loves
us . . . We all know the story.

Some men lash out and leave marks, the black eyes and broken noses
that send women to the emergency rooms and from there to the kindly
social worker and the battered women's shelter. But the real devils are
the ones who hide the traces, who practice constant psychological abuse
until the woman is all but destroyed.

It could be happening to anyone. Your coworker. Your best friend. And you
have no idea. Sometimes the secret comes out too late. And sometimes
just in time. A woman—a mom—may try to escape and be driven to do
something extreme before she can get help.

What to do? Make your voices heard. Let our lawmakers know that women
need to be protected by law. Volunteer at a shelter. Raise your sons to be
men who would never mistreat a woman.

And if it's happening to your friend?

Do anything she needs. Help her in any way you can.

Okay, moms, enough heavy stuff. I'm starting a chain so you can share your own abuse stories and let me know what you think about this subject.

Love,

Stephanie

38

EMILY

I should have wanted them both dead. I don't know why my rage collected around Sean and not around Stephanie. Maybe because, once
again, Stephanie's naive, dopey malleability meant that she could help
me get what I wanted. And Sean seemed like an obstacle blocking my
path.

To start, I wanted revenge on Sean. And why was I willing to plot
against him with the so-called friend he was sleeping with? Because I
knew it would work.

Also I wanted my ring back. Not because I stole it from Sean's mom
or because it had any sentimental associations with him, but because
it was the last thing that touched my sister.

Even as I confronted the guy from the insurance company and set
up a meeting, I knew exactly how I was going to fit Stephanie into my
plans. Stephanie owed it to me for sleeping with my husband. And
also . . . she was born to be the fish.

I suppose I felt a little guilty, making the abuse story up. The lying
itself didn't bother me, but I was pretending to have a violent husband,
which is a real problem for many women. I felt bad for faking it to get
the result I wanted.

But I was obsessed. I couldn't rest until I'd made Sean pay for betraying me and ruining our plans for the future. For *forcing* me to kill my sister.

I let Evelyn die because her death would help me and Sean. And now there was no "me and Sean." There never had been. He was always in it for himself—even while I was letting Evelyn go. There had been me and my sister, and now there was me and my son.

I was in it for me and Nicky. I wanted to raise my son alone—without the "help" and "support" of a man I didn't love and couldn't trust.

It would be tricky, making Sean give Nicky up. But I could do it. And Stephanie would help. All I had to do was mention the words *abuse* and *violent,* and she would drop Sean in a heartbeat and forgive her long-lost best friend for whatever she imagined I did. All I had to do was make her think that we were figuring this out together, when in fact I'd figured it out long before our tearful reunion in the bar.

I altered some details to make my story more credible. I told her that Sean was under pressure for failing at work, but actually he was doing quite well and had almost gotten back up to speed after working from home for a while following my disappearance. I had practice in controlling information, changing details. Spinning the truth was what I did for a living.

And oh, poor Mr. Prager. He was collateral damage. Wrong place, wrong time, wrong profession. He asked too many questions—too many of the wrong questions. Silencing him and getting Stephanie to help me dispose of the body killed two birds, as it were, with one stone. It solved my Prager problem and regained and ensured Stephanie's loyalty, once and for all. There is no bond as tight as the bond between partners in crime. Thelma and Louise. Hilarious. Stephanie would die for me if she had to. Fortunately for Stephanie, I don't expect that will be necessary.

The next thing I did was call Dennis Nylon. I talked my way up the food chain. I got as far as Adelaide, his bitch of a personal assistant.

She said, "How did you get this number? Emily Nelson is dead, and this is a tasteless joke. Whoever you are, you know Emily's dead! What you're doing is repulsive."

I told her to calm down, and I revealed several facts about Dennis's various crises and stints in rehab that only I—Emily—would have known. I could practically hear Adelaide's jaw drop. Then I said, "Cut the shit, Adelaide. It's me. Emily. I'm not dead. Put me through to Dennis."

Dennis said, "I knew you weren't dead. My psychic told me she couldn't reach you on the other side—so you must still be here."

"You must have quite a confident psychic," I said.

"The best money can buy," Dennis said.

"I need to come see you," I said.

"Cocktail hour," he said. "I'll be waiting."

I found him lying on the couch at one end of his cavernous loft/atelier. He put down the coffee-table book on Mughal miniatures and rose and kissed me on both cheeks.

Adelaide came in with a tray and two martini glasses filled with Dennis's favorite mezcal-mango cocktail. The rims of the glasses were frosted with chili powder. They were much better than what I'd been making for myself at the Hospitality Suites.

"Cheers," I said. "This is delicious."

"Right back at you," said Dennis, raising his glass.

"It's good to be back," I said.

Dennis drained his glass in three swallows. How did Adelaide know to reappear with another cocktail and remove his empty glass?

"I knew you would have to do something heroic to get out of that marriage. But I had no idea you would have to fake your own death. Everyone around here was devastated. Everyone except me. I knew it was all a charade, just like I knew the happy marriage was a fraud."

"How did *you* know?" I said. "I didn't."

"I don't mean to sound cynical, but most marriages are. And in your case . . . the whole world knew. By the way, some of the kids who work here were saying that you were having an affair or had a drug habit or something, and that you'd asked them to help you get a fake ID. I don't know why you didn't come to me. I could have found you the best fake credentials. The British husband was cute, but he didn't have the brains or the stamina to keep up with you, to swim with a shark like you, dear. We all knew you'd get bored. You would have been out of there years ago if it weren't for that beautiful son, who can now become a much more interesting child, the product of a broken home."

A pang of missing Nicky shot through me.

"I need a favor," I said.

Dennis said, "If you want your old job back, you've got it. We haven't hired a permanent person. Life in the war zone hasn't been the same without you."

I said, "Really, that would be great. But I have a little . . . red tape to cut through first. Some things I need to take care of. I'm not totally sure yet, but I might need to talk to a lawyer. I know we have good ones on retainer."

"A divorce lawyer?" Dennis said.

"I don't know," I said. "Domestic."

"I know a great one," said Dennis. "When that crazy male stripper was suing me, this guy made him go away. Consider him at your disposal. The psychic too, if you need her."

"Thanks," I said. "I'll let you know. Meanwhile I need something fabulous to wear."

39

STEPHANIE

I still don't know how it happened, but Emily made it clear that we were never *ever* to talk about the dead insurance investigator. Our vow of silence—her gag order, you could say—started immediately after we pushed his car over the ridge.

I took Emily to her car. She told me to follow her for a while. We kept going along the back road until Emily pulled over at a diner, and I turned into the lot.

We got a table by the window, far from any other customers. Emily ordered coffee and a grilled cheese. That sounded fine. Perfect, in fact. I ordered the same. I shouldn't have been hungry after all the potato skins I'd eaten in the bar, but I was.

I was thinking how to begin to say what I wanted and needed to say when Emily said, "That never happened."

"Excuse me?"

"What just happened never happened. Mr. Prager . . . the car . . . none of that occurred."

I thought about it. "All right." That certainly solved a lot of problems. "Someone's going to find out. There have got to be consequences."

"*Consequences.*" Emily rolled her eyes in a way that made *con-sequences* sound like the stupidest and most offensive word in the language. We fell silent when the waitress brought our food and ate in silence.

Emily seemed so confident. But I was sure that someone would track us down. I had gone to help a friend. And I had become a criminal, an outlaw. I imagined the Wanted poster with my face on it. The tape that Emily recorded beside the submarine ride was nothing compared to what she had on me now.

We were not allowed to talk about that, either.

"It didn't happen," Emily said. We finished our meal and got up and left the diner.

And after a week and then another week of nothing happening—no consequences—I was almost willing to believe that she was right.

Nothing happened. There were no consequences. Maybe it had all been a bad dream. Something I'd imagined.

But now, when I picked Miles up at school, when I read to my son and put him to bed, I was no longer the same person. I was a mom and a blogger and an accessory to a murder.

40

SEAN

The first alarming thing was that there were two cars parked in my driveway. One was Stephanie's. That was strange in itself because a week had passed since she'd moved out. And though we still, so to speak, shared custody of the boys, ferrying them back and forth from house to house, and though she still picked them up at school in the afternoons, I hadn't seen much of her.

Our relationship, if you could call it that, was doomed from the start. And there was no way it could have survived Prager's visit. The chance—the fact—that Emily was alive would have made it impossible. I was furious at Stephanie for not telling me that my wife had a sister. And Stephanie was enraged at me . . . I didn't want to tally up the things about which Stephanie had every right to be angry.

Well, I wasn't all that sorry. I didn't mind not having Stephanie around force-feeding me and Nicky her nourishing meals. It was fun to be just two guys again, father and son grabbing a pizza on the fly. It was good to be home, where we only had to deal with each other and we got along fine.

I got back in touch with Alison, so I had someone to pick up the slack when I had to work at the office and didn't want Nicky to stay with Miles.

So now the fact that Stephanie was in my house was a little unusual. It made me uneasy. Well, maybe she'd come to retrieve something she'd forgotten. But whom did the other car belong to? Had Stephanie and whoever it was come here together? Another insurance investigator? I hadn't heard anything from Prager since that initial visit, and I didn't like that, either. No news was not necessarily good news.

The other car was an old brown Buick with Michigan plates. I didn't know anyone in Michigan, except Emily's mother, and I couldn't say I knew her. We'd never met.

Maybe it was Emily.

I'd had a bad day at work. I'd found it hard to concentrate. That was understandable. I had a lot going on.

Carrington, the VP of international real estate, the guy who'd brought me into the firm and whom I felt I could depend on, perhaps because we're both British, had given me several hints of impending trouble. The broadest hint was over lunch at the Oyster Bar. We had three scotches each and oyster stew. He said he hoped I wasn't off my game, or that I would soon get back on it. I'd been working hard and, I thought, doing well. But on the day I came home to find the two cars in my driveway, I'd seen a project that should have gone to me assigned to a kid from Utah who'd just come to work for the firm.

As far as I knew, Nicky was spending the night at Stephanie's, and I'd bought a bottle of good scotch with which I intended to curl up in front of the flat screen and stream *Inspector Morse*.

I unlocked the front door.

"Hello?" I said. Some guardian angel or helpful instinct prevented me—saved me—from calling out a name.

I walked into the living room. Stephanie and Emily sat side by side on the couch. I told myself: Focus, Sean, focus.

Emily said, "We thought this would be fun. Don't you think it's fun?"

I said, "What's going on? Why are you here?"

"Ask Stephanie," Emily said. "She's the one who's been living here."

I looked at Stephanie. I thought, Tell her you've moved out. Tell her we're not together anymore. As if that would save the situation. As if that would make any difference at all. No doubt Emily already knew.

"Where are the boys?" I said.

"Playing in Nicky's room," Stephanie said. "Let them be."

Who was Stephanie to tell me to let my son be? I looked at Emily for support. It seemed unlike her to sit back and let another woman tell me what to do about Nicky. That was worrisome. And not just another woman. Stephanie was the fish we'd found to help us with Emily's crazy plan.

Emily glared at me. Why was I asking Stephanie where Nicky was? Emily's dark cloud of hatred and scorn glided over Stephanie and hovered above my head.

"It's disgusting," Stephanie said.

"What is?" I said.

"That you could have abused your amazing wife."

"*What*? I never 'abused' her." I couldn't stop myself from hooking quotation marks around the word, though I knew it was a bad idea. "You know that as well as I do."

"I saw it," said Stephanie. "You slapped her in front of me."

"You're lying" was all I could say. It was two against one. He said, she said . . . and she said.

"And what about what you did to my sister?" Emily said. "How am I supposed to ever forgive you for that?"

I said, "I never even *met* your sister. How the bloody hell could you be married to me for six years and not even tell me you *had* a twin sister?"

Emily turned to Stephanie. "Don't you just hate the way the British curse?" Then she turned back to me. Her eyes, which I'd always thought were so beautiful, which had once looked at me with what I'd imagined was love, had become two glittering disks of ice.

"You knew about her all along. You'd met her dozens of times. Your not knowing that she existed was another act. Another lie. I'm talking about how you treated her the last time we were all together in the cabin by the lake. And when she showed up unexpectedly at the cabin on your birthday weekend, you couldn't have been more annoyed. You teased and baited her, telling her she wasn't fit to live, that she should die, that she should do her sister a favor and die, that she had nothing to live for, that the world would be better off if she died. Until she finally believed you. It took months, maybe, but it worked. When I went back without you and met her there, in the middle of the night, when I was asleep, she took all those pills and drank all the booze in the house and walked into the water."

"I was never there when your sister was," I said. "You know that, Em."

"Don't call me Em," my wife snarled. "I *told* you never to call me that. That was *her* name for me, and now because of you, she's dead."

I said, "I don't recognize the person you seem to think is me. The monster you're inventing, you, you—"

"You crazy bitch," Emily said.

"You crazy bitch," I said. "Your words."

Stephanie gasped.

"Crazy bitches," said Stephanie. "Did you hear him? That's us. Crazy bitches."

Emily and I wheeled to face her, both thinking, Shut *up*. So at least there was that. I felt as if I was gazing at the three of us from a great distance above. How small and pathetic I appeared, fantasizing about forgiveness, searching desperately for signs that Emily might still be on my side (we both wanted Stephanie to shut up!) when the ugly truth was Emily was making accusations that could get me put in jail.

"Tell that to the coroner," Emily said. "Ask if they can date the time of death with that much precision. Ask if they can positively say that you weren't in the cabin around the time Evelyn killed herself."

I knew that what she was saying made no sense, that it wasn't logical, that I could prove my innocence. But I couldn't think. "That's a lie. It's all lies."

"You're the liar," said Emily. "And I don't want our son growing up to be a liar like you. You said we were in this together. And obviously we weren't."

"Sean, your doctor warned you that those sleeping pills could make you psychotic," Stephanie said. "You could do things and not remember that you did them. You could take a trip and not remember. You could bully someone to death and have no idea that you did that . . ."

Emily looked at Stephanie like a teacher regarding a dull student who'd said something unexpectedly smart. Stephanie must have come up with the part about the sleeping pills on her own. If I had to, I could prove that my doctor didn't prescribe them until quite a while after Emily disappeared. Would I really need to prove that?

"I want Nicky," Emily said. "Now. Can I make that any clearer?"

I recoiled from the sight of Stephanie beaming at my courageous wife.

Emily explained why she'd returned, very calmly and coolly. She was determined to take Nicky. Stephanie was going to help her. They were both determined. Emily's story would hold up. She had a witness. I'd slapped her. I'd hounded her twin sister to death. I'd forced Emily to disappear and pretend to be dead. I'd planned to defraud the insurance company, and I'd made my terrified, battered wife go along with my plan.

Having two women conspire against me was a classic male horror fantasy, but I never saw myself as the kind of male who had fantasies like that. I like women. I'd never been afraid of them—until now. In any case, this wasn't a fantasy. It was real. These women would do anything to separate me from my son. They would lie. They would perjure themselves. God knows what they would do.

Stephanie said, "I'm only telling the truth. About what I saw you do." And then, to my horror, I understood: She *believed* what she was saying. I had no idea how she'd convinced herself, but she had. It had been wrong, from the start, to put our fate in the hands of a woman who had no thoughts, only feelings.

"You can't get away with this," I said. "I'll get a lawyer. There's already an insurance investigation under way, and this time I'll tell them the truth, no matter what the consequences are—"

I was bluffing, but so what? I half wished that Mr. Prager would ring the doorbell right then. He'd see the three of us together; he'd sense the mood, and he'd get it. He'd figure out the truth. Settle things once and for all. He was too smart to be fooled by Stephanie and my wife. It would be great to have another man present. Seeing all of us in the same room would crack his investigation wide open!

"Go ahead," said Emily. "Get a lawyer. I've got Dennis Nylon's legal staff on my side. They'll tell the authorities that you threatened to take Nicky if I didn't go along with your insurance-fraud scheme. And I agreed, out of fear. Or . . . there's another version we could go with. I needed some time away from the family, and you panicked and called the cops. A huge miscommunication. Sorry! And the fact that you'd taken out the policy was just a coincidence. No fault, no blame. No payment. I'd be glad to go with the second version if you will just go away and leave Nicky with me."

I couldn't. I couldn't give up my son and let my wife—my *crazy* wife—raise him. There had to be another way.

I said, "I'm just trying to understand. Look, can everybody just take a deep breath and slow down and—"

The two women exchanged long looks.

Stephanie said, "We know what you did to Emily. And Emily knows how she wants to proceed."

"Oh, *please*," Emily said impatiently. "Everyone knows everything. That is not the point."

I was afraid to leave them like that. To leave things in that state. But I needed air. Only now did I realize that I hadn't even taken off my coat.

"I'm going out for a moment," I said. "I can't listen to this. But first I want to see Nicky."

I walked past them to my son's room. He and Miles were building a parking garage with Legos.

"Hey, guys," I said. "That's cool."

The boys hardly looked up.

"Hi, Dad," Nicky said.

"Hi," said Miles.

I kissed the top of my son's sweet head, and grief washed over me.

"Mom's home," Nicky said, matter-of-factly. As if she'd never been gone.

"I know that," I said. "Isn't that great?"

"Is *my* mom still out there?" Miles sounded worried. Did he think it was *his* mom's turn to disappear?

I only wished that Stephanie *would* disappear, though I wouldn't wish that on Miles.

I said, "Your mom's in the living room with Nicky's mother."

My home didn't feel like home anymore. It had been invaded and destroyed by my wife and her friend. I couldn't get them to leave without resorting to the kind of violence they'd accused me of. I needed to get out. I went to my room and pulled together a suit, a change of clothes, some travel stuff, my sleeping pills, and my laptop.

I said goodbye to my wife and Stephanie. They didn't answer. They didn't seem to hear me. They'd poured themselves glasses of white wine and were stretched out on opposite ends of the couch.

I drove to the station and took the first train back into the city. I checked into the Carlyle. It was way more expensive than we could afford, but I told myself that times like this are what money is *for*.

I called in sick to the office and spent the day in bed. In the evening I went down to the magnificent Carlyle bar, with the Ludwig Bemelmans murals. I've always thought it was one of the most stylish and sophisticated places in New York.

I needed style; I needed sophistication and service. My life had gone dark and lonely and rough. I didn't want to think about how much happier I'd been when I'd believed that Emily was dead.

I ordered a civilized martini (straight up, extra olives) from a civilized waiter, and when it came, chilled perfectly, I looked around at this civilized place and, after the second martini, imagined that things between me and Emily—and now, I guess, Stephanie was in the mix—could be settled in an amicable and civilized way.

I went back to my room, took two pills—twice the recommended dose—and tumbled into a dreamless sleep.

The next morning, I showered in the luxurious bathroom and used every expensive bath product. I smelled like a floral bouquet. I ordered coffee from room service, tipped the waiter well, and dressed.

At work I went straight to Carrington's office.

I was dreading this conversation. I was going to ask if Carrington knew a lawyer who might (I'd have to be circumspect about this) take my case, if needed, at company rates.

What would I tell the lawyer? Once again, I couldn't think straight. My wife had scrambled my brains, as it were.

Carrington tilted back in his chair and rolled away from his desk.

He said, "Good God, Sean. Are you the only person on the planet who hasn't seen this?"

He spun the monitor around. In order to read the screen, I had to lean over or squat in front of his desk. It was all terribly awkward.

On the screen was a Facebook page. The profile picture was of Carrington's wife in her garden with an armload of rhubarb. It was Lucy Carrington's page.

A headline said,

MOMMY BLOGGER SOLVES MYSTERY.
Hear what this mom has to say about her friend's disappearance.

Carrington handed me the mouse.

"Click on it. Wait. Come around. You can sit in my chair. I don't have to be here when you read it."

I said, "You can forward it to me."

He said, "I don't know how to do that."

He left. I followed the links to Stephanie's blog.

41

STEPHANIE'S BLOG

MYSTERY SOLVED!

Hi, moms!

First let me say that I hope you're sitting down. Comfortably. At your desks and kitchen tables. For those of you who need catching up, I'm linking this to the post about my friendship with Emily, and then to the series of posts about her disappearance and death. Or anyway, what we all *thought* was her death. But I'm getting ahead of my story. By the time you're done reading those posts, you'll be pretty much caught up.

Anyway, the latest installment blows everything out of the water.

Moms, are you ready for some big news? Some shocking news?

Emily is alive!!!

I'll skip a couple of steps. I'll leave out my vague suspicion that Emily really wasn't dead. Let's call it my mom intuition. That maternal sixth sense that once again turns out to be right.

When I wrote that post about the afterlife, that post which so many of you reposted, I was actually trying to get in touch with Emily in case she *was* alive somewhere and could somehow read it. I wanted her to know that I hadn't stopped thinking about her and praying for her.

Emily was the friend I was writing about when I wrote about the friend reaching for our help and about how we know whether or not it's real. (link)

Let me say it as plainly as I can: *Her husband was abusive.*

She was so afraid of him that she faked her own disappearance and death. It was worse than that. He'd come up with a fraudulent scam to collect a fortune in insurance money after she disappeared and supposedly died. It's the sort of thing you see on TV, but I guess it happens in real life.

In fact it was her twin sister who died, a desperate measure to which Emily's sister was pushed (to be fair, partly pushed) by her cruel, unsympathetic, abusive brother-in-law.

Sean Townsend.

If it seems surprising that the nice guy and responsible dad I praised on my blog should have turned out to be a terrible person, all I can say is it happens. Hustlers and even serial killers prey on loving women. Not that I am implying that my friend's husband is a killer. Not literally, I mean.

Sean is a very bad person. I don't know what the insurance laws are. But according to Emily, a Mr. Isaac Prager has been spearheading an investigation. He tracked down Emily and got in touch. He offered her a deal and agreed that she would not be implicated in the case if she told him the truth. And of course she referred Mr. Prager back to Sean. The last

Emily heard from Mr. Prager, he and Sean had arranged a meeting about thirty miles from our town.

Emily and I are friends again. She was brave enough to reach out for help, and I was a good enough friend to be there for her. Once again, we're moms united in the same struggle. So here's to the moms and to good friendship.

Love,

Stephanie

42

SEAN

Carrington waited outside his office door the way a doctor waits for you to get undressed before entering the examination room.

"Bad stuff," he said as he walked back in. "Women! You have my sympathy, dear fellow." Whether he believed in my innocence or not, I was grateful that he was polite. Civilized. It was just occurring to me that I'd taken too many pills last night, that maybe in a few hours none of this will have happened. But I knew I hadn't taken *that* much. This was real.

I said, "It's all lies, I swear. Isn't this cyberbullying? Blackmail? What are the libel laws in this country? None of this is true."

I gave him my version. I made one trivial departure from the truth. I pretended I hadn't known that my wife was planning to commit insurance fraud. It made the story less embarrassing. Less complicated. I said I'd seen no connection between the policy I'd signed up for and her subsequent disappearance until the detectives pointed it out. Whatever happened was her idea. She'd always been the thrill-seeking type, always needing to play the bad girl. I said this was not a quality that was going to wear well as Emily aged.

Carrington yanked at his cuffs, sign language for *too much information. We're British.*

And yet I think he believed me.

Carrington said, "I'll ask one of our men in Legal. Apparently the internet isn't like print. There are lots more gray areas. Meanwhile, what do you need? What can I do?"

It was one of those "road less traveled" moments when one has to choose this route or that one. You only hope you feel guided, that you *are* guided. And I did. I was. Maybe the pills were a good thing. They kept me from overthinking.

First thought, best thought, as they say. Though not the absolutely best thought, maybe. I should have mentioned Prager.

I said, "I need distance and time."

Emily had taken time off. It was my turn. Get away. Go somewhere else. Think. Wait for the dust to settle. All the signs and portents were pointing in that direction.

Carrington said, "This has been reposted on Facebook. There have been hundreds of likes. It's gone viral, as they say. Mildly viral. Treatable, perhaps." His chuckle was dry and mirthless. "The so-called truth is beside the point."

"Dear God," I said.

"Dear God indeed," said Carrington.

"What does all this mean? For me?"

"It means that even as we speak, somebody is figuring out if they can prosecute you. And if they decide to do that, things could happen rather quickly."

"Bloody hell," I said.

"Bloody hell indeed." Carrington had a habit of waiting till someone else cursed and then repeating it.

He said, "You're lucky that I like you. And that I believe you, except for the part about not knowing about the insurance scheme, which doesn't bother me, myself, though it would have generated some unfortunate publicity for the company if you'd been caught. Meanwhile I have an idea. We need someone to handle the sale of a plot of land on the Irish coast where a client is planning to build a retreat. Not a big client, not a big retreat, maybe a bit of a tax dodge, but everything perfectly legal. Perhaps you could arrange it. A temporary relocation. The golf in that part of the world is supposed to be outstanding.

"And as you said: Distance and time. As soon as matters are sorted out, we can work on the question of your return."

There were several things that Carrington didn't need to say. I was a British citizen. No one was going to extradite me for suspicion of spousal abuse or assisting a suicide or even attempted fraud. The insurance company would be thrilled not to have to pay. Prager could move on to another assignment.

Carrington was a good man, a nice man. I recognized his offer. The rope thrown to the drowning. The rescue from the burning building.

Carrington said, "The position would start immediately." He couldn't look at me, which was just as well.

"Excellent," I said. "Thank you. Really and truly. Thank you."

"Once is sufficient," Carrington said.

I knew that it was temporary. I needed distance and time. I'd go away and come back and get Nicky. His mother and I could still work things out in a more or less civilized way.

Civilized? What did that word even mean when I was talking about Emily, my wife, the woman I'd loved and thought I knew. What I knew now was that, most likely, she wasn't done with me. Did she still have some evil plan in store to punish me for what she'd imagined I'd done. I couldn't help thinking that she wouldn't rest until she'd made me suffer more than I already had.

There was nothing to do but wait. To hold my breath and wait.

43

EMILY

Sean rolled over, in an email. He'd been assigned to a project on the coast of Ireland. He didn't know how long he'd be there. It was a great opportunity. He asked me to give Nicky all his love. He said he would be in touch about Nicky as soon as he knew how long he'd be gone and when he was coming back. It was very surprising. I thought that he'd fight harder.

But I wasn't complaining. It was what I'd wanted. I couldn't imagine a better way for things to have turned out.

There was one bad night. Maybe the fear was all in my mind. But no one could have told me that then.

It was the first night after Sean moved out. I'd moved back into the house. I'd spent the day restoring my home to its pristine pre-Stephanie condition, throwing out the disgusting teas with which she'd filled the pantry, restocking my wine cooler, dumping the repulsive "Bless Our Happy Home" cross-stitched pillow she'd had the gall to bring over from her house and put on *my* couch, and arranging for the priceless design pieces and my personal items to come out of storage.

Then it was only Nicky and me. The two of us. We had a delicious dinner of crusty, perfect mac and cheese I'd made from scratch. Nicky chattered happily. The kitchen was warm. I'd been living like a hunted animal, but I was again a human being. I'd risked everything. I'd played hard. I'd won.

I knew that I had never been happier. I vowed to make this last, to do everything in my power to overcome the impulse to tear my life up into tiny scraps and fling the pieces in the air. I promised myself that I would make it work, that I would never get restless again, that I wouldn't let everyday things bore or annoy or scare me, that I'd stop trying to control the truth and instead live in the truth.

For as long as I could.

That first night, I'd put Nicky to bed, and I was finishing the Highsmith novel I'd started all that time ago. *Those Who Walk Away*. I assume my subconscious picked *that* right off the shelf.

Maybe reading that particular book alone in the house (except for Nicky) was a mistake. I'd just read a spooky part about the vengeful father of the dead woman following the son-in-law, whom he plans to kill. The older man lurks in shadowy alleys of Venice like the creepy red dwarf in that sexy horror film with Julie Christie and Donald Sutherland.

I was reading on the couch when I got the feeling that someone was out there. Watching me from the woods. Maybe I only thought that because I'd been the one watching the house. Poor Stephanie. I'd tormented her. What a waste of energy. Neither she nor Sean had been worth it.

I wanted to think I knew what a person might sense if someone was out there. I knew I would have been more aware than Stephanie and Sean had been. I'd been the watcher, I was being watched.

I heard a noise. A rustling in the woods. Sean was out there. I could feel it. I sensed his presence. His anger. His malevolence. Was he going to come in the house and try to steal Nicky back? He would convince himself that I deserved it.

I heard whistling in the distance. The sound got louder—then stopped. Nearby.

Did Sean whistle? Why did that tune sound familiar? Maybe it wasn't Sean at all—but a stranger, a killer. The angry ghost of Mr. Prager.

I wanted to look outside, but I was afraid. I turned off the lights and peered into the moonless, opaque night. Then I was afraid to be in the house with the lights off, so I turned them on. Suddenly I hated having so many windows. Why had we thought that we needed so much light?

I could have put Nicky in the car and driven somewhere safe. To Stephanie's, as much as it would have cost me to ask for her company. Her protection. Maybe I'd caught her paranoia, imagining a vengeful husband.

But finally, waking Nicky and leaving seemed like so much trouble . . . for nothing. I decided to take one of the sleeping pills Sean left. He'd never needed them when he was with me! But to be fair, I hadn't yet disappeared and died, and he hadn't moved someone else into my place, and I hadn't threatened him with my alternate versions of the truth.

I lay down next to Nicky. Sean would have to wake me first if he tried to take my son.

Just as I was falling asleep I remembered Stephanie saying that Sean's pills could make someone psychotic. Maybe he'd gone insane. Maybe he'd lost it—and he really was out there.

Or maybe *I* had. I'd taken one of those psycho pills. I was wide awake, my heart slamming against my rib cage. I took another pill and passed out and slept until Nicky woke me the next morning.

Daylight streamed in through the windows. I was in Nicky's bed. I'd fallen asleep with all my clothes on. Sunlight splashed onto the bedroom floor.

"Good morning, Mom," Nicky said.

I kissed his damp, smooth forehead, and we snuggled under the covers. It was bliss.

I want Nicky to have a father. I'll stay in touch with Sean. Meanwhile

I'll file for divorce. For full custody. Just in case. These international transatlantic lawsuits can take ages to settle.

I don't know what Stephanie expected from me. Perhaps she imagined we'd become *real* best friends now. That we'd pool our resources and children and live together in some experimental cooperative-kibbutz kind of thing, dividing up childcare and laundry.

That was never going to happen. Even living with Sean would have been better than that.

I went back to Dennis Nylon and negotiated a *substantial* raise which I used to hire a full-time nanny. I persuaded Dennis to support a foundation that rescues and shelters street kids, and we named it after my sister. I've also worked out more flextime that I can spend with Nicky and that allows me to work part-time from home. I suppose that sometimes you have to leave to make people appreciate you, though this approach can backfire as I discovered with Sean.

I never would have imagined that I could be satisfied with a life like the one I'm leading now. Home, motherhood, work—minus that terrifying boredom, that unstoppable urge to cause trouble, to make something dramatic and awful happen for myself and for everyone around me. I'm doing a pretty good job of fending off that sense that I'm not fully alive unless I'm in control, in flight, or in danger. Maybe all the suffering I've been through—losing my sister, being separated from Nicky—has taught me a lesson and brought me some sort of wisdom. Or maybe not. It remains to be seen how long this truce with my demons can last. But for now it seems to be holding. Who knows how long I can keep this up—or what the future will bring.

Nicky and Miles are still friendly, but they don't have many playdates. Our new nanny, Sarah, drops Nicky off and picks him up at Stephanie's house.

I'm in occasional contact with Sean. I plan to set up a time in the (not-so-near) future when he can fly over and see Nicky, but that will have to wait until I feel that he is sufficiently sorry for what he did, for forcing me to disappear and to pretend that I was dead—and for contributing to my twin sister's death.

I haven't yet decided how—and how much—I plan to make Sean suffer. At the very least I still want him to suffer as much as I have.

I like being back at Dennis Nylon. Everyone there seems glad to have me back after all my adventures. I like being home to have dinner with Nicky or at least to put him to bed. I like my privacy, my solitude.

I couldn't be more pleased with the way things have worked out.

44

STEPHANIE'S BLOG

ALL IS WELL

Hi, moms!

All's well that ends well. Though of course motherhood never ends as long as we and our kids are on this earth—and it lasts longer than that, as I've blogged about in the past.

Emily and I are neighbors again, raising our sons to be the happiest, healthiest little people we can. Sean is out of the country, and it's not clear when (or if) he'll return. I assume, though the details of this are beyond me, that he might be facing some kind of legal trouble when (and if) he comes back. And knowing Emily, I'm sure she plans to make him pay— pay dearly—for what he's done.

I don't see Emily as much as I'd like. She's working so hard and being such a great mom, making up for lost time. But friendships wax and wane, and I know a time will come when we'll again hang out on her big, comfy couch, if she still has it. Miles tells me that Nicky has some new stuff in his house, different from when we lived there. I don't press him for details. There are some things, plenty of things, I don't want to think about.

Miles is doing splendidly at school, Nicky trailing only slightly behind.

We've all been through a lot. But little Nicky is the one my heart goes out to. He paid the highest price. Losing his mother and getting her back and then losing his dad. How will he ever learn to trust?

The only comfort is how strong kids are. How brave and tough and resilient. Nicky will survive this and grow from it—and grow up into an even more thoughtful, compassionate, wise adult. A more interesting person.

There will come a time when each one of us will be able to move on and put this behind us, when we learn to live with our secrets, to value them. Because they are a part of us too.

I couldn't have gotten through this challenging time without the love and support of the moms community.

God bless you, moms everywhere. Keep strong. Stay beautiful. And if you have a story like this, I encourage you to post it.

More soon.

Love,

Stephanie

45

EMILY

A month or so after I moved back into my own house, a police car crawled up the driveway and stopped in front of our door.

I told myself: This means nothing.

Two plainclothes cops got out and rang the doorbell.

The woman extended her hand first. "I'm Detective Meany," she said. "And this is my partner, Detective Fortas."

I said, "I'm Emily Nelson."

"Yes, we know," said Detective Meany.

"Would you like to come in?" I said. I had nothing to hide.

They came in and sat on the new couch I'd bought to replace the one Stephanie sat on.

"I don't think we ever officially met," said Detective Fortas. "But we worked on your case. We met your husband—"

"My about-to-be-former husband is in the UK at the moment."

"I see," said Detective Meany. "That probably shouldn't have happened. Someone will probably need to interview him at some point . . ."

I was curious to know at what "point" that would be. But I kept my curiosity in check. I assumed I would find out, sooner rather than later.

"Look," I said, "I want to say . . . I'm so sorry I put you to all that trouble. It wasn't entirely my fault. My husband worked himself into a frenzy, pushed the panic button when I went off the radar. But all I needed was a little time off to mourn my sister's death. I *really* needed to unplug, to get *way* off the grid. It was a *huge* miscommunication that unfortunately intersected with an insurance policy I'd forgotten Sean had taken out." I smiled.

"I remember," said Detective Fortas. "We also interviewed a young woman, a friend, the mother of one of your son's friends . . ."

"Good memory," I said. "That would have been Stephanie. Not my least neurotic friend, if you know what I mean."

Detective Meany smiled. She'd met Stephanie. She knew what I meant. The two cops laughed mirthlessly, as if they weren't sure why they were laughing or if they should laugh at all.

I said, "I don't mean to be rude, but can I ask why you are here?"

"Just a conversation," said Detective Fortas. "A preliminary conversation. Over the last few days, someone found a wrecked and burned-out car not far from the interstate. Not that far from here. And in the car were the cremains of a man we believe to have been a Mr. Isaac Prager. This house was on the list of calls he made in the weeks before he disappeared. And naturally we connected this with your apparent disappearance, which, as we said, we investigated."

"How amazing!" I said. "What a coincidence!" I was flirting with both of them. I needed them to believe me.

Detective Meany said, "There wasn't much evidence left in the wreckage. Most likely, it was an accident. But there are some suspicious and . . . intriguing aspects here. And they did find a piece of jewelry at the scene that seems unlikely to have belonged to Mr. Prager."

She handed me a photograph. I knew exactly what I was going to see.

Of course, I was aware that I'd lost Sean's mother's ring. But because I'd gotten out of the habit of wearing it, several days had passed before I noticed it missing. And the funny thing was I didn't care. It had only belonged to my sister for . . . I didn't want to think how long. Before that, it had been mine for a while. And before that, it had belonged to

Sean's mother. Now, when I thought about the ring, I heard Sean's mother's maddening voice, whining and complaining about her life as she did the dinner dishes in that smelly, beastly kitchen.

I'd told myself not to worry about where I lost the ring. There were plenty of places it could have been beside the spot where I pushed a dead man's car into a ravine. It seemed unlikely that the ring would be there, especially because I had worked so hard to convince myself (and Stephanie) that the whole thing had never happened. No crime, no consequences.

I must have taken off my gloves after we finished pushing his car. But I didn't remember doing that. A lot of things about that day were blurry, difficult to recall with any certainty. I'd done my best not to think about it, and until now I'd succeeded.

"Funny thing," said Detective Meany. "My partner has a phenomenal—superhuman—memory for details. So when this image came up on the screen, this ring . . . my partner remembered a similar ring in the autopsy report. When they found the corpse that they thought was yours."

We both looked at Detective Fortas as if to see what wondrous kind of human being would have mental powers like that. But all we saw was a rather dull-looking fellow with a spray of pimples on his forehead and a wispy blond mustache.

He said, "The ring that they found in Michigan and, we understand, they gave your husband, in the case—"

"I know which ring you mean." I heard myself talking through clenched teeth. The cops were smart enough to remember a picture of a ring they saw months ago but not smart enough to realize in advance that the "corpse" they'd mentioned was my suicided sister. My beloved twin. Only now, too late, they got it. Detective Fortas blushed an unattractive pink.

"We're sorry for your loss," said Detective Meany.

"That's all right," I said. But it wasn't. And they knew it.

"The funny thing is," said Detective Fortas, "I remembered the first time we interviewed your husband. And your friend. And they were describing you. And both of them mentioned this ring." He jabbed at the printout. "We're pretty sure it's this ring."

It was crucial not to hesitate. Not to flinch. Not to falter.

I said, "My husband gave it to me when we got engaged. Later, my sister stole it to pay for drugs. Which is how it turned up in the lake."

Were they sorry for my loss? I was sorrier than they were.

I said, "Let me ask you something. When you talked to my husband, in the midst of that . . . misunderstanding about my disappearance . . . you said you talked to him and a friend . . . Stephanie."

"That's right, Stephanie," said the memory prodigy, Fortas.

"Well, did you know that she subsequently moved in with my husband? Did you know that they planned to get married? Do you know that he gave her his mother's ring, *my ring*, and that they both felt just great about that? They thought that my husband giving my ring to my best friend was something I would have wanted. Can you believe that?"

"My God," Detective Meany said, sounding horrified by my husband and my best friend's treachery. "I assume you have this . . . Stephanie's current contact information."

"Her number and her address," I said. "I can tell you that without even needing to look it up. And if you need more information about her relationship with my husband, I can give you a link to her blog. My impression is that he's dumped her by now, but that's no longer of any interest to me, as you can well imagine."

The police could well imagine. They wrote everything down. They had Stephanie in their sights.

I was remembering another thing that the poker champs told me about the fish. You know the fish is going to lose, but not when. You never know which hand is going to catch the fish and leave it flopping, gasping on the ground.

If the police had been less incompetent, less bumbling, they would have arrested me right then and there, on suspicion. Or at least they would have asked me to come in to answer more questions. Instead they left—hot on Stephanie's trail, I imagined—and politely asked me not to go too far. I promised that I wouldn't.

After the police left, I waited a little while. I took several deep breaths to clear my mind. Then I went into Nicky's room and took out some of his things and began to pack. It was time to leave. It was time for Nicky and me to head into the sunset, or sunrise, whichever. To go off the grid for a while. We would take a break, see what happens.

I got Nicky's passport and both of mine—the fake passport and the real one—just in case we needed them. Maybe we would visit Sean for a few days. Maybe I'd toy with him. Torment him. Maybe I could be the cat again—with yet another mouse.

I'd been expecting this. Planning this. Preparing for something like this, for a very long time. For my whole life, you could say.

I'd never been less scared. I felt young and excited and brave.

I felt happy to be alive.

ABOUT THE AUTHOR

DARCEY BELL was born in 1981 and raised on a dairy farm in western Iowa. She is a preschool teacher in Chicago. This is her first novel.